I magine a man clipping away up the smooth highway of his life; until, that is, a beautiful redhead makes him turn off into a side road full of potholes and other unpleasant surprises.

Well, my dear friends, this tale is about a hard-boiled detective who walks right into such a situation.

While investigating an unusual death, our good man meets a strange woman. She seems to know him while he has no recollection of her. The lady pierces her way into the most sensitive parts of his heart and then vanishes without a trace.

Our detective checks her background but finds only that a young coed with the same name had disappeared many years ago.

As he follows her trail, he runs into the business end of a slimy government conspiracy. His adventures take him within inches of death on more than one occasion and into...

I won't give anything away by revealing that in the world he finds himself the "game" has new rules. He navigates this parallel universe by the proverbial seat of his pants until...

Well, my dear friends, you have to read the tale to find out how it ends.

Two Highways

A *Science Fiction Mystery Yarn*

by

Andrei V. Lefebvre

Arthur & Bocci

First Printing

ISBN: 978-0-578-03629-8
Published by Arthur & Bocci
Los Angeles

to Mom and Dad

Contents

Contents

"... Just as a mirror may be used to reflect images, so ancient events may be used to understand the present..."

Chinese proverb

Prologue

y name is Marty Greenblatt. My private eye certificate fills the empty white wall behind my desk.

What do I investigate?

Well, I don't know where to begin... And please, my dear reader, don't touch this picture! It has a sentimental value and can't be replaced.

Who is the redheaded woman in this picture?

Hmmmmmm...

She's someone I used to know.

Were we married?

Interesting question... Yes and no.

Please, my dear reader, wipe that all knowing smirk off your face and wash your gray matter out with soap to boot. This situation is not what you are thinking...

How do I know what you are thinking?

I am a detective.

!?

Okay, I see that I got your attention now. So, let me spin my tale.

Our story begins one January day in the year 1993 with a scientist by the name of Walter Kurz and a rock. Yes, my dear reader, a rock. There is nothing remarkable about this two-pound piece of a basalt formation. It is flat with a sharp edge on one end. The scientist, however, is a remarkable man. He is a throwback to that early Twentieth Century type who still believes in the Science with the capital "S." For many decades, Walter toils in a variety of laboratories with one goal only—to test his subatomic theories.

In 1993, he works for the Uncle Sam in one of his super secret think tanks developing weapons of the future. On this particular morning he is in his lab. The solidified lava—which is what the basalt formation is—is part of his experiment and he watches it intently. The rock, however, can care less about Walter and sits on a stainless steel lab table with not a small measure of errogance.

The scientist stabbs at a computer keyboard several times and adjusts the dials on a large electronic device. The rock begins to fade into thin air slowly. Walter works with the dials some more. The rock disappears completely.

"Well, it looks like you dispatched it away, Dr. Kurz," says a female lab assistant, who stands behind Walter. "Let's do the transmitter next."

Walter puts the plastic egg-shaped radio transmitter on the stainless steel table. He fiddls with the dials on the electronic device and drums his fingers on the keyboard. The radio transmitter does not disappear.

"Why isn't it working?" asks the lab assistant impatiently. Her young voice echoes back from the bare white walls of the lab.

"Something is interfering. I can't even promise you that the rock reappeared by the target beacon," Walter says, his German accented voice full of detachment. "I've tried this procedure six hundred and fifty-one times. We had positive results in less than two percent of the time."

He types up another sequence on the keyboard and synchronizes the dials on the electronic device.

"I have the right beacon, the power is there," mumbles Walter under his breath.

He adds another sequence and presses the Enter key. Suddenly, Walter feels nauseous and observes a faint silvery fog appear in the lab. He looks at it and sees the image of himself staring back. The fog thickens into a solid cloud and Walter's image multiplies into infinity. Just then, the lights go out and the ground shakes under Walter.

Outside, major rockslide blocks a nearby highway and the entrance to an abandoned silver mine where Walter's superiors built the lab for him. Soon, the nausea goes away but he can see nothing still; the power is out. Walter gropes for a flashlight in his desk's drawer, finds it, turns it on, and looks around. The electronic device hums along as if nothing had happened; it has its own power supply. Then, he sees his lab assistant on the floor in a pool of blood. The two-pound rock came back and crushed her skull. Walter bends over the body and examins the wound carefully. The sharp edge of the rock penetrated deep into the scull. Pieces of brain and bone litter the floor. In his almost eighty years on this Earth, Walter had seen enough carnage to know that this woman is dead.

He walks up two flights of stairs and tries the front door. It does not move since the rockslide buried the main entrance. Walter, being a wise and pragmatic man, guesses that this is the case and decides to try another path. He descends three floors and uses a fire axe to break the lock on a back door. It leads into a splinter shaft of the old mine. He walks for forty-five minutes before reaching the surface.

There, torrential rain greets Walter. He slides down a steep hill to the highway. A light show of the fire trucks and police cruisers greets the old scientist. A huge mass of rocks and other debris dominates the scene. It blocks the highway and has Walter's car underneath.

He fishes out a cell phone from his wet jacket and places a call. Ten minutes later, a young sheriff's deputy comes up to Walter.

"Are you Dr. Kurz?" the deputy asks with much respect of in his voice and adds after Walter nodds. "I am ordered to take you home, sir."

Walter remains quiet all the way to his house. His unseeing eyes look straight ahead but his mind is on the dead lab assistant and the silver fog with its multiple images.

* * *

While Walter Kurz does his scientific magic in the lab, another drama unfolds some twenty miles away. A cold, shower-like in

intensity, rain torments two men. They seat

still on the roof of an old brick building downtown San Bernardino. Usually, this old Southern California city, of about 200,000, sports a magnificent mountain view. Today, however, the men see the rain and the gray clouds only.

They maintain total silence for four hours now. Every so often, the shorter, stockier man with dark hair brings his field glasses up to check a parking lot across the street. Every time he does that, the other man—thin with blond hair—clutches his M40A1 sniper rifle tighter, ready to bring it his shoulder. A waive of disappointment rocks both men every time they fail to spot their targets.

Finally, the spotter sees a door on the side of a building, across the street, open and three figures in black leather jackets exit. The darkness of their clothing blends in perfectly with the gloomy day.

"Seven o'clock," the dark-haired man whispers the targets' location to the thin man with the rifle.

The sniper brings the M40A1 to his shoulder and exhales slowly. A loud repot obscures all the other sounds. The dark-haired observer looks through his field glasses and sees the target in the middle drop, his head a bloody mess. His comrade to the right picks up a knapsack off his shoulders and makes a few steps back, towards the building's front door. The blond sniper fires again. The second target freezes for a fraction of a second and falls backwards. A pool of dark blood develops around his head.

The third target does not panic. He catches the knapsack before it hits the ground and makes it to the door. The sniper has time to fire once more, but misses.

"Son of a ..." he uses a string of expletives.

The shooting team springs forward and slides down an external fire escape within seconds. Thanks to bad weather, the traffic is light and they run across the street unobstructed. The blond sniper leaves his rifle behind on the roof and has his .45 Colt Commander at ready now. Without saying a word, he points to a half-opened door, into which the target had disappeared, and then at his partner. The dark haired man nods and makes a half circle with his left hand. Their silent conversation means that while the spotter will go in after the target, the sniper will cover the back door.

At one time, this one-story structure had been a medical clinic. For many years now, it stands empty, waiting for renovation. The spotter creeps noiselessly through a darkened corridor straining his hearing. His ears pick up the sounds of labored breathing and hurried footsteps. He hears a door open somewhere in front of him.

The spotter sprints forward, Smith & Wesson Model 59 in his right hand. Within seconds, he comes to a rear entrance and sees his partner through an open back door. The sniper seats in a huge puddle of rainwater while his gun slides away on a slick hardtop. Their target managed to knock the blond man down somehow. The bad guy reaches into the flap of his leather jacket and his hand pulls out a revolver. The gun's blue steel finish glistens menacingly.

Just as the spotter's sprint carries him outside, a faint silvery mist appears in front of him. He is startled to see the images of himself and the two other men in it. Just then, an egg-shaped plastic device—yes, my dear reader, you guessed it; it is the transmitter from the Walter Kurz' lab—hits him on the back of his head. And, as if Lady Fortuna decides to add insult to injury, a wave of nausea overcomes the spotter.

He wills the pain away but loses a few precious moments in the process. The silvery fog, meanwhile, solidifies into a thick cloud and the images, it contains, multiply into infinity. The countless figures of the target point the multitudes of blue steel finished revolvers at the innumerable doubles of his partner.

"Allah akbar!" all the bad guys yell in a thunderous chorus and the myriad of revolvers go off.

Four Die In Wild Street Gun Play Downtown S.B.

Feds Look For Experimental Weapons

Barry Roberts
News-Record Staff Writer

SAN BERNARDINO (Feb. 19, 1993) – An undercover Federal investigation resulted in the death of four men, a San Bernardino Sheriff's Department official said privately.

For some time now, the local law enforcement agencies have been receiving confidential warnings from Washington D.C. about an undercover operation in the Inland Empire, conducted by an unidentified Federal agency.

"We were told that the Feds are in hot pursuit of some experiential weapons from the old Warsaw Block," said a News-Record source in the Sheriff's Department, who has direct knowledge of the advisories. "We were told that a violent crew of international weapon smuggles took possession of some dangerous technology."

The same source attributed recent fatal shooting in San Bernardino to this Federal operation. Four men died in a barrage of gunfire last month. The Sheriff's Department has been unusually vague about this incident, refusing to provide any details. Moreover, a federal judge had sealed all of the reports and issued a gag order in connection with the shooting, News-Record learned. The newspaper, however, obtained a draft of the official police report prior to the court's actions. In it, the investigating officers refer to a White House-ordered project titled "Operation Remove Claws" and described the shooting incident as part of the operation.

Part One

Highway's Noise

"… Death's at the bottom of everything…
Leave death to the professionals …"

Graham Greene (1904–1991), British novelist, and Carol Reed. Major Calloway (Trevor Howard), in The Third Man (film) (1950).

Chapter One

Mortal Men Don't Die Twice

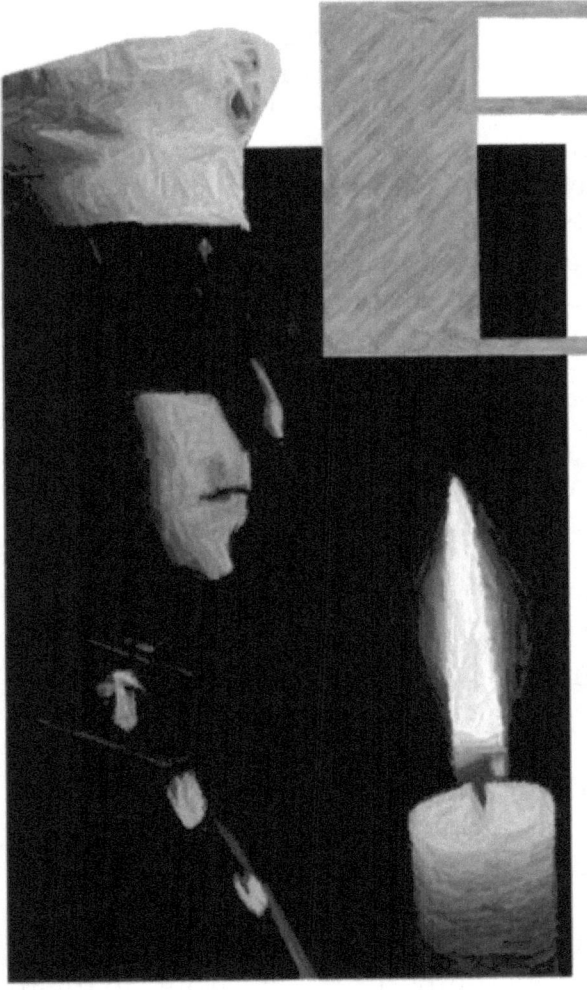

Eleven years later my cell phone rang.

"Greenblatt," I said into this evil gadget to stop its wining demand for my attention.

"Is this Mr. Marty Greenblatt?" asked a timid woman's voice.

"The one and only," I said jovially.

"Sir, I wonder if you can make some time for me," the woman continued. "I don't know who to turn to and someone said that you help people in unusual circumstances."

"How far away are you from Silver Springs?" I asked. Silver Springs is the one-horse town where I live and work. My home carries the double duty of my office.

"I don't know where it is," she answered. "Can you come over? I am in Riverside."

We agreed to meet the next day in the morning.

The woman's house was in an old suburban neighborhood. This part of Riverside went through some rough times in the late Eighties and the early Nineties. By 2004, however, the real estate prices rose insanely. A flow of people, escaping the urban gridlock of Los Angeles, flooded Riverside and surrounding areas. They consisted of a "young upwardly mobile" kind. In no time at all, the newcomers brought the neighborhood back into the middle class conformity.

The house of my destination sported the Spanish Stucco style of the early Fifties. The front lawn looked freshly cut and I saw no vehicles in the immaculate driveway. As I parked in front of the house, someone peered through the living room curtains. A tall Hispanic woman opened the front door before I had a chance to ring the bell.

"Mr. Greenblatt?" she asked.

"Yes, ma'am. I am," I said with much respect in my voice. The woman's face spoke of great strain and recent tears.

"My name is Rose Perez," she said, her voice betrayed a California native. "Thank you for coming."

She ushered me inside a small living room. The heavy curtains covered the windows and the room would have been completely dark if not for the scores of candles. The wicks burned brightly on the mantelpiece. More little flames illuminated a large photograph—on a small table full of pictures—depicting the upper torso of a man in the United States Marine Corps dress uniform.

"Mi niño pobrecito," she whispered and crossed herself Catholic style. I mentally translated from Spanish, "My poor baby."

Rose motioned for me to sit down. I made myself comfortable in a soft couch while she sat on the edge of a large leather armchair.

"I asked you here about my son Jack," she said pointing to the picture of the Marine.

I guessed her age to be fifty something. After my eyes adjusted to the darkness of the living room, I noticed that it was spotless. The smell of fresh roses caressed my nose and I spotted several vases with these flowers throughout the room. The Catholic saints looked down at me from the walls. I glanced at the small table with the pictures again. In addition to the large formal photograph of the Marine, smaller snapshots of the same man showed him at the beach, riding a horse, and washing a truck.

"Mr. Greenblatt, losing one's child is the worst thing that can happen to a mother," Rose continued. "Jack died five years ago in a traffic accident."

Her dark brown eyes, full of tears, reflected the flickering candlelight.

"We buried him here in Riverside. He was a good boy. Good son. Good Marine. The honor detail came to the funeral. Everybody loved him," Rose's voice remained strong but the tears ran down her face.

She stood up and walked into the kitchen only to return shortly with a box of tissues.

"Please, forgive me," she said, wiping her face. "Even though the wounds of his death will never heal, I had learned to live with it. But something happen recently which brought all of it back."

She blew her nose into the tissue, discarded it into a small trashcan under a coffee table, and continued, "The reason I am falling apart now, after learning to live with it, is because the Los Angeles police called me two weeks ago and told me that they found a dead body they think was my son. I told them that Jack was dead and buried but this Detective Samuels insisted that I look at pictures of this body. I went to L.A. and I looked at the pictures. Except for the beard, the dead man's face looked just like my boy's. He looked a little older and had some scars I never seen before. But he had the tattoo of a mermaid on his forearm. I was so pissed at Jack when he got it his senior year in high school. The man they found dead was Jack. I have no doubts."

I took my notebook out. "Rose, did you remember the body you buried five years ago? Are you sure that man was your son?"

The woman sat silent for awhile, her gaze fixed prominently to the ceiling to her left. She blew her nose again and gave me a tired look.

"I don't know what to think. Five years ago, I had no doubts that it was my boy I was burying. But now..." Rose cocked her head to her side and looked at me as if trying to penetrate my thoughts. "Now I am not sure of anything."

Then, she lowered her eyes and sobbed. "Mr. Greenblatt, can you find out what happened to my boy?" she asked through the tears.

"Why do you need me? Isn't police helpful?" I asked.

"At first they were," Rose said regaining control over herself. "But yesterday, Detective Samuels called and said that they made a mistake and that this dead man can't be my son. He was rude. He told me to forget it. But I can't."

* * *

On my way back, I dialed a Washington D.C. number. I had a contact among people who have access to the databases which store the information about any of us. I asked him to check out one Jack Perez.

The man called me back within fifteen minutes.

"Juan Alphonso Perez was born June 19, 1969," he said. "He graduated from the Arlington High School in Riverside, California in 1987. After that, Cal State Fullerton ROTC. Commissioned as second Louie into USMC in 1991. Navy flight school. Assigned to the Third Aircraft Wing, El Toro California. Fighter pilot. Honorable discharge in 1999 in the rank of Major. Killed in a traffic accident the same year."

"Do you have any indication that he may not have been killed?" I asked.

"I found no special tags on any of his records," my source said. I thanked him and clicked off. "Special tags" were indications that a person was involved in intelligence work.

The traffic bunched up at the intersection of 91 and 60 freeways. While my Nissan Pathfinder crawled along at two miles per hour, I called the LAPD and asked for Detective Samuels. After transferring me several times and getting a different number, I finally reached him.

Samuels agreed to meet with me the next day. The detective worked out of Wilshire Division which took me to the West Venice Boulevard in Los Angeles.

He asked me to stop by at 9:30 AM. I arrived early. An unformed clerk asked me to cool my heels in the lobby after I informed her of the reason for my visit. Samuels kept me waiting for almost one hour. Finally, a door with the "Police Personnel Only" sign opened and a tall black man in a sharp blue suit came out. He eyeballed me for a short

while and then motioned to follow him. He guided me inside one of the interrogation rooms and closed the door behind us.

We stood facing each other.

"Are you packing heat?" he asked without preambles.

"Not this very minute," I said sensing something amiss.

"Do you mind if I frisk you?" he asked and put his large meaty paw on my shoulder.

"Yes, I do mind." I said and gave him a hard stare.

"I wasn't asking," Samuels said and tried to turn me around by my shoulders.

I flexed my muscles and resisted. When Samuels realized that he can't easily force me to turn, he reached under the table and pushed the "officer needs help" button. Within seconds, the room was full of uniformed cops.

"Samuels, I need to see the watch commander now," I said calmly.

The uniforms gave the detective questioning looks. The "officer needs help" button is for the situations when suspects get violent inside the interrogation rooms. Since they observed no violence, they did not know what to do.

I could see that Samuels was lost too. For some reason he wanted to take me down a notch but it backfired. He could not back down in front of the witnesses but the same witnesses precluded him from being too forceful.

"Samuels, you have to make up your mind," I said. "If I'm a suspect in some crime, arrest me. If not, let these officers go and let's discuss Jack Perez."

Detective bit his lower lip and lowered his head slightly. I could read him like a book now. He had no cojones for an all out confrontation with me and was ready to backpedal.

"Code four," he said in a loud voice, allowing the uniforms to go back to where they came from.

"Pull up a chair, Samuels," I said arrogantly, and sat down behind the desk.

The detective lowered himself down into the suspects' chair slowly. "Greenblatt, before I tell you anything I need to know what is going on."

"Mortal men don't die twice," I said. "I checked with some people. They believe that Jack Perez has been dead awhile. Cold dead, not paper dead. He was, as far as I can determine, a civilian. His mother asked me to find out why she was shown a dead body which looked like her son. Up until that time, she was convinced that he died five years ago."

"I can't tell you much," said Samuels squinting. "I received direct orders from my brass to turn the investigation over to the Homeland Security a week ago."

"May I see your report," I asked.

"There is no report," Samuels frowned. "I am not even sure that a crime has been committed."

"Why?"

"The man walked inside a medical clinic on the Olympic Boulevard and died in the waiting room three weeks ago. The reason I got involved was because the clinic's staff thought he might have been poisoned."

"Was an autopsy done?" I asked.

"I don't know or care," Samuels said. "Now you have to leave."

He escorted me back to the lobby.

"By the way, I will report your visit to the Homeland Security," he said when I was half way out of the front door.

"... For conspiracy,
I know not how it tastes, though it be
dished
For me to try how..."

**William Shakespeare (1564–1616), British dramatist, poet.
Hermione, in The Winter's Tale, act 3, sc. 2, 1. 71-3.**

Fall 2004

Chapter Two

The Odor of Conspiracy

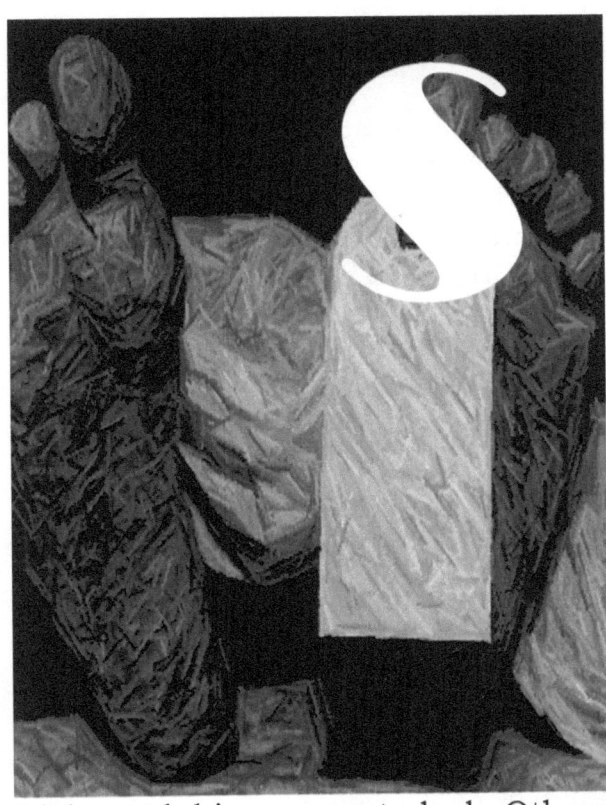

corching rays of the September sun blinded me as I came out of the Wilshire Police Station. While I stood still, waiting for the eyes to adjust to the bright light, my gray matter examined the results of the meeting.

Samuels is scared stiff, my common sense told me. The Homeland Security people must have frightened him a great deal. Otherwise this, seemingly robust, cop would not have overreacted with the panic button like that.

I stopped by a random Mexican food stand and ordered two fish tacos with a bottle of Coke. I ate in my Pathfinder. Samuels intrigued me. Prior to our conversation, I expected to find some bureaucratic mix up which resulted in a misidentification of the body. Now, however, the case obtained a conspiracy odor.

I finished my tacos and lit up the Arturo Fuentes Double Corona. The sharp tobacco smoke made my thoughts crystal clear. I chased the rough taste with what was left of the Coke and drove to the Olympic Boulevard. This street traverses Los Angeles from the beach all the way past downtown. Samuels did not tell me in which medical clinic he found the dead body. However, the facility must have been inside the Wilshire Division's geography. I decided to check all clinics along this stretch of the Olympic Boulevard. I found the right place on my fourth try.

"Yes, I remember when this man died in our waiting room," said a young receptionist. She looked no older than twenty and appeared ready to gossip. "He came in early in the morning. It must have been seven o'clock. He had an old ID. It was expired like five years ago and he had no insurance. I told him that he needs insurance but he showed me a roll of money this thick." The receptionist spread her well-manicured fingers, with long purple nails, two inches apart.

"He didn't look good," she continued. "He said that his belly hurts and that he's passing out. I started filling out the paperwork and told him to sit down and wait to be called. I turned around to make a copy of his ID. When I finished, he was on the floor. I called Dr. Patel. But the poor man was dead."

"Did the doctor say what he died of?" I asked.

"I donno," the receptionist shrugged. "The cops and paramedics came, but he was dead by that time. Why don't you ask Dr. Patel? He's here today."

She picked up the receiver and talked into it. I did not make out what she said because she kept her voice at a conspiratorial whisper. The content of what she said made no difference anyway because the doctor came out right away and shook my hand. He examined my private detective's ID and badge carefully.

"How may I help you?" he asked, heavy dose of the Indian sub-continent in his voice.

"Dr. Patel, the relatives of the man who died in your clinic are trying to find out what has happened to him," I said. "What did he die of?"

The doctor looked me in the eyes and said nothing. After a long pause he invited me to his office. The look on Dr. Patel's face was unmistakable. He was ready to talk but he wanted something in exchange.

"I am a man with many connections," I said. "Is there anything I can do for you?"

"I have a patient who owes me some money," Dr. Patel said. "Do you do collections?"

"How much does he owe you?"

"Eight hundred dollars," the doctor said and leaned back into his chair.

I took out two one hundred-dollar bills and put them on his desk. "This is all the money this patient had on him."

As Dr. Patel reached for the cash, I placed my palm on top of it. "Let me see the file and talk to me."

He pulled the bills from under my hand carefully and said. "At first I thought that he may have been poisoned. Before I came here, I consulted the police in my own country. I have seen many poisonings. His appearance was consistent with the oral ingestion of Oxalic Acid."

"What is it?"

"Oxalic Acid is found in some home cleaning agents. If ingested, it produces abdominal pains and kills the victim by removing calcium form the blood. The man had slight muscle tremors, rapid respiration, and mild convolutions just before he expired."

"Do you know if anyone tested him for this poison?" I asked.

"No, I don't," said Dr. Patel. "The police took over and I am not even sure they knew I was a doctor. However, I know why he died."

The doctor stopped and rustled the one hundred-dollar bills in his hand. I shook my head; I wasn't going to give him any more money.

"Okay, I'll tell you anyway," he said with disappointment on his face. "I tested the body liquids he left behind. His bowels emptied *post mortem*. I wanted to protect my other patients and staff from anything this man my have been exposed to. I am glad I did because the culture test showed a common *Vibrio Cholerae* strain. I had to close the clinic for four hours and disinfect the whole building."

"You mean he died of Cholera?" I asked.

"Yes. The symptoms are very similar to Oxalic Acid poisoning: painful intestinal cramps, muscle cramps which result in tremors. The patient dies of massive loss of fluid and electrolytes as well as severe potassium depletion which results in a circulatory collapse."

"Where would this man contract Cholera?"

"I have not seen one case since I came to the United States fifteen years ago," Dr. Patel said.

He left and came back with a file. I watched him open it. A personal information form on top caught my eye. It has been filled out in shaking block letters. Blue paperclip

attached a plastic rectangle of the California Drivers' License to it. I reached across the desk, closed the file, and tried to put it under my arm. Dr. Patel, however, held on to it tight. With my free hand, I pealed one more one hundred-dollar bill from my money clip and dropped it on the desk. The doctor released his grip.

"How come you didn't give the ID to the police?" I asked him.

"You know, they were so self-righteous. They really did not want to talk to any one of us in the clinic. They found some other ID in his pocket. Also, he had those metal things hanging around his neck."

"What metal things?"

"You know, army men wear them."

"You mean dog tags?"

"Yes, dog tags," Dr. Patel said.

"Did you get a close look at those dog tags?" I asked.

"No."

* * *

I fought traffic all the way home. My house sits on a wooded hillside, lost in the ocean of pine trees. I parked in front of my garage and walked inside. My belly demanded food. The fridge greeted me with its welcoming coolness. I fished out some salami, cheese, and sweet pickles. I combined it all with French roll and made a sandwich. After I placated my stomach, the rest of my body wanted attention too. I shed my clothing and took a long bath.

Refreshed, I walked into my den, which serves as my office, donned latex gloves, and opened up the file I took form Dr. Patel. The standard patient information form bore the name "Jack Perez" scribbled in blue ink. The address, the dead man wrote, was that of Rose Perez. I put the form to the side and examined the drivers' license. It appeared to be a genuine product of the California Department of Motor Vehicles issued in the name of Juan Alphonso Perez. It had Rose's address also. The date of birth matched her son's and it has been expired for seven years now. The DMV mug shot looked me in the eyes. The young man's face showed hardness and determination. The mouth formed a snickering half-grin and the eyes bore into mine with some chilling ruthlessness. This was not a man to trifle with, I decided.

I broke open my fingerprint kit and dusted the license with a fine graphite powder. Several prints came through prominently. I placed a piece of clear adhesive tape over the powder, lifted the prints, and put the tape onto a

cardboard. I counted three white good prints and another four partials.

Then, I placed the license in a plastic bag, put the lifted prints away, and changed gloves. My attention shifted to the patient information form. I looked at it from different angles. The fingerprints covered most of the edges. I repeated the dusting procedure, using a fine brush. The black graphite set the prints into focus. Instead of lifting the powder, I placed the clear tape over the fingerprints, taping it to the form and preserving the prints.

The setting sun hit the den's window hard, tuning the white walls pastel pink. I looked west. The sun's crimson disk shone between the trees, making the high clouds glow in rich gold color. I love this time of the day. Wonderful things happen just before the sun sets. While I took the beauty of the sky in, my next move became obvious. I knew several law enforcement types who could run the fingerprints through the identification process. My choice, however, fell on Deedee Wilson. The City of San Bernardino employed her as a crime scene tech. She had access to the databases and was discreet. She was also a tad more than just a police contact.

"Hi, sweetcakes," I said after dialing her cell phone.

"Hi, Marty. I haven't heard from you in a hundred years," she said trying to sound severe. "What makes you think I will talk to you after you ignored me for so long."

"I am sorry honey," I said using a mockingly exaggerated tone of a guilty man. "But you went back to your husband. I've been nursing a broken heart ever since."

Deedee laughed. She had been separated from her husband for three years now. We never became a real couple. Yet, we enjoyed each other's company every so often.

"So, what are you up to these days?" she asked in a friendlier tones.

"I need a small favor," I said. "I have a few unidentified fingerprints you could help me with."

"Oh, you're not even interested in me anymore," she said with disappointment. "It's all business now. Is this how it is?"

"Sweetcakes, it's just an excuse to see you," I said. "I was hoping to stop by tonight so I can spank you cute little bottom."

"You're such a dog!" Deedee exclaimed. "What makes you think I let you take my pants off again?"

"I'll be over in one hour," said I ignoring her question.

"Okay, but make it two, I'm still at work and I want to take a shower before you get here."

"...Lust is to the other passions what the nervous fluid is to life; it supports them all, lends strength to them all ... ambition, cruelty, avarice, revenge, are all founded on lust...."

Marquis de Sade (1740–1814), French author. Juliette, in L'Histoire de Juliette, ou les Prospérités du Vice, pt. 2 (1797).

Chapter Three

Duty Calls

Spending the night with Deedee is an experience I would not suggest to the fainthearted. A year before her fortieth birthday, she discovered the erotic pleasures of Marques de Sade. Promptly, she became a devoted follower of his love making style. When her husband refused to keep her tied up and corporally punished during their infrequent intimate moments, Deedee kicked him out without hesitation. We met shortly after her separation. Our friendship had developed into a passionate affair, bent on exploring the "darker" side of erotica.

My pocket watch told me that the time was 6:47 P.M. when I rang her doorbell.

"Hi Marty, you like?" Deedee greeted me at the door of her ranch style home and made a graceful turn like a runway model. Her black see-through negligee left very little of her tanned voluptuous body to the imagination. Deedee handled the four-inch stiletto-heeled slippers like a pro. Her large bust bounced alluringly and her soft rump wiggled in the most enticing way.

"Sweetcakes, you can drive a man into taking a belt out his trousers," I said and gave her a light slap on the shapely butt.

Deedee smiled provocatively and pulled me inside. I put both of her small wrists in my left hand and led her to the bedroom. There, an assortment of leather whips, floggers, and paddles greeted me from a rack on the wall. On a shelf to the side, Deedee displayed a collection of clamps, handcuffs, and other objects designed to augment her erotic ecstasy.

I walked my sex-slave-for-the-night to a sturdy bedpost--which I reinforced with a steel rod two years ago—and started a binding ritual. I decided to fashion her in the Shibari syle. I broke open a 100-foot roll of white cotton rope, I picked up on the way to Deedee's, and began. Shibari is a Japanese form of bondage art, which combines the hard physical sexuality with the visually erotic display. The beautiful restraining rope patterns are designed to provide submissive woman with sexual pleasure and to make her body an eye-pleasing living sculpture.

I bound Deedee's wrists and forearms to the bedpost. At first, she protested ritually, repeating that she was a "good girl" over and over. And I, ritually, told her over and over that "good girls don't invite strange men over to have sex." By the time her arms disappeared under the orderly rows of white coils, her words turned into carnal moans. I worked my way down patiently. The ropes had to be tight enough to hold her still, but with adequete slack to keep her blood circulation out of jeopardy. I spent almost an hour paying attention to her abdomen, navel, and thighs. Since this was not the first time we've done this, I knew her erotic secrets. So, I teased her mercilessly, making her cry in a fiery ecstasy of multiple orgasms. By the time my rope work of art was done, time tick-tacked to 10:47 PM.

At this point, I retreated to the wood chair, Deedee had at her arts and crafts table. Here she was, in front of me, making my blood boil with excitement. The pristine white coils pushed her large bosom up, leaving the prominent nipples—with brass clamps attached—stand out. The rope forced her bottom out and wrapped her thighs tightly around the roundness of the thick wooden bedpost, just as if she rode a giant phallus. While I took my La Gloria Cubana Pyramid and got it going, Deedee moaned though a red ball gag loudly.

"Not yet, Sweetcakes," I said enjoying the flavorful tobacco and watching Deedee wiggle her exposed bottom, as much as the ropes allowed. "Don't be impatient, you'll get yours soon."

My dear reader, what followed was not for those who prefer the missionary position. By the time we finished, the watch reported 1:07 AM. I put the leather tools of pleasure back on the rack and untied Deedee with care. I placed her on the bed and gave her a deep muscle massage. Deedee smiled and kissed my hands.

"Why can't my ex- do what you just did to me?" she asked.

"Different men do different things," I said.

"You know Marty, I am still in love with him. But unless he learns how to please me in bed, I can't be with him," Deedee lamented.

"...Mystery is in the morning, and mystery in the night, and the beauty of mystery is everywhere; but still the plain truth remains, that mouth and purse must be filled..."

Herman Melville (1819–1891), U.S. author. The Confidence-Man (1857), ch. 37, The Writings of Herman Melville, vol. 10, eds. Harrison Hayford, Hershel Parker, and G. Thomas Tanselle (1984).

Chapter Four

Strange Visitors

hen I left, Deedee slept undisturbed by my movements. I placed an envelope with the fingerprints on the pillow, next to her head. The early morning sun brought in another day. It produced some considerable heat already.

The dashboard clock showed 6:06 AM when I parked in my driveway. A surprise waited for me. Three men sat on my large porch and three horses stood in front the porch, tied to the railing.

"Mornin' Mr. Greenblatt," said one of them while all three got up. I looked at them hard and found the men unfamiliar. They sported full beards and wore wide-brimmed straw hats. They had nearly identical clothing which consisted of baggy shorts cut from a desert camouflage cloth, military boots, and Hawaiian-style shirts. All three had—what looked like—M-16 rifles slang behind their backs. Their horses stood still, saddled with the Western saddles over the Indian blankets. My visitors had an air of rugged outdoorsmen about them, more congruent with the old Wild West rather than the Twenty First Century. In any other part of the Southern California they would have stood out like a sore thumb. On the western slope of the San Bernardino Mountain, however, you can run into a wide variety of weekend warriors playing cowboys in Indians. Still, today was a weekday.

"Forgive our intrusion but I'd like to talk to you," the older man continued. Neither he nor his companions exhibited threatening body language. If not for the rifles, I could have safely assumed that these men came to proselytize some random religious movement.

"Why don't you come inside, gentlemen," I said.

We entered my living room and arranged ourselves around the coffee table. The men looked slightly uncomfortable as if they did not want to be here, but had to. They took off the straw hats letting me see their faces clearly. The one who spoke looked to be in his fifties, much gray in the long thinning hair and bushy beard. The other two had their heads shaved and their beards could have passed for the severe five-o'clock shadows. They looked to be in their early twenties. I saw enough resemblance between the three of them to justify a conclusion that they were a father and two sons.

"My name is Juan Robertson," the older man said extending his hand for a shake and, confirming my familial conclusions, continued. "And these are my boys Jake and Andrew."

"Would you like anything to drink?" I asked after the handshakes. "Coke, beer?"

"Coke would be fine for all three of us," Juan said and looked at his sons who no longer appeared stern but showed grins. "It's too early for beer and we haven't tasted good pre-partnership Coke in a long time."

"Pre-partnership?" I asked while taking the cans from the fridge and tossing them to the men.

"Just a figure of speech, Mr. Greenblatt," said Juan as if catching himself after saying something he shouldn't have said.

"What we came here to ask is..." Juan hesitated and then went for it. "Do you know who Jack Perez is?"

The man looked sincere and I could see that Jack Perez was important to him.

"I never had the pleasure of meeting the man. But we have some commotion around the name," I said. "First he dies in 1999 and then his mother hired me to find out if he died again three weeks ago."

"I'm not interested in Jack Perez in 1999," Juan said impatiently. "I need to know where he is now."

"I can't be one hundred percent sure but I think he died again in Los Angeles," I said.

The news was an obvious shock to Juan. His hand gripped his M-16 tightly and his nose made a sound as if he was suppressing tears.

"How sure are you that he died three weeks ago?" he asked.

"Pretty sure," I said.

"How did he die?"

"I am told it was Cholera," I said.

Juan looked me in the eyes with an obvious effort to discern if what I was telling him was true. I took his hard probing in stride. His inquiry did not have the feel of an idle curiosity. Few moments later, Juan got up and his sons followed.

"We need to go now. Much obliged for the Cokes and for talking to me strait," he said and shook my hand hard. "You're the same everywhere. Your reputation is in tact as a decent man."

The men put the straw hats on and mounted their horses. "Mr. Greenblatt, forget we came by. Our affairs are ours and you shouldn't be involved," he said from the saddle and the three horsemen trotted away down the hill.

* * *

After the trio melted into the hillside, I turned my stereo to a jazz station and took a shower. My thoughts jumped from Jack Perez to Juan Robertson with his sons and back. None of it made sense. The shower water refreshed me. Thanks to Deedee's demanding nature, my head was completely clear of useless clatter. Her radical erotic games had a way of making me very creative and productive afterwards.

This time, however, my mind remained blank. I had no theory which would explain the Jack Perez situation. Covert operatives fake their own death sometimes to remain in deep cover. I had ran into a few such "ghosts" in my career. The method of operation for such a premise was all wrong, however, too crude. Jack Perez circumstances felt more like a fugitive trying to get away. Samuel's reaction, in this scenario, was strange as well. He acted scared rather than being smug. A reek of conspiracy overwhelmed me.

I put the Jack Perez mystery aside and started on my other cases. By the time my watch reported 4:16 PM, I had finished a background investigation. It was contracted by a lady who planned to marry and wanted to know more about the man. I e-mailed her the bad news, her bridegroom-to-be was married already, at least three times. I also made much headway into a confidential request by a corporate executive to gather some dirt on his rival. My police contacts told me, off the record, about the two—hushed up—drug arrests which never came to trial. The rival, apparently, had some serious political pull on the local level. I also had a promising telephone conversation with a Foothill Boulevard madam. For the right price, she was willing to tell all about his cocaine-infused orgies with her prostitutes. She also claimed to possess a video record of the debauchery. I e-mailed my corporate client about my progress with an estimation of the madam's tell-all fee.

The sun began to disappear behind the hill to the west of my home. I made myself comfortable in a rocking chair on the porch and got the Onyx Churchill going hot. The bitter cigar taste made me close my eyes in enjoyment. I chased the bitterness with a cup of coffee. Then, I heard the sound of an approaching car and lifted my eyelids. Deedee's red Corvette pulled up to my garage. She stepped out, not bothering to bring the ragtop up on her convertible. I walked down and took her into a bear hug.

"Marty, thank you for the warm welcome but you're breaking me," she whispered breathlessly as I heard something fall from her hands. I picked up the manila

Andrei V. Lefebvre

folder, I left on her pillow this morning, and threw it into the rocking chair on my porch. Then, I led her to my bedroom, ripped her clothing off as fast as I could, and ravaged her soft generous body for quite a while. Since I do not possess the abundance of bondage and punishment toys, I made do with what I had. Please, my dear reader, don't press me for details.

A few hours later, I was exhausted, stretched on my bed in my birthday suit. Nude Deedee tucked herself under my right arm as if making a nest.

"How come you never kiss me?" she asked.

"This is not the nature of our association," I said.

"What is the nature of our association?" she pressed.

My free hand spanked her delicious bottom and I hugged her hard.

"You should go back to your husband. I'm not your marriage material. Too mean. Too used to being single."

"Why can't we be a regular couple?"

"Is what we do regular?" I asked.

"Well, some couples do that," she said, somewhat unsure.

"Sweetcakes, you may be submissive in sex, but in the everyday life you are one bossy broad. Am I wrong?"

"Well, yes," she agreed.

"So, the reason I don't kiss you is because I don't want to fall in love with you," I said almost convincing myself of this fact. "If we bring in such tender emotions, we'll make each other soap opera miserable rather than porno flick happy."

Deedee gave me a smile, an all-knowing grin really. She navigated this saturation better than I could ever. After all, my dear reader, women always gain an upper hand—after a while—when they start sharing our beds.

"Marty, you're such a dog!" Deedee exclaimed and did a few things which made me plunge into the sweet torture of our erotic pleasures for the rest the evening.

Andrei V. Lefebvre

"...My rule of life prescribed as an absolutely sacred rite smoking cigars ..."

Winston Churchill on dining with the abstinent King Ibn Saud of Saudi Arabia, *Triumph and Tragedy* Houghton Mifflin 53

Chapter Five

The Bucket of Worms Gets Deeper

By the time Deedee drove off in her convertible, my alarm clock reported 12:07 AM. I looked in my humidor and found it almost empty. I had a choice—Arturo Fuentes Double Corona or Bolivar Belicoso. I picked the Bolivar and took my time lighting it. As the Cuban tobacco's sweet taste caressed my pallet, I looked though the manila folder Deedee brought back.

She found that the drivers' license contained the fingerprints of three people. One of them was Juan Alphonso Perez. The patient information form had his prints too. In addition to the fingerprint ID slips, Deedee enclosed copies of the accident report and the death certificate.

In 1999, Jack Perez lost control of his Kawasaki Ninja ZX-9R motorcycle on his way to Las Vegas on the I-15. California Highway Patrol found him westbound in the number two lane. The death certificate stated that the lethal end came as a result of the severe trauma to his head and neck.

Deedee also printed out a one-page bulletin from the NCIC system for me. It read:

"Juan Alphonso Peres aka Jack Perez, even though Death Cert. filed with San Bern. Cnty Calif. if stopped or

observed contact DHS. Approach with caution. Subject armed and dangerous. No current warrants outstanding. Maintain all contacts in confidence."

"So you didn't die in 1999 Jack," I said out loud. "Or did someone assume your identity?"

I love mysteries. This one was worth getting my teeth into. I slept well that night. When my eyes opened, the alarm clock showed 7:08 AM. I showered and dressed within twenty minutes.

My first stop was Lee's Convenience Market—about a mile from my home—at the bottom of the Silver Springs Hill. As I paid for the new supply of cigars, a green Ford Explorer parked in front of the store. Through a large plate glass window, I saw a woman and two pre-teen girls get out. The girls looked like any other kids. The woman, however, attracted my attention. She appeared to be in her early thirties with an attractive face. She was thin; blue jeans and white t-shirt flapped as she walked slowly through the front door of the store.

I looked her in the eyes on my way out. Her pale, sickly face contorted into an expression of fear. She gave me a furtive double take and turned around.

"Back in into the Ford," she ordered the two girls who complied instantly.

She climbed back into the Explorer with visible difficulty and sped away. By the time I decided to record the license plate, the vehicle was too far for me to see. At that time, I did not think much of the incident, my stomach demanded food. But you, my dear reader, make a mental note.

In another fifteen minutes, my posterior hit the stool at the Blue Lyon's Diner. I ordered three eggs, bacon, and hash browns.

While waiting for my order, I grabbed the front page of the San Bernardino News-Record. Before I had a chance to read past headlines, someone large sat on the stool next to me.

"I was hoping for find you here," a familiar deep voice greeted me. I looked over the paper and recognized the man.

"Good morning, Edward," I said and shook his huge paw. Edward Oline stood almost seven feet and bent the scale at over three hundred pounds. He managed several family-owned new car dealerships in our county. I had done a number of internal fraud investigations for his company and we became buddies.

"Marty, thank you for helping Rose Perez. Her husband Bud, until he died from a heart attack, worked for my dad. I gave her your number," he said and ordered the steak and eggs breakfast. "Were you able to figure out what happened to her boy?"

"Strange case," I said. "On one hand, I have no doubts that Jack died three weeks ago in L.A. However, I dug up a death certificate and a CHP report showing him to die in 1999."

"Do you have any theories?" asked Edward.

"Yes, a few. But before I start shooting my mouth off I'd like to interview the chippies who found the dead body back in 1999."

Our food arrived and we ate in silence. Out of the corner of my right eye, I saw someone enter the restaurant and sit down in one of the booths. I turned my head and recognized the woman from the Lee's Convenience Market. She was the same one who came in with the two girls and ran off when she saw me. Now the woman and the girls made themselves comfortable in the window booth. I guess she felt my gaze because her eyes locked with mine. This time, the woman's face turned dark crimson. I smiled and expected her to smile back. Instead, she got up quickly and left the diner with the girls. I followed them to the parking lot only to see the trio get into the green Ford Explorer and hightail up the Highway 38.

Edward finished his food by the time I came back. "Marty, I think I can help you with the CHP," he said.

"How so?"

"I know one of the officers who did the traffic accident investigation back in ninety-nine," he said. "He's a good ol' boy. He's retired and runs a hunting ranch in Montana now. Great elk. He also stocks wild boar."

* * *

Later the same day, I found myself in the co-pilot's seat of Edward's Douglas DC-3 on the way to Montana. The Gooney Bird's two Rolls-Royce Dart engines pushed us North at 200 miles per hour. Three hours into our flight, Edward climbed to 20,000 feet taking us above the cloud cover. He took out two H. Upman Churchills and offered me one. I accepted, obviously, and we lit up. This was the true Cuban tobacco, not the Honduran version of the same label.

"I am taking a box of these to Remy," he said.

Remy Hensley was the retired chippie we were flying to see. Edward showed his eccentric side by inviting me to go hunting to Montana, right then and there, in the diner. I barely had enough time to get my Marlin 336 .30-30 caliber hunting rifle and a backpack with the camping essentials.

"We're going to bag ourselves a boar, have Remy's guys dress it and barbeque it," Edward continued while puffing on his H. Upman. "Beer, veggies and we'll have a great party."

"Sounds like a plan," I chimed in.

We talked about the guns, liquor, and cigars all through the rest of the flight. Even though, both of us knew that the only reason for our trip was to interview Remy about the Jack Perez accident, we pretended that we had no other business but hunting. My watch showed 10:16 PM when our plane touched down on a private airstrip about 200 miles west of Great Falls. Remy and his adult grandson met us and helped with the luggage.

Both Hensley men stood almost as high as Edward. The three huge figures made me feel like a fairytale character lost in the land of giants. After a brief introduction they took us to our cabin. It had two bedrooms and a sitting room. The sanitary facility consisted of a log outhouse fifty yards away.

Next morning, Edward woke me at 4:01 AM, according to my watch. Our hunt was not much of an adventure. Remy and his grandson drove a herd of elk towards us. So, instead of a boar, Edward shot a nice fat buck. I purposefully held back my fire, wanting my buddy to enjoy himself. After all, he picked up the tab for our trip and Remy was his contact.

I spent the next three hours skinning and boning the elk. I used my machete to chop the carcass into the venison t-bone steaks. They came out much smaller than their beef version. Since the wild deer has much lighter fat content—and the taste of meat is in the fat only—than domestic animals, I cut slits in the steaks and stuffed the meat with garlic, basil, and pieces of salt pork. Then, I made a whiskey and balsamic vinegar marinade.

While Edward and I drank beer, ate potato chips, and told each other tall stories about past hunting trips, the venison marinated quietly. When the time came to 3:38 PM, Remy's grandson got the wood barbeque pit going hot and threw the steaks on the grill. Within twenty minutes he served us a plate full of meat. He also brought out sliced cucumbers, tomatoes, and some raw onion. We stopped bragging, our mouths too busy with the food.

When the last steak disappeared, Edward passed around his H. Upman cigars.

"I know that you didn't come to hunt only," Remy said, addressing Edward. Without shifting his gaze, he threw a can of Budweiser my way. "You friend Marty here don't look like the rich idiots you entertain usually."

He looked me in the eyes and winked, letting me know that no offence was meant.

"Marty, if had to guess, you're some sort of a dick in search of something I may be able to tell you." Remy winked again, but his face lost the friendly smile. "Ever since you arrived I've been trying to figure out which one of my past deeds had caught up with me."

"Remember Bud Perez' boy?" asked Edward.

"Oh, yes. Terrible. Terrible. He was a pilot I think. Nice kid. Rode his bike to Vegas on I-15 one night and lost control. The boy died before he knew what hit him. Broken neck, half of the skull caved in," Remy said in a quiet voice.

We puffed on our cigars and drunk more beer. A cold wind gust made the coals in the barbeque pit glow bright red and I heard a coyote's howl in the distance.

"Why are you interested in Bud's boy so many years after he died?" Remy asked.

"Marty here thinks that the man you found dead on I-15 may not have been Jack Perez," said Edward. "He found another body whose prints ID as Jack's. That man died three weeks ago."

"Oh," said Remy and took a deep drag from his cigar.

The darkness enveloped us completely by now. The coyote howled again, this time much closer. Several other howls answered and I felt the evening light up with the excitement of the predatory energy. Dogs started to bark angrily somewhere not too far away. All four of us gut up. I picked up my rifle and made a few steps away from the barbeque area. In the darkness, I felt transformed into another world. The dogs continued to bark and I heard one of them squeal.

The primeval desire to hunt made me ran towards the sound. I glided through the grass effortlessly, my Marlin at ready. Within two minutes, I came upon Remy's two dogs. A pack of five coyotes cornered them between the oak trees. In silence, the wild canines lunged forward together, took a few quick snaps at the dogs, and retreated. The sound of barking and squealing filled the air. I identified the pack's leader quickly. He looked big for a coyote, eighty pounds possibly. The rifle felt great in my hands as I caught his head in the scope's crosshairs. He looked directly into my eyes. The reflection of his mirror-like retinas made his eyeballs flash with a surreal white light.

He stood still for a fraction of a second and moved quickly, with much grace, out of my sites. The rest of his pack followed. The dogs barked a few more times but did not chase their wild cousins.

"I've never seen them come this close," I heard Remy's voice from behind me.

I lifted my rifle up and turned towards the voice. Remy and I stood along under a huge sky. The moon's quarter made the world around us barely visible.

"What I'm going to tell you now, Marty, is for your ears only. Our buddy Edward does not have to know," Remy said. "Perez kid was no accident. I think someone waited for him and knocked him off the bike on purpose. There were no skid marks you see usually when kids lose control over their motorbikes. He was pushed backwards by something. I found some broken headlight glass which did not belong to his Kawasaki. I also found a witness who saw a Humvee sit in the freeway's center divider facing oncoming traffic. When Perez approached, the truck gunned the engine and hit him head on."

"How come the report said 'lost control'?" I asked.

"Assistant Commissioner of CHP field operations called me into his office a day after the accident and had a short conversation with me. He gave me a typed up accident report, with the diagrams and everything, and ordered me to sign it. Then, he told me that the whole case is closed now and that our meeting did not take place," Bud said.

"Why did you agree?" I asked.

"We all have our price," he said with sadness. "I've been caught doing something stupid. By playing ball I wiped my slate clean and was able to retire with full benefits."

"Who saw the Humvee?" I asked.

Remy looked me in the face, gave me a tired grin, and told me.

* * *

Edward flew us back to California the next day. My Pathfinder greeted me with glee—at least I imagined that it did—when I got inside it. The dashboard showed 1:42 PM and my belly demanded food. I picked up a burger at a local drive through joint. I ate it while I drove home, up the Highway 38. Just before my turn, a solitary figure of a woman, walking on a shoulder of the highway, attracted my attention. She was about a quarter of a mile ahead of me and beyond my turn. I stopped the Pathfinder and picked up my Nikon Monarch Binoculars. The heavy rubberized optical instrument brought the woman's head within arms' reach. Her red hair moved from side to side as she walked. She turned slightly to adjust the weight of her large backpack and her face came into my field glasses clearly. She was the same woman I had run into inside the Lee's Convenience Market and the Blue Lyon's Diner. I thought about catching up with her and offering a ride, but decided against it.

Once home, I went straight to my computer and began a news search for the name Remy had given me. The witness had been an up-and-coming television actor who died five years ago. I found tons of news coverage. The police had discovered his dead body—riddled with 9mm slugs—in the living room of his Malibu home. I checked the dates carefully. Someone had ran Jack Perez off the motorcycle three weeks earlier.

The Los Angels Sheriff's detectives found the actor's murderer quick. The Hollywood media described the killer as a "sadistic gay lover" of the victim. Bryson Milroy had pled guilty to the second degree murder charge. I kept looking through the news stories. Apparently, two years into the eight-year sentence, he committed suicide. My mouse continued its travels through the e-world until a jailhouse interview, Milroy had given just a few weeks before his death, caught my eye. This bucket of worms was getting deeper and deeper.

Jollywoodgosip.com

Q – Bryson, are telling us now that you did not kill your boyfriend?
A – I loved him, man (crying). I wouldn't hurt a hair on his head. I worshiped him.
Q – Why did you confess to the murder then?
A – It's complicated. I owed money to these people. These radical dudes, you know. So they tell me that if I to set up a meeting with my boy and them, just social picture taking type thing, they'd give me a pass.
Q – Did you set up the meeting?
A – Yaaah (sobbing). We waited for them to come to our Malibu pad. Instead of my dudes some other dudes in green camouflage uniforms busted in and shot the place up. I hid in the closet but they pulled me out and put this gun in my hands and laughed. "You tell the cops you killed him," they said. "Or we'll come back for you next..."

"...Do not tell secrets to those whose faith and silence you have not already tested..."

Elizabeth I (1533–1603), Queen of England (1558-1603). As quoted in The Sayings of Queen Elizabeth, ch. 11, by Frederick Chamberlin (1923).

Fall 2004

Chapter Six

Secrets

The day turned into an evening quickly. My body trembled with energy but my mind failed to find a comfortable place. As if they had an ability to make decisions on their own, my feet took me out of my home and up my favorite foot trail. It runs in the back of my property, all the way up a pine-wooded hill. I climbed eagerly in the darkness and all my senses came online—if you pardon my computer analogy, my dear reader—big time. This is how I imagined our primeval ancestors felt before the civilization separated us from the wilderness. For countless millennia they were along against the tremendous force of elements. "What if the wilderness was all there was? Would I survive?" I asked myself while my legs carried me up the trail.

The answer came in a form of a memory. Good Lord gives us pop quizzes once in a while, my dad had told when I was a kid once. On that occasion, thirty-five years ago, eight-year-old me put some glue in my eye rather than on a school project. I remembered the pain and my father's low frequency voice, "Pull yourself together, big guy. It will hurt like a son of a bitch. But you'll take it. This is your test. God gives those to us without warning, we have no time to prepare. So clinch you teeth and act like a man."

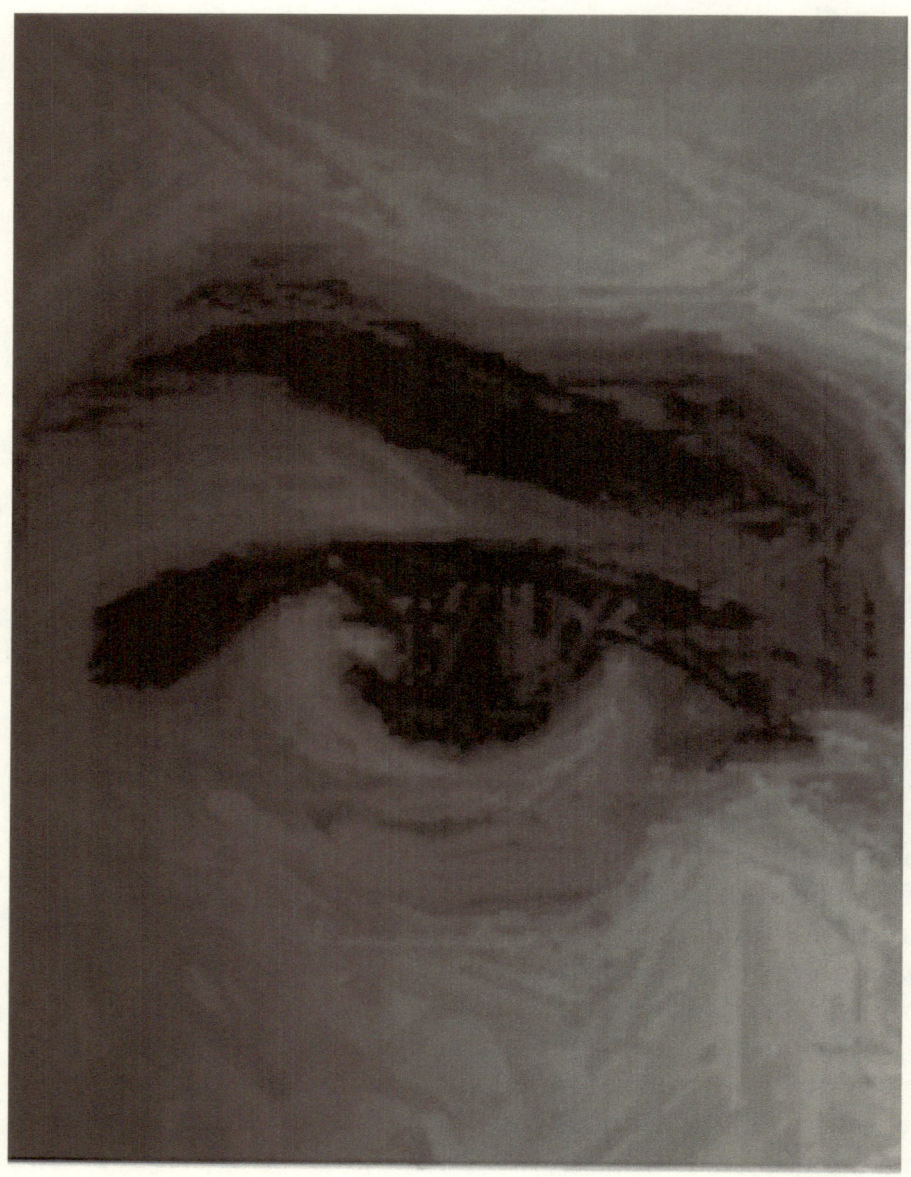

The memory of my effort to "pull myself together" made my legs move faster, with more energy. The incident had concluded when an emergency room doctor removed a small piece of solidified glue from my eye. I had sustained no permanent injury. What the physician could not remove, my dear reader, was the philosophy of the pain. It is a rich and interesting subject. The pain can hurt, and it can bring pleasure, and it can...

But I digress...

I was in pain now. The kind which hurts but not the variety which attacks our flesh. No. The pain I felt went deeper. If you see our world as one busy highway, my life was taking it's place on the shoulder. I saw many a man pass by in the fast lane—prestigious jobs, good looking wives, smart kids. These people hired men like me to clean up their messes so they could keep speeding down that highway, happy and proud.

"Why can't I be like them?" I asked myself.

"Because you're not willing to give up something. That something which lets you do things which those fast-lane men can't," the answer came.

My mind wondered in various directions until it stopped at the strange woman I had seen in the market and the diner two days ago and, then, on the Highway 38 earlier today. She seemed familiar somehow. My gray matter came up with no memories, however.

By the time I reached the crest of the hill, the pain left, replaced with fatigue. I went down a different path. When I entered my home again—three hours after I left—Alicia Keys CD went into my stereo. While her throaty voice reverberated in my eardrums, I eased into the hot bathtub.

* * *

Rose Perez called next morning, 9:02 AM.

"Marty, I want you to work for me no longer," she said.

"How come?" I asked.

"It has nothing to do with you. You've been great. Some cops came over earlier and explained that all of this was a mistake. Jack died in 1999 and that's that. I already mailed you your fee," she said and hung up.

I shrugged my shoulders and tried to let go of the case. Surprisingly, the case did not want to let go of me. I had too many unanswered questions. I hate injustice. My gut told me that Jack Perez found himself facing the business end of some slimy government intrigue. His two deaths were no mistake. Someone was covering up something unpleasant. But, Rose fired me and I had no reason to continue. I cleared my mind and started on the cases with clients.

By the time the hands of my watch showed 10:16 AM, I craved a La Gloria Cubana Pyramid something terrible.

Since I smoked my last one yesterday, I had to make a trip to the Lee's Convenience Market again. When I parked in front it, a black Chrysler 300 pulled up behind me—blocking my exit—and two men in dark suits came out of it. I stepped out of my Pathfinder and faced them.

"You are Marty Greenblatt, aren't you?" one of them enquired.

"Who'd like to know?" I asked rudely.

"Homeland Security, Mr. Greenblatt," said the other one and showed his ID.

"What do you want?"

"Please follow us to San Bernardino," the first Homeland Security agent said. "Our supervisor wants to have lunch with you."

Our destination turned out to be the plush El Deseo Hotel, downtown San Bernardino. The man, I was brought to see, waited for me in the hotel's restaurant. His minions stayed back as he got up.

"My name is Stanley Greene," he introduced himself. The man looked to be in his sixties, thin with distinguished air about him. "I am the Under Secretary for Science and Technology in the Department of Homeland Security."

I shook his hand hard. Greene looked the part of a Washington D.C. bureaucrat. I had no love for his class of people, but I knew also that I can't afford to show my disdain. We had a polite conversation about weather and sports all through the lunch. He ordered grilled chicken salad and I asked for a porterhouse steak.

"You must wonder why I brought you here?" he asked finally.

"The question crossed my mind."

"You had touched on a raw nerve when you started asking questions about Jack Perez," Greene said.

"Why?"

"Let's say that the name of Jack Perez transcends the regular way business is done in our country and takes us somewhere where we shouldn't go," he answered cryptically. "I know who you are. You have a great reputation. You have served your country well in the past and I have no doubts that you will do so with distinction again, if called upon."

The Under Secretary looked at me with the expression of a football coach who knows that he needs to bench one his best players but finds it difficult.

"Mr. Greenblatt, for the time being, forget about everything you found out about Jack Perez. It is a problem for the people like me to handle. Who knows, we may need your help on this one some day. But I hope not."

Before we parted, Greene put a slip of paper into my breast pocket. "If you ever encounter something which defies explanation on the global level," he said. "Contact the man whose information I just gave you."

Andrei V. Lefebvre

Part Two

Highway Picks Up Speed

"...Imagination is built upon knowledge, and his dreams will rest upon his facts. He is worth to the world just about what he has learned from it, and no more ..."

Elizabeth Stuart Phelps (1844–1911), U.S. novelist and short story writer. Chapters from a Life, ch. 11 (1897).

January 2008

Chapter Seven

The Morning Call

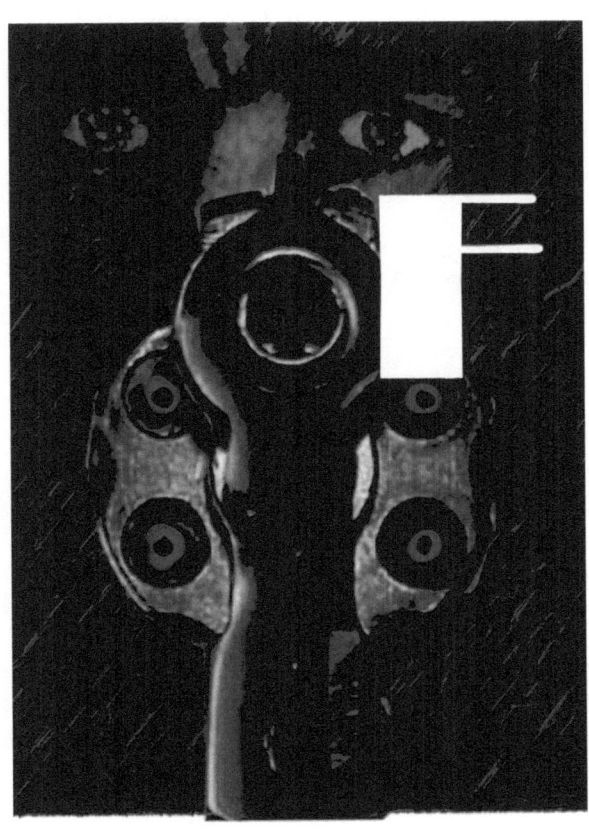

our years passed since my lunch with the Under Secretary. The Jack Perez affair faded from my memory as the new cases took up the front burners of my mind. I continued my way up the highway of life without a clue that the fog of the unknown concealed something huge blocking the road just ahead. As always, the change came when I least expected it.

An upbeat jingle of my cell phone interrupted a bad dream one winter morning. The nightmare—which I have often—echoed what had happened years ago. In the dream, the young me is in hot pursuit of a dangerous man, I worked for the Uncle Sam then. All I see of him are his eyes—dark, wide open, and menacing. I also eyeball the void of his pistol's business end pointed at my partner. I know that I need to step forward for a better aim and fire first. I never do because something hits me on the back of my head and a feeling of nausea freezes me. The bad guy's muzzle explodes into an orange ball before I react. The dream never goes anywhere after that because I wake up at this point in cold sweat.

During the actual incident, fifteen years back, my partner sustained a fatal wound to his chest. I never could shake the guilt off. Even the fact that I came out of my stupor and pumped the killer full of the government-issue lead altered nothing.

The cell phone, just like a nagging wife, demanded attention though. I fumbled for it and growled into this self-important gadget while clearing my throat, "Greenblatt."

"Marty, did I wake you?" a mocking voice of Bobby DiCesare came through crisply and jeeringly. "I am soooooo sorry my little dear."

He let go a hearty laugh.

Bobby and I go back a long way. When we were twenty-year-old punks with no brains, we served in the same Special Forces unit. Later, both of us bootlegged for a supper secret government agency. Since it was kept hidden from the Congress and funded covertly from less than reputable sources, we had some very interesting missions. One of those had resulted in my reoccurring nightmare, by the way.

"What do you need this early in the morning?" I asked Bobby.

"Some people want to talk at you."

"Who?"

"Can't say on the air," Bobby's voice turned serious. "Be in my office in two hours. Bye."

Bobby clicked off before my acknowledgment. I opened my eyes and the bedroom came into view. The four bare walls wished me good morning. The radio clock, on my nightstand, reported that the time was 4:53 AM. I looked at the old framed picture of my parents which stood next to the clock. Something in my mother's eyes made me uneasy. I felt like she was trying to warn me about something.

I shook my head, getting rid of the uneasiness, picked up an Arturo Fuentes Double Corona, and struck a long wooden match. The cigars like to be warm before you take the first drag. Why? Well, my dear reader, it's a subject for another tale.

As I glided the flame under the tobacco, I analyzed the phone call. Bobby would not yank me out my slumber just for fun. Something heavy duty must have fallen on his lap. Furthermore, this something must have been unexpected. My cigar happily burned as I puffed on it.

While taking a shower, I searched my memory for any red flags. I could find nothing which would trigger a call like that. My slacks and a white dress shirt did not have an opinion on the subject either. I decided against a necktie but put on my wool sports jacket. Before leaving, I walked into my den, which served as my office, and checked the e-mail. Nothing.

My private investigator's license on the, otherwise, bare wall, had an idea. The embossed California state seal reminded me that Washington D.C. time ran three hours ahead of the West Coast. Bobby must have gotten a call from his friends in that time zone. This was a workable theory. Since I have done nothing recently to provoke the East Coast's powers that be, my internal alarm bells went off. I put on a shoulder holster and picked out Smith & Wesson Model 59 from the gun safe.

When I got behind the steering wheel of my Pathfinder, the dashboard clock showed 5:29 AM and the San Grigonio Mountain still concealed the unstoppable rise of the January sun. I live at 4,000 feet above the sea level. The city of Silver Springs snakes along the Highway 38. The Los Angeles area suburbanites use this road as a back door to a popular skiing resort at the Big Bear Lake.

I drove down my dirt driveway—which traverses much of my four-acre lot—coasted down a winding mountain road, and made it onto the hardtop of the Highway 38. Even at this early hour, the highway packed busy traffic. The winter snow had attracted skiers from the Southern California's beach cities. Thankfully, today was Tuesday and most of the cars sped uphill, whereas my destination was the City of Redlands, at the feet of the San Bernardino and San Grigonio Mountains.

As my Pathfinder rolled downhill, I checked the rear view mirrors. I saw no tail. This fact did not mean that no one was following me. But I felt better nevertheless.

Twenty minutes later, the Highway 38 became Lugonia Boulevard, a major thoroughfare of the City of Redlands.

Bobby's office was on the top floor of one of the Redlands' few office buildings. As I parked the Pathfinder in front of this four-story structure, my pocket watch—I hate anything on my wrists—told me that the time was 6:18 AM. I was about forty minutes early. My calculations paid off, Bobby's Jaguar was parked in the parking spot which sported a sign "Reserved for Guzman, Swartz, and DiCesare Partners Only." I walked up to the fourth floor and ushered myself into Bobby's suite.

"I am glad you got here early," he greeted me.

Bobby wore a dark pinstriped suit with a bright yellow power tie. He looked like a shark lawyer that he really was. We walked into his private office and I saw a vaguely familiar man sitting in a visitor's couch. He wore dark blue cotton slacks, dusty cowboy boots, and cream-colored shirt. A bulge on the right side of his beltline suggested a sidearm.

"Bobby, you know Jose Gonzalez," said Bobby and the man stood up.

We shook hands and I remembered him. Jose was a few years younger than I and had joined my Airborne unit about six months before Bobby and I had left the regular service.

"Hey, Marty," said Jose and tapped his index finger on my left lapel, "I see you are packing too."

"Jose is with the Treasury," said Bobby easing his posterior into a plush leather chair behind a massive lawyer's desk. "He's with the Secret Service to be exact."

He opened a huge mahogany humidor on his desk and offered cigars. I picked out a La Gloria Cubana Pyramid and fired it up with my lighter. Jose did the same to his Onyx Churchill.

"The reason I called you both into the office before our guests show up is because I don't want either one of you to be blindsided," said Bobby. "Jose, let Marty know what you have and I'll fill in the rest."

Jose pulled out a thick file from his briefcase and thumbed through it.

"I've been working with the counterfeit currency for the last ten years," he said in a low voice. "About nine years ago we intercepted almost one hundred thousand in the U.S. one hundred bills. Neither me nor anyone else at the Treasury have ever seen such perfect fakes."

Jose handed me several photographs depicting the bills.

"Not only the printing is perfect but the paper is the same cotton based pulp used for the real bills. We analyzed the ink. It came up identical to the Treasury specifications too," Jose stopped to take a deep drag from his Onyx Churchill.

"How did you know that these dead presidents were counterfeit then?" I asked.

Jose gave me a hard stare and then looked at my lawyer friend.

"Remember when Sean Smith bought it?" asked Bobby, referring to my nightmare's dead partner. "You and him worked some super secret 'if I tell you, I'll have to kill you' operation no one ever wants to talk about. But you know that obviously. What you probably don't know, however, is that during the same time another super secret operation had confiscated almost three million in one hundred-dollar bills. The money was put into the evidence vault here in the ATF office in Redlands. The reason I know is because I placed it there."

Bobby paused to light up his cigar and pointed it at Jose to continue the story.

"We ran a routine serial number check and it redflagged on the cash which came from Bobby's dirtbags," Jose said. "We thought it was that money. I went and checked. That money was still in the vault but all of the fakes' serial numbers duplicated the real cash."

I took a long drag from my La Gloria Cubana. "So far so good," I said.

"Not that good," Bobby retorted. "The Secret Service had found your fingerprints on the fake money. Your friends in the high and low places vouched for you back then and you were never officially a suspect in anything. Officially. But now..."

"Tell him who else left prints on the fake money," interrupted Jose.

Instead of answering Bobby stood up and looked through a large office window.

"They are here," he said.

U.S. Department of Homeland Security

TOP SECRET

Confidential Memorandum

To: Stanley E. Green
From: Vincent Lee
Subject: Greenblatt A2 (Project Mark Foxtrot)

Per request from the Secretary of the Science and Technology, I have conducted a discreet background investigation of the subject Martin A. Greenblatt A2 (referred bellow as GREENBLATT). Here are my findings:

GREENBLATT's full name is Martin Andrew Greenblatt. He is a single (never married) man, 5 feet 11 inches tall, and approximately 180 pounds in weight. He has no unusual identifying marks with Light completion, dark brown hair, and hazel eyes. GREENBLATT prefers to be called Marty.

He was born on Dec. 8, 1963 in Los Angeles, CA to Joseph A. Greenblatt and Laura V. Greenblatt (Ozerski/maiden name). GREENBLATT graduated from the Fairfax High School (Los Angeles) in 1980 and immediately enlisted into the U.S. Army. After basic training, he entered the Special Forces Training Program at Fort Bragg which he successfully completed.

Our subject served with distinction until 1988 as an active duty enlisted man and non-

commissioned officer, reaching an E-6 pay
grade. Even though the record of his orders
remains sealed as of the day of this
memorandum, our Pentagon assets report that he
has been assigned missions in the former Warsaw
Block territories and Arab Middle East.
Furthermore, we know from a public copy of his
military service record that he has received
two Purple Heart medals, the Legion of Merit,
and the Department of Defense Distinguished
Service medal.

After his honorable discharge, dated Nov 17,
1988, GREENBLATT has attended the California
State University Long Beach campus until June
16 1989. After this date, neither I nor any of
my investigators have found any records of his
whereabouts until Feb. 19, 1994 when GREENBLATT
took residence in Silver Springs, California.

Our Treasury Department asset believes that he
has been involved in the Remove Claws Operation
(conduced off the books by the White House).
Our Langley asset had confirmed this
assessment, even though his information is
third- or forth-hand.

Side Note : *It is my belief that the Remove
Claws Operation lies at the crux of Mark
Foxtrot. GREENBLAT may be in the focal area of
the mark's Alfa Point since he shows a
significant variation in his divergence from A1
during this period.*

Two Highways

Since Feb. 19, 1994, GREENBLATT has maintained residence in the rural Silver Springs. He has obtained a California Private Investigator's License. GREENBLATT's listed office is his residence. He does not advertise his services and has few clients. GREEBLATT's primary source of income is a retainer agreement with the Guzman, Swartz, and DiCesare law firm in Redlands, California (15 miles away from his residence). Pre-M/F Robert D. DiCesare (one of the firm's major partners in A2TL) and our subject have served in the same Special Forces unit, according to DiCesare A1. Moreover, the same A1 believes that DiCesare A2 has never left the U.S. Government employment but provides services in the "unofficial" capacity under the cover of his law firm.

DiCesare A2 and A1 (who converged positively) are against bringing GREENBLATT into M/F confidence. The reason given has nothing to do with the GREENBLATT's potential contribution to the project, but is based on a sentimental desire to shield an old friend from harm. I am convinced, however, that GREENBLATT can become an invaluable asset.

I have no reason to believe that GREENBLATT has ever converged with his A1 (who no longer exists) nor is aware of Mark Foxtrot. As such, my recommendation is to treat him as "friend" and use his skills and expertise accordingly.

"...Our village life would stagnate if it were not for the unexplored forests and meadows which surround it ..."

Henry David Thoreau (1817–1862), U.S. philosopher, author, naturalist. Walden (1854), in The Writings of Henry David Thoreau, vol. 2, pp. 349-350, Houghton Mifflin (1906).

January 2008

Chapter Eight

Our Visitors

T wo identical older model black Cadillac stretch jobs and one white Ford Crown Victoria sedan parked in front of the building. Four crewcutted men in dark suits got out from the Crown Victoria and fanned out throughout the parking area, assuming the century duty. Four more of their clones stepped out from the stretch jobs. Two of them walked inside the building and into Bobby's suite. They nodded to Bobby slightly and examined Jose and I with suspicious, probing looks.

"I need take you weapons for the duration of the meeting," one of the men told us in a deep emotionless voice.

I looked at Bobby; he smiled faintly and winked.

"Okay," said Jose and handed the man his Glock.

I forced myself to smile and surrendered my Smith & Wesson. The crewcuts seemed to relax somewhat. Just like dutiful hounds, they went through Bobby's suite checking every room for danger.

"Clear," said the taller man into his throat mike, after they finished. He gave Bobby, Jose and I a disapproving look. "You have to get rid of your cigars. She don't like the smell."

"Forget the cigars, chief..." Bobby said with a steel edge to his voice. "Let's get the show on the road. You came to see us, we didn't come to you."

Moments later, the two bodyguards ushered a distinguished looking woman into the suite. I recognized her immediately. Even though I have never met the lady before, I knew who she was. Our guest of importance was a highly-placed White House official.

"Where are the Stanleys?" she asked.

Stanley Greene, the Homeland Security Undersecretary, came in right behind her and smiled. Then, I saw another man walk in. I had to blink several times before I agreed with what I saw. The second man looked exactly like Under Secretary Greene. Identical!

"Let's sit down and talk, gentlemen," the second Stanley Greene said in a raspy voice.

Bobby, both Under Secretaries, White House official, and I walked inside a large lawyer's conference room. The doors closed behind us. Everyone else, including Jose, stayed outside.

"No need for introductions, we know who we are already," said one of the Stanley Greenes—I couldn't tell which one anymore, they looked too much alike—after we sat down behind a long conference table. The lady White House official had a blank expression on her face.

"We need your help desperately," Greene continued. "We found ourselves in a circumstance where we can trust only a handful of people."

"What exactly can we do for you?" asked Bobby.

"Imagine a situation where any of the people—you have grown to depend on—may not be who they actually are," said another Stanley Greene. "Further, imagine that some of these people may be in the highest positions of power."

Bobby got up and opened a small refrigerator, snugly hidden in the corner of the room.

"Soft drinks, or something more potent?" he asked with a smile.

"Coke, please," the lady White House official said.

No one else spoke.

"Mr. DiCesare is one of the people whom we trust completely. This is why we asked him to contact you," she said, after taking several sips and looked me in the eyes. "I know that you Mr. Greenblatt is our friend too."

"I can't give you the big picture, because ..." the first Greene said with the pained look of a man trying to explain the birds and the bees to a child. "... because," he paused again, "... you need to figure it out by yourself to believe it."

He smiled at me and took the thick-lens glasses off.

"Mr. Greenblatt, you have a reputation of a man who can solve problems which defy solution..." he continued and left the sentence fade into silence.

No one spoke for exactly one minute and forty five-seconds. I timed the absence of conversation using the second hand of a fancy wall clock in the room. I took several deep drags from what was left of my cigar. It glowed embers for a while and then went out.

"How can I be of help?" I asked reluctantly, breaking the uncomfortable halt in the conversation.

"Mr. Greenblatt, we need you to do an intense search for a very dangerous object. A number of important people are involved. Your inquiries may produce some political implications and ferret out some unpleasant people. You need to find this object, we refer to it as 'the beacon,' quick. You've been down this road once already," the same Under Secretary said.

He looked at me waiting for a reaction. When I said nothing, he asked, "Remember Operation Remove Claws?"

Since the mission he referred to never took place officially, I kept my mouth shut but nodded ever so very slightly.

"You will find that your new assignment may parallel, if you will, the Remove Claws," Stanley smiled.

"Were do I start? What is this beacon?" I asked.

"The beacon is a part of a network we inherited from the Cold War. I don't know what it looks like exactly. To what it is ..." Stanley paused in indecision. "Well, let's say it can produce some unusual effects."

"Marty, listen," Bobby cut in, looking like a man who would rather be anywhere else but in this meeting. "Start checking for weird incidents along the Highway 38 from Redlands all the way up to Big Bear in recent months. This situation of ours is so sensitive, you can't be cleared to hear the details. But I know how you do things. You'll figure it out yourself soon and leave us room for the deniability of involvement."

"Thank you, Mr. DiCesare," both Greens said in unison, visibly relieved.

"And now, Mr. Greenblatt, please wait outside; we need to discuss something in confidence with Mr. DiCesare," the lady White House official said with a smile.

The conference room remained silent as I walked out and closed the door behind me.

* * *

The explosion came at me in the form of a reverberating air concussion. My eardrums did not pick up the sound. My body, however, felt the tremendous disturbance of the air. The time slowed down as soon as my eyes saw a bright, glinting yellow light expand into a white-hot ball and scorch my face with its edges.

As the shock wave slammed me into the wall, I saw my guardian angel for a moment. I shall tell more about him in another tale, my dear reader. This angel must have worked overtime, during these fractions of a second, because I did not lose my connection with the real world completely. Nevertheless, my vision blurred and the sounds of the heavenly trumpets rang in my ears. I shook my head to clear out the interference and the suite's reception area came back into better focus. The ringing in my ears did not stop but the report my eyes gave me turned my self-preservation instinct on.

My shaking hand reached for the Smith & Wesson and I was stunned to discover an empty holster. My eyes closed in disbelief but the memory of the taller crewcut taking my gun away emerged slowly. Now, his lifeless torso was on the—once plush—carpet. His partner was dead too, not too far away. Both men took the full brunt of the explosion. Their blood and body parts littered the reception area.

After picking through the gore of the mutilated bodies, I found the small leather bag where the crewcuts had stored my gun. The cool hardness of the Model 59 grips stopped the ringing in my ears and brought me back to the real time. I looked around for Jose, but found only the blood soaked pieces of his Hawaiian shirt.

Moments later, Bobby emerged from the conference room, his .44 magnum cannon in hand. His eyes scanned the reception area carefully and an adrenaline-induced smile of excitement lit up his face.

"Take our guests to the roof," said Bobby in a business like fashion, as if asking me to make a food run. "I'll deal with the situation here. Your job is to keep them in one piece. I was ready for something like this and planned another exit avenue."

My peripheral vision picked up movements to the right. They came at us quick. My body reacted by diving on the floor by pure instinct. A swarm of nine-millimeter slugs whined through the space my torso had occupied just a fraction of a second before. I plopped on the blood soaked carpet and—on the way down—my eyes registered the three men in green camouflage fatigues. Their arms vibrated with the recoil of Heckler & Koch MP5 submachine guns. They made a mistake by keeping the selectors in the automatic fire setting. Such choice proved unfortunate for them. The gunmen could aim only the first round accurately, the rest went astray. Under the traditional combat conditions it was acceptable. In the close-quarter fighting situation, however, such choice was a kiss of death. As soon as I could site my Smith & Wesson, I squeezed two rounds into the first camouflaged forehead. He fell backwards into the second gunman, forcing him to stop firing. Bobby let the hammer fall on his Ruger Super Redhawk from somewhere to my left. His .44 slug entered the second gunmen through the cheekbone and took the back of his head away on exit.

The third gunman continued spraying the suite with his submachine gun but began backing out. I heard some faint yelling coming from the outside. The bad guy fired one more automatic burst and fled.

"Okay Marty," Bobby said, his adrenaline smile still on. "Change in plans. I'll take our guests to the roof. You cover me."

He motioned for the lady White House Official and both Stanley Greenes to follow him. Their four figures disappeared into the stairwell leading up to the roof. I, in turn, began my slow descent down. Thankfully, no unpleasant surprises waited for me.

The parking lot looked like a

battle field. One of the black stretch jobs burned profusely. My guess was that it had sustained a direct hit from an anti-tank grenade. The other limousine sat on four flat tires, body and windows full of bullet holes. Four black-suited crewcuts sprawled dead on the pavement. I looked around for the white Crown Victoria but found it gone.

Before I had time check the condition of my Pathfinder, a "tap, tap" sound of the helicopter's blades came from the top of the roof. Three General Electric CT7-6 turbo shaft engines made a swishing noise as the EH101 bird descended and picked up our guests. The turbine's wine increased in intensity and pushed the helicopter up off the roof. It clipped away into the westerly direction.

I heard footsteps behind me. "Stand down Marty," said Bobby, no longer sporting his smile of excitement. "The fun's over. Now we wait for the cops."

The Redlands Police Department did not keep us in suspense. A chorus of sirens came from all directions. Soon, a red-blue-and-yellow light show of the police cruisers surrounded us. Bobby and I greeted the cops with our open hands in the air. The last thing I wanted was to be shot by a trigger happy rookie.

We were frisked, relived of our guns, handcuffed, and placed in the back of separate police cars. Since we were the obvious suspects in a carnage before them, the police followed an age old tactic of separating the defendants to prevent the collaboration of stories.

My imprisonment did not last long. A tall uniformed cop with gold lieutenant's bars on his navy blue lapels opened the back door of the police sedan and let me out. His brass nameplate read "Cook." He unlocked my handcuffs in silence. A cop with the sergeant's stripes freed Bobby, who walked over to me.

"Mr. DiCesare and Mr. Greenblatt, what we have here is crap," the Lieutenant said in a quiet voice, doing his best to contain his fury. He appeared to be his late forties, tall, fit, with the look of a man experienced in the law enforcement politics. "I happened to know who both of you are. What took place here is reprehensible. Redlands is a nice quiet community. I can't have firefights in the middle of my city."

He shook his head violently. "The Chief called me personally and assigned me to control this bucket of worms. Clean yourselves up and come to my office tomorrow morning. Early. Don't stiff me. I have ways of making your life miserable if you don't help."

The man made a parade-perfect about face and marched towards the cluster of cops at the entrance to the office building.

"…Than smoke and mist who better could appraise
The kindred spirit of an inner haze?"

Robert Frost (1874–1963), American poet. "A Cabin in the Clearing."

January 2008

Chapter Nine

Two Girls and a Horse

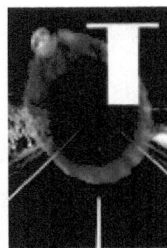he scorching shower babied my body until the hot water ran out. To my surprise, my morning adventure left me with minor injuries only, a few bruises and a long scratch on my neck. When I started drying myself with a huge bath towel, the wall clock in my bathroom reported 11:37 AM.

The shower brought all my senses back full force and a vicious headache started its evil work on my right temple. I took three Tylenol with Codeine capsules, cleared my mind, and stretched on the couch in my living room.

Soon, the pills' opiates closed my eyes and the dreams took over. My parents sat at the kitchen table in the house I grew up in. I was a boy again and my dad and I discussed baseball. My mom said nothing in this dream but looked at me with her soft brown eyes full of the unconditional love. More dreams came and left without leaving anything memorable behind. Finally, the dangerous man from many years ago menaced my partner with his gun again and I stood paralyzed, unable to move a muscle. Just then, the familiar upbeat tune extinguished the nightmare.

For the second time today, my cell phone woke me up before the dream's bad guy fired his weapon.

"Greenblatt!" I yelled into the hated gadget.

"Marty, are you okay?" a friendly baritone inquired.

"Do bears crap in the woods?" I answered with an attempt to sound jovial. As the words came out of my mouth, I recognized the voice. The man on the other end of this call was Eddie Sobaleff. This upwardly mobile young detective was in my "good people" file. He worked for the San Bernardino Sheriff's Department and made a detective four years ago. He had a sharp mind and great political instincts. If I was a betting man, and I am, I would have bet—and I had in more ways than one—that Eddie would be elected Sheriff some day.

"Marty, we need to talk," Eddie's friendly voice had a hard edge to it. "I'm standing in your driveway. Open the door."

The wall clock showed 4:11 PM when I let him in.

"Sorry to wake you up, partner," said Eddie and I think he smiled; the darkness of my house made it difficult to see.

I drew the drapes back, letting the late afternoon sun in, and offered the detective a La Gloria Cubana Double Corona. Without saying a word, Eddie lit up with his silver lighter and took several deep drags. I started a cigar of my own. The taste of tobacco woke me up completely.

"What have you gotten yourself into?" Eddie asked, giving me his all-knowing grin. Eddie was an experienced interrogator. He used such friendly facial expression to stimulate suspects into talking. He wasted it on me, though.

"I wish I knew," I said truthfully.

"Do you realize that this is the first multiple homicide in the City of Redlands since... since a long, long time? Longer than my memory takes me," Eddie said turning his grin in to a formal smile.

"Why does the Sheriff's Department lose sleep over the incorporated city problems?" I asked because Eddie was a deputy sheriff serving the unincorporated county's geography. The City of Redlands had its own police force.

"Ordinarily, we wouldn't give a flying rat's banana," said Eddie and let out several smoke rings which gracefully rose to the ceiling, increasing in size. Just like portals to another world, a thought popped into my mind. "Your shootout in the Okay Corral, slash downtown of the bedroom community capitol of our county, is huge news. I had a meeting with one of the Sheriff's right-hand men. He told me that the Redlands P.D. found some radical crap at the crime scene. Also, some heavy duty East Coast spook crew came down and sealed much of the evidence in the name of the 'national security.' I was told that the Redlands' Chief of Police is having kittens over this situation. All this crap makes my people edgy too, and my people include more than just the Sheriff. You have to understand that such crimes and the Fed's involvement upset the local political status quo."

We talked for an hour before Eddie left with an obvious disappointment written all over his face. I gave him no details about the morning's shooting. I felt disappointment as well. Today's events did not give me the warm and fuzzy filling of safety and security. My pocket watch showed 5:03 PM when I saw the taillights of Eddie's unmarked Chrysler disappear into the early evening's darkness.

Ten minutes later, I started down the hill to the convenience market on foot—police impounded my Pathfinder as evidence—and reflected on the Eddie's visit as I walked. He was right, the local powers-that-be could not allow shooting wars in their streets. I had no doubts that the San Bernardino County politicians had busied the phone lines to the Washington D.C. all day. When the calls produced no results, they had to send Eddie to pump me for information. I gave him—and them consequently —nothing. But, I too, knew nothing. Yet.

My destination was a mile and a half away, at the foot of the Silver Springs Hill. There, the Silver Springs Avenue, the sole public street of the town, runs into the Highway 38, just like a minor tributary feeds a large river.

Walking requires much different navigation skills than driving. The community of Silver Springs has no streetlights. The darkness, exacerbated by the shadows of the pine trees made the street indistinguishable from the long driveways forking away. I had to stop and turn around several times because I had taken the splinter paths, mistaking them for the street.

The memory of a fifteen-year-old manhunt came to my mind. It took place about the same time of the year. It was the incident which started my nightmares. Back then, I had been a part of a secret and, more than likely, illegal spook mission. My orders were to recover a device, believed to be a prototype energy weapon. Since all the information was given to my team on the "need to know" basis, I have never learned the origins of this wonder gadget. The people, purportedly in possession of the device, were a shadowy terrorist crew. For the same "need to know" reasons, I was never told what kind of terrorists they were. Sean Smith, my old partner, died when we caught up with one of their associates.

My gait turned into a military marching step as I remembered that nauseating feeling—I had experienced during the shootout—which stopped me from moving forward, putting the killer into my gun sights, and squeezing the trigger. Only a superhuman mental effort, during those few seconds, had helped me brake through the daze. Once in full control of my body again, I shot my target twice in the heart and once in the back of the head. Too late! Sean had expired by then. The sad part about the whole affair was that his death had been in vain. We found no exotic weapons on the guy I shot. The only thing we recovered was the bad guy's backpack. It contained several conventional firearms, a change of underwear, shaving kit, and a large clumsy electronic apparatus which looked like an old radio with several dials. I had no idea what it was. But I knew what it was not. That device could not have been an energy weapon.

There was an odd part to this shoot out. Just before shooting my partner, the terrorist threw a plastic egg-shaped radio transmitter at me. Actually, I never saw him throw it, it just struck me on the back of my head and I assumed that he threw it. The stupid thing was too light to cause injury and it broke apart on contact.

Before I knew it, the Lee's Convenience Market came at me like a brightly lit island of civilization in the middle of the primordial darkness. This small trading post, on the shoulder of a busy highway, offered the standard staple of canned foods, liquor, and excellent selection of tobacco products. I nodded to Mr. Lee, the proprietor, and dove into the moist paradise of the temperature controlled walk-in humidor. The treasure-throve of fine cigars greeted me from the shelves. I let my nose focus on the exquisite tobacco fragrances and my eyes feast on the perfections of the cigar shapes. The combination of these two powerful stimuli diverted my attention from the outside world. Not for long, however, because my ears picked up Mr. Lee's voice. I could not make out the words but the irritation came through loud and clear.

I walked closer to the glass door of the walk-in humidor. From this position, I could see the front counter clearly. Mr. Lee stood behind it, gesturing with his hands and saying something angrily to two girls in front of him. The older one looked to be in her early teens. She stood with her right arm extended, a roll of green bills clutched in her hand. The other girl appeared to be eight or nine. She held her hands pressed together to her chest as if whatever she and her older friend wanted held a great significance. Both of the young ladies were dressed in blue jeans, cowboy style boots and denim jackets with fake white fur collars. The fact that the back of their bell-bottomed jeans covered the heels of the boots, Texas style, made me think that they were acquainted with horses. When I walked out of the humidor, my equine theory became stronger because of a faint horse manure smell emanating from these girls.

"But, Mr. Lee," pleaded the older girl. "Let me have all four cases. I'm payin' ain't I?"

"You should've called me and told me that you're coming. I can't let you have all the Spam and canned pork with beans I have," Mr. Lee grumbled. "My delivery is not 'till two days after tomorrow. I can't have empty shelves."

Just at that moment both girls heard my footsteps and turned their heads. I found nothing remarkable abut their faces until I saw the eyes. Their eyes reached deep into me. I felt as if I have seen both of them before. A powerful notion—that I knew the girls well—ran through my mind like a loud sax note through a lullaby. No matter how much I strained my gray matter, however, no such memories surfaced. What made the situation even stranger was the fact that they seemed to be as shaken as I was.

"It's not really him," I heard the older girl whisper to the younger girl, who kept staring at me with the expression of hope and sadness on her face. We stood still for a few more moments, frozen in a mutual discomfort.

"Mr. Lee, please take the boxes to the back where our cart is," said the older girl finally and pulled the younger one out of the convenience store by her hand.

"I'll be back soon. It won't take long," Mr. Lee said to me, frowning. He, then, put the girls' money into the cash register and walked to the rear of the store. I heard him grunting in the back, as if he was picking something heavy up. I felt a cold draft, which was probably set loose by the open back door. A loud crash of the same door slamming shut made me jump. I paid for my cigars and left the store as soon as Mr. Lee returned.

The darkness made the Highway 38 look surreal. Its sparse traffic appeared distant and foreign. I saw the irony of our vain human belief in the superiority of technology over the magnificent power of nature. The people driving uphill to the ski resort were enveloped in the civilization's thin veneer, ending abruptly outside of their luxury cars and trendy sport utility vehicles. As I walked on the highway's shoulder—towards the turn which was to take me back home—I put fourth a theory to myself, just as if there were two of me philosophizing. I postulated that the San Bernardino Mountain had its own life. I further proposed to the other me that such life existed outside of our time frame. And, I concluded that the mountain did not care much for the self-centered two-legged creatures who imagined that they could rule it. The other me agreed and the power of the mountain's contempt overwhelmed both of us.

Two Highways

The headlights of a passing Mercedes erased my philosophical contemplations in an instant. The beams sliced through the dark air and let me see something absolutely unexpected. I saw a bay horse, pulling a small wagon. The wagon contained two silhouettes. The light illuminated the figures just for a fraction of a second. This brief moment, however, was enough for me to recognize the two girls from the market. They were about five hundred feet ahead of me, making a turn into the old—now abandoned and bypassed—stretch of the highway. Fifteen years ago, a large rockslide closed that road section. Instead of clearing it, Cal Trans curved the highway through the other side of the hill. A chain with the "Closed To All Traffic" sign blocked the entrance to the old path. I traveled it once, nevertheless, and found it obstructed hopelessly by the rocks about a quarter of a mile up.

The horse-drawn wagon went around the chain and entered the old highway. Curiosity made me followed it. When I entered the abandoned stretch, the cloudy sky opened up a hole for the full moon to shine down. I saw the outline of the wagon clearly in the bright moonlight. It climbed uphill slowly but with a deliberate purpose. Soon, the old highway veered to the right sharply and a steep hillside blocked my view of the wagon.

I picked up the pace of my walk. After about ten minutes, I saw the horse and the wagon again. I also spied something which made me slap my face to make sure that I was awake. A huge hollow circle of silver mist, a close cousin of the tobacco smoke rings Eddie blew earlier today, opened up in front of the horse. It floated in the air silently as the moonlight outlined the shadowy edges of this cloud-like formation. The girls drove their wagon right through the middle of this phenomenon and disappeared. I ran towards it. When I was within thirty feet, however, the nausea took me over and I had to let go of the sandwich I ate earlier. When I could lift my head up again, the wagon and the cloud were gone.

"... Phenomenal nature shadows him wherever he goes. Clouds in the staring sky transmit to one another, by means of slow signs, incredibly detailed information regarding him. His inmost thoughts are discussed at nightfall, in manual alphabet, by darkly gesticulating trees. Pebbles or stains or sunflecks form patterns representing in some awful way messages which he must intercept. Everything is a cipher and of everything he is the theme ..."

Vladimir Nabokov (1899–1977), Russian-born U.S. novelist, poet. "Signs and Symbols," Nabokov's Dozen (1958).

January 2008

Chapter Ten

Lt. Cook Asks For Help

The pocket watch reported 5:24 AM when my rear end touched the comfortable cushions of the Blue Lyon's Diner corner booth. Bobby had e-mailed me last night about the 6:00 AM meeting with Lt. Cook here. I found his message in our, seldom used, emergency Yahoo e-mail box. It read simply, "600hrs morning chow w/cook watch ass." In our private code, the "morning chow" designated the Blue Lyon's. I did not like the "watch ass" comment. It meant that Bobby thought I might be under surveillance.

Since police still held my Pathfinder as evidence, I had to put my old, 1978 vintage, Datsun pickup truck back in use. It had close to 300,000 miles on the odometer but ran well nevertheless.

I checked the truck's battery last night, after coming home from my amazing detour into the abandoned highway. It was low on juice, so I charged it overnight. In the morning, the starter fired the power plant up like it was fresh from the factory floor.

The Blue Lyon's Diner was only fifteen minutes away from my home. I, however, had taken a long, zigzagging rout, checking my rearview mirrors constantly for a tail. I had seen no one following me.

During the drive, my mind kept going over the events of last night. Since I could find no logical explanation for the cloudy phenomenon, I decided to tell no one and to tackle this mystery at a later date.

The human thinking process, my dear reader, is not so controllable, however. The restaurant's corner booth offered a great view of the parking lot. As I looked for Bobby and Lt. Cook, a thought hit me like a sledgehammer. I remembered something about last night and had to shut my eyes to be sure. Without lifting my eyelids, I took my

small notebook from the back pocket, opened it, and jotted down the information which had struck my gray matter with so much force. When I finished, my lungs exhaled the air—I held my breath all that time—and looked at what I had written down. My eyes confirmed the accuracy. Yes, my dear reader, my pen had recorded everything correctly.

I put the notebook away and scanned the parking lot again. A smoke Cadillac Escalade pulled up and parked in the handicapped zone by the front door. I saw four men inside. One of them was Bobby, riding shotgun. He left the truck, came inside the restaurant, and joined me in the  corner booth. The Escalade's driver stayed put while the other two men followed Bobby and took the booth by the window, not too far from us.

"Mornin', chief," my friend greeted me with a happy smile.

"What's with the muscle?" I asked nodding towards the Bobby's obvious bodyguards.

"Things are getting rough," he answered. "I didn't want you involved, but I don't make all of the decisions. I will disappear after today until this mess is cleaned up. Use our Yahoo box if you want to talk but I don't promise quick responses."

Gloria, the waitress, came over and took our orders.

"You have to work blind, chief," said Bobby, after she walked away. "I know that you will find the answer to our situation. Start with the crime scene in my office and anything unusual you can find along the Highway 38."

"Give me something to hang my hat on. What is going on?" I asked.

"You'll have to figure it out by yourself, chief," Bobby said and got up to greet Clay B. Cook, the Redlands Police Lieutenant, who just walked through the front doors.

He turned out to be far more interesting than I expected. At the crime scene yesterday, I pegged Cook for a career moron climbing up to the top over the proverbial dead bodies. As I ate my eggs-with-bacon breakfast and listened to him, a realization came upon me that this man was a shrewd politician and could not be dismissed as just another hack.

He, apparently, had some good contacts who told him about Bobby's and mine spook connections. His demeanor changed completely. Yesterday's intimidating fury turned into a polite, professional assistance request.

"Gentleman, these murders are not going to go away quick," Cook told us and ordered the same bacon and eggs Bobby and I were having. I, my dear reader, always psychoanalyze the human micro reactions. His breakfast choice looked like an olive branch offer. "The press is all over my department. The FBI is not in the picture yet, but the Sheriff is making behind-the-scenes noises. He wants the Redlands City Hall to contract his agency to provide the police services. As you may imagine, such turn of events will slow down, or even end, many careers of competent police administrators within our department."

Bobby nodded and continued his love affair with a huge breakfast plate.

"Lieutenant ..." I started.

"Clay, please," Cook interrupted.

"Okay. Clay, you are sharing a meal with just a pair of private citizens who inadvertently found themselves caught up in some strange circumstance," said I.

He gave me a conspiratorial wink and laughed. "I respect your position. However, you have some very ..." Cook paused looking for a way to say what he wanted to say, "... some very specialized skills which could be relevant to our problem." He put much emphasis on the word "our."

Bobby finished his plate, wiped his mouth with a paper napkin, and said in a quiet crisp voice, "Clay, my new friend, I'll be gone for a while. But Marty here is at your disposal. All I ask of you is that he is not to be abused. He does have some special skills you'll find useful." Bobby put the same hard inflection on the word "special" as Cook did on his word "our."

* * *

After breakfast, I followed Cook to the Redlands Police headquarters. He invited me into his office. As soon as I sat down in front of his desk, he picked up the phone.

"Rich, get everything you have on the yesterday's one-eighty-seven multiple and bring it into my office," he ordered and punched several buttons on the phone again.

"Brenda, I'm indisposed unless the Chief wants me," he said in much softer tones.

We did not have wait to long for Rich. He turned out to be a young detective in a sharp gray suit with a silk, hand-painted tie. He brought in five  large boxes marked "EVIDENCE."

After he sat the last box in front of Cook's desk, the young man extended his wiry hand in my direction.

"Detective Rich Mendoza," he said as I shook it. "I heard many interesting things about you, sir."

"All lies," I smiled because I liked this young homicide dick instantly. "I am just a private citizen doing my duty."

The detective and Cook laughed politely. "Rich, tell Marty what you have found so far," Lieutenant said.

"At least five suspects are involved," the young detective started his narrative as if reading a police report on a witness stand. "Between five and six hundred hours yesterday, the said suspects introduced explosive devices into the lobby and parking lot of the Guzman, Swartz, and DiCesare law firm building. Out of the nine victims, the explosions rendered seven dead and two walked away with minor injuries only. The victims DeCesare and Greenblatt fired upon the suspects with their personal handguns and killed two of them... "

"Do we have any ID's on the bodies," Cook interrupted from behind his desk.

"Yes, sir. We identified one of the victims. He is, I mean was, a Secret Service Special Agent Jose Gonzalez. The rest of the bodies ID's are still pending."

"Marty, can you use your special skills to help the ID process?" Cook asked, stressing the word "special."

"Gentlemen, I can do many special things," said I. "But to do all the wonderful things you want me to, I need a different setting. I need a large private room into which you can fit a picnic-size table so we can arrange the evidence in an easy visual way."

Cooked picked up the telephone receiver and started making arrangements. By the time he had one of the basement storage areas emptied and two long tables brought in, my pocket chronometer showed 1:26 PM.

I bought Rich and I sandwiches from a deli across the street. We ate our lunch in silence. When we finished, the detective and I donned latex gloves and began going through the evidence boxes. We organized the plastic bags, files, and firearms according to the crime scene location they were found in. I drew an outline of the crime scene with a black marker on a white board. Then, I used a blue marker to superimpose a grid. When I was done, the crime scene sketch was divided into six-inch-by-six-inch squares. We examined each item and recorded the location where it was found on the board. After that, we organized the plastic bags, files, and firearms on the two long tables. My watch showed 5:56 PM when we finished.

"Is this all of the evidence we have?" I asked Rich.

"No. Two men with the Homeland Security credentials came in yesterday and went through the evidence. They seemed to know what they were looking for and carted away two boxes," he answered.

"Do you remember what was in the boxes?"

"From what I saw, some folders. They looked like court jackets. Some of the files were stamped with letters NAHP."

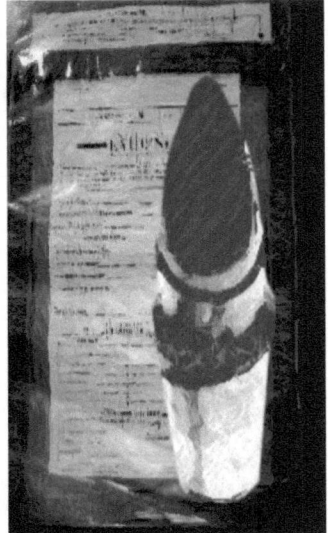

"Did these people say why they were messing with the one-eighty-seven evidence?"

"They said 'national security,'" Rich frowned. "Lt. Cook called to verify their bona fides. It must have checked out because he okayed whatever they took."

"Time to go home and rest," I said. "I'll meet you here tomorrow at eight hundred hours. We have a lot to go over and I want both of our minds fresh and rested."

"... Women are supposed to be deep—why? Because one can never get to the bottom with them..."

Friedrich Nietzsche (1844–1900), German philosopher, classical scholar, critic of culture. Friedrich Nietzsche, Sämtliche Werke: Kritische Studienausgabe, vol. 6, p. 63, eds. Giorgio Colli and Mazzino Montinari, Berlin, de Gruyter (1980). Twilight of the Idols, "Maxims and Arrows," section 27 (prepared for publication 1888, published 1889).

January 2008

Chapter Eleven

Strange Woman

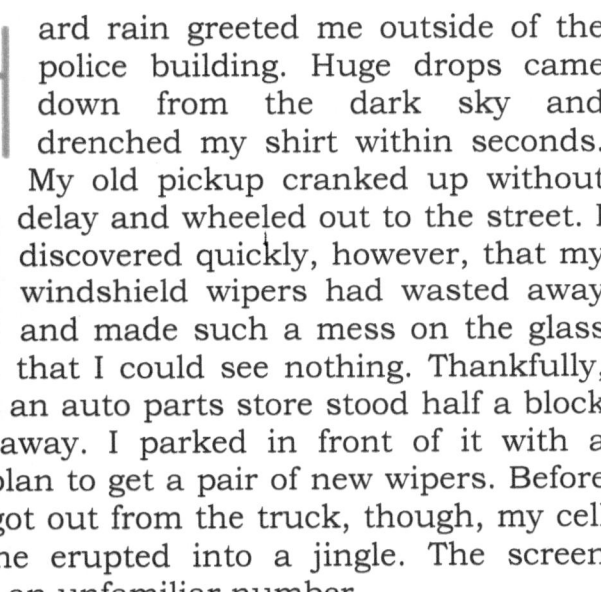

Hard rain greeted me outside of the police building. Huge drops came down from the dark sky and drenched my shirt within seconds. My old pickup cranked up without delay and wheeled out to the street. I discovered quickly, however, that my windshield wipers had wasted away and made such a mess on the glass that I could see nothing. Thankfully, an auto parts store stood half a block away. I parked in front of it with a plan to get a pair of new wipers. Before I got out from the truck, though, my cell phone erupted into a jingle. The screen displayed an unfamiliar number.

"Greenblatt," I said into it.

"Hi. Is this Marty Greenblatt?" a barely audible female voice asked.

"Yes. I am him."

"Well..." the voice paused. "I don't know how to begin..."

"The beginning is the best choice usually," I said and heard the woman, on the other end, take a deep breath. When the pause became long to the ridiculous, I decided to introduce some humor.

"Please, relax and tell me at least something. You don't have to worry, I don't bite unless specifically directed to provide such services," I said.

The woman did not laugh, but sighed and said, "I used to know someone who said similar things."

"See you can talk to me," I said cajolingly. "Give me at least a hint of what you're calling about."

"Marty... May I call you Marty or do you prefer Mr. Greenblatt?" she asked, her voice much louder now.

"Marty's fine."

"I wanted... Well, what I needed... Mr. Greenblatt, I mean Marty, can we meet in person? I'll be less nervous then."

"Okay. Where? When?"

"Well... Marty, please, help me with this, it's very awkward for me ..."

"What's your location?"

"I'm not far from you. I'm in Big Bear."

"Do I know you?"

"Well... No. No you don't," the woman stressed the word "you."

"But you do know where I live, the exact location where my house is?" I asked, surprised.

"Yes."

"Meet me there in one hour."

"Okay," she said and waited for me to click off.

While I purchased and installed the new windshield wiper blades, my mind examined this phone call. Strange it was. If someone wanted to do me harm, would such a person use a phone call like this to set me up? The logical answer was "yes." But set me up for what? Assassins and kidnappers rarely telegraph their intentions. They rely on surprise.

So, what is going on here?

My gray matter had no clue.

After I turned onto the Silver Springs Avenue from the Highway 38, I switched my lights off and put the pickup's manual transmission into the first gear. I drove up slowly in the darkness, watching for anything unusual. I spied no unfamiliar vehicles. I got to my driveway, parked, and entered my house through the back door. An almost invisible black string, which I placed strategically in the door jam, was still there. It would have been broken if someone had opened this door after I left this morning. I found the front door string undisturbed as well. A quick search of the living room, bedroom, and my den produced nothing unusual.

I turned the inside and the porch lights on. Then, I got back to the truck and drove down. I parked at the intersection of the Silver Springs Avenue and Highway 38 with my engine running and lights off. My appointment did not make me wait long. I saw a green Ford Explorer, of the mid-nineteen-nineties vintage, turn into the Silver Springs Avenue. The interior of the vehicle was dark. I could not see who was driving it and if there were any passengers.

I followed the Explorer up to my house with my lights off. The Ford parked in my driveway. I stopped about twenty feet behind it. The rain, sparse up until this moment, started up in force again. I saw a woman exit the Explorer and ran up to my porch. I left my truck too and did not slam the door shut but closed it carefully, without making a noise. I walked quickly to the Ford, my hand on the .357 Magnum Colt Python in my waistband, and looked inside it. It was empty.

"Here I am," I called to my visitor who had her hand on my door knocker.

"Marty?" she asked, her voice muffled by the rain.

"Yes. The door is unlocked," I said. "Walk in. I'll catch up with you in a second."

She entered my house.

"Welcome to my castle," I said after walking inside my living room behind the woman and extended my right hand.

She gave it a hard squeeze with her small cold fingers and smiled. "My name is Judy. Thank you for seeing me on such a short notice."

She was close now—medium height, attractive, mid-thirties, shoulder-length dark red hair.

Blue jeans, hiking boots, and khaki ski jacket covered her pleasant curvy figure. Her face was rather round with high cheekbones. Judy's green eyes darted around my living room and I noted her discomfort, caused by my probing gaze.

"Coffee or something stronger?" I asked.

"Well... Do you have any tea?"

"I happened to be a tea fanatic," I said and smiled. "What kind do you like?"

"Oh, English Breakfast, if you have it."

"Do bears ..." I started my smart reply, but stopped myself.

Judy laughed anyway. I guess she knew how that one ended. She helped me start the fire in the fireplace and I put a kettle with water on the stove to boil.

"You don't have to fuss on my account," she said, more comfortable now.

"Oh, it's my pleasure."

Cold rain, laced with snow, drummed its wild tune on the roof of my house. My living room, however, became nice and toasty thanks to the fireplace burning intensely. Judy took off the ski jacket revealing a green sweater which could not conceal the swell of her breasts and complimented the color of her eyes. She sat into my couch and stretched. I served her tea in a large glass mug, the way I saw it done in Eastern Europe. I poured more tea into another mug for myself and eased into my armchair. The fire made the pine logs crack contently in the fireplace while we sat in silence, enjoying the hot drink.

"I was so nervous about meeting you," she said finally.

"Why?" I asked.

"This is the hard part. I am not very good with men. But I knew that I needed to meet you. I know everything about you. I have been studying you for a long time and only got my nerve up today to call you."

"I have never seen you before, or have I?" I asked needing time to make sense of what she said.

"Well, we have run into each other, once or twice, a few years ago. But I could never figure out how to meet you without looking stupid, so I stayed out of your way."

As she said that, a slow recognition came. Judy was that strange woman I saw four years ago, once in the

Lee's Convenience Market and then in the restaurant. She gained some weight and did not look pale and ill anymore. I thought about what she had told me so far and what her body language projected. The only conclusion I came up with was that this female had romantic inclinations towards me.

Odd.

I looked for the micro-furtive movements which betray evil intentions.

Nothing.

Her posture projected shyness and embarrassment only.

"Or do I see what I want to see?" I asked myself.

"You just want to get laid tonight, horndog," my self laughed back.

I didn't like my internal conversation; but that's what women have always done to me—brought confusion. I have never been married nor have I ever came close to matrimony. More than ten years had passed since the last time I had a steady girlfriend. Don't misunderstand me, my dear reader, I love ladies. And some of them—Deedee for instance—actually liked me back. Most of the women, though, seemed to annoy me enormously after just a short time of dating. Once I had figured out this little quirk of mine, I had stuck to the one night stands and the ladies who did not look at me as their primary male companion.

I have to admit that Judy did not annoy any of my perceptive faculties. She, however, was not the type of a female who should have been interested in me. She spoke in a quiet educated voice and projected the impression of a woman well-acquainted with the cultural things in our life. The females, who found me attractive, were much less refined usually and wore their easy virtue on the sleeve.

"How did you even know that you wanted to meet me?" I asked.

"Well, I can't tell you just yet. What I can say is that we have many mutual friends, sort of speak," she said and put her hands to her hair, fussing with it. "One of them pushed me really hard to contact you. Your number is listed, so I called you."

Could she be a flim-flam artist? The obvious answer was "yes." I guess Judy was perceptive enough to read my thoughts.

"I learned enough about you to know that you are a super suspicious type. This is why I had memorized something which would prove that I am not a dangerous coo-coo woman," Judy said giggling. "Well, I may be coo-coo, because I barge into the man's home who doesn't know me at all and tell him such things, but I am not dangerous."

"Okay," I said intrigued.

"You are Uncle and I am a nesting bird," Judy said and blushed.

I understood her gibberish. "Uncle" was my old handle. I used it three times during covert missions years ago. "Birds nesting" was another old code for a situation without danger. If the "birds" would "walk," "run," or "fly," they would describe the various degrees of peril. The only other two people who knew the code were Bobby DiCesare and Sean Smith. The latter was long dead.

"Hmm... Interesting. Were you one of the claw removers?" I asked, referring to the old but still super secret "Remove Claws" operation.

Judy's face went crimson and she lowered her green eyes down to my hardwood floor. "I don't know what or who 'Claw Removers' are. The person who told me about the uncles and the nesting birds did not go into details. I don't know what it all means. He told me that you would understand and trust me if I said it."

"Do you know who Bobby DiCesare is?" I asked.

"No I don't," said Judy. The tears were in her eyes now. "If I am making you uncomfortable I will go away."

She made no attempt to get up, however. I decided to let my self-preservation instinct stand down. But it did not mean I couldn't enjoy playing the game. I seemed to be in control now. With ladies though, my dear reader, any notion of control is a self-delusion.

"No," I said and put some hard edge into my voice. "Consider yourself my prisoner. You've picked my interest too high. Let me have your car keys."

"What do you mean?" she asked with some fear in her voice as she handed me the keys, which I put in my pocket. "What are you going to do with me?"

"I haven't decided yet," I gave her my honest answer.

"So, what are we going to do now?" she asked nervously and raised her beautiful green eyes to mine.

"I don't know about you but I am going to take a relaxing bath," said I and gave her a wink. "You may want to join me."

I walked into my bathroom. There, I opened the faucets and began filling up my huge bathtub, the only luxury item I owned. I bought it on e-Bay and paid a small fortune for it. The bathtub was a scaled up replica of the old Nineteenth Century bathhouse tubs. It stood on the four lion's paw-shaped legs and could hold two people comfortably.

While the water ran, I brushed my teeth and undressed. Then, I eased my tired body into the torrid water. I must have dosed off because I did not hear Judy walk in. When I opened my eyes, I saw her standing over me.

"Please, don't look, Marty," she whispered.

I did as she asked but then lifted my right eyelid ever so slightly. Judy turned off the lights and lit a large candle she held in her hands. I recognized it. This candle was a present from my mom. I kept it on the mantelpiece for more than ten years now. Judy undressed and a dancing candle flame made her white body look translucent, just like one of the Francisco Goya's classic nudes.

"Keep your eyes closed, you mean man," Judy whispered and stepped into the bathtub.

"...Morning has spread again
Through every street,
And we are strange again ..."

**Philip Larkin (1922–1986), British poet. "Morning has
spread again."**

January 2008

Chapter Twelve

Judy

ext morning I woke up to the Kenny Gee's soprano saxophone. His rendition of "Chestnuts Roasting On An Open Fire" brought me out of my slumber slowly. First, the tune blended in with a forgettable dream about something. Then, the real world started to intrude. I understood that my alarm clock radio had gone off while my whole being rolled with the beautiful sax tune.

As my pineal gland adjusted the levels of melatonin to the wake cycle, I became aware of something warm, soft, and breathing rhythmically to my right. When I tried to turn, I found that Judy had appropriated my right arm. Lost in dreamland, her head rested on my shoulder while her sleeping hands held on to my right forearm, as some children clutch a teddy bear. My movements woke her up and she rubbed her nude bubble-butt against my hip. The touch of her soft skin caused another one my glands to adjust the levels of a much more flamboyant substance in my bloodstream. This particular chemical had nothing to do with the sleep-wake cycle, however.

I turned her around by the shoulders and gave her a wet French kiss.

"Marty, what are you up to?" she whispered her question and kissed me back with much passion.

"Listen to me, my little missy," I growled. "Once you climb into my bunk, you're on your own."

"It wasn't a bunk. It was a bathtub," Judy cooed and caressed my face. "But I guess I am still a nasty little girl. What do plan to do about it?"

The radio played on. As the Gypsy Kings worked the strings of their guitars, I turned my intense carnal attentions to the beautiful willing female in my bed and showed her what I had in mind for the self-admitted "nasty little girl." What followed was enjoyable to the extreme. When we were done finally, my alarm clock radio showed 5:32 AM.

I gave Judy the last slap on the bottom and walked to the bathroom, her moans of ecstasy ringing in my years. I shaved and took a quick shower. When I opened the door to come out, a smell of frying bacon hit my nose hard. Judy stood in my kitchen, wearing my white dress shirt, and fussed around the stove.

I let the towel drop, came behind her, and took her in my arms. "You're such a wet Sasquatch," she said laughing. "Let me finish cooking."

I didn't let go, but held her while she served us the two plates of bacon, hashbrowns, and eggs. Judy fried my eggs over-medium, exactly how I liked it. I made myself comfortable at my small kitchen table and sat her down onto my lap. We fed each other breakfast just like two infatuated teenagers during their first morning after.

"Were you serious about keeping me as your prisoner?" Judy asked. Her green eyes looked at me with a transparent hope that I will confirm her captured status.

"Yes," I answered, obviously. Would you, my dear reader, say anything else under the circumstances?

"May I have my keys back anyway?" she asked, looking relieved. "I need to buy us some more food and a few female type knickknacks for me."

"Great," I said, walked to the bedroom, and gave Judy a one-hundred-dollar bill. "Here's some money."

"Oh, I have enough," she started to protest but took the money after I growled at her. "Do you want anything special?"

"As a matter of fact I do want something special. I want to know who you are?" I asked trying my best to sound severe.

"Shhhhhhhhh... you mean furry Sasquatch," she put her finger to my lips and kissed my hairy chest. "I can't tell you yet."

"I'll find out anyway, my little missy," I said.

Unexpectedly, Judy started to cry. She buried her face in my chest and I heard her faint whisper through the sobbing, "Don't mind me, Marty. I'm just emotional. The words 'my little missy' mean something to me. I got used to hearing these words from you until..." she stopped, pulled back, and covered her mouth with her hand as if she said something she did not want to say. We stood in silence for a short while until Judy put her hand down with a visible effort and gave me a forced smile through her tears. "I always wished that you would call me that too some day."

"Who was calling who what?" I asked confused, knowing that my grammar sucked.

"Oh, you'll find out soon enough," she smiled again, happy this time. "Just promise me that you won't toss me out before I get a chance to make you fall in love with me head over heels."

"I promise," was all I could say and lit my first La Gloria Cubana for today.

She had the upper hand now. My experience in being pursued by an attractive, smart woman could be summarized in three words: zip, zero, nada.

"...The investigation of the truth is in one way hard, in another easy. An indication of this is found in the fact that no one is able to obtain the truth adequately, while on the other hand, no one fails entirely, but everyone says something true about the nature of things, and while individually they contribute little or nothing to the truth, by the union of all a considerable amount is amassed. Therefore, since the truth seems to be like the proverbial door, which no one can fail to hit, in this way it is easy, but the fact that we can have a whole truth, and not the particular part we aim at shows the difficulty of it ..."

Aristotle (384–322 B.C.), Greek philosopher. Metaphysics II.1: 993a27-993b7, Complete Works of Aristotle, trans. by W.D. Ross, ed. Jonathan Barnes, Princeton University Press (1984).

January 2008

Chapter Thirteen

Dead Bodies Reveal Secrets

y pocket watch showed 6:17 AM when I tore myself away from Judy and walked to my truck. I jotted down her Ford Explorer's VIN number as I passed it by. My old Datsun truck cranked up right away, ready to go places. I drove down to the Highway 38. Instead of making the left turn to Redlands, I turned right and soon was at the entrance to the abandoned stretch of the highway. Just like the horse-drawn wagon from two days ago, I wheeled around the chain and drove up to the rockslide. I let the engine run and got out.

The rain had done a sloppy job of washing away the evidence. The faint hoof prints between two parallel lines, the wagon's wheel tracks, ended abruptly at the rockslide. I examined the impressions. The horse hoof prints were unremarkable. The wagon wheel marks, on the other hand, looked like the fourteen-inch all-weather tire tracks. My hand reached for my small notebook where I recorded something which I had remembered in the restaurant yesterday. Before I looked at it, though, I studied the tracks left by my Datsun. These impressions were from the fourteen-inch all-weather tires too.

Hoping that I am wrong, I opened my notebook and compared the seven-digit number, I wrote down yesterday, to the license plate's digits of my own truck.

The numbers matched!

I slapped my face hard. The sharp pain let me know that I was awake. I closed my eyes and brought up the memory of the horse-drawn wagon up from the deep recesses of my gray matter. My eyes had seen the back side of the wagon only. Its rear end had some faint lettering which read "Datsun." Not only that, but I also remembered a blue California license plate as well. I opened my eyes and compared the numbers in the notebook to the ones on my truck's plate again.

Match!

What I saw two days ago was not the back of horse-drawn wagon but the tailgate of my own truck with a horse pulling it.

Unbelievable!

The excitement of this discovery sent a powerful signal to my suprarenal glands which pumped my bloodstream full of adrenaline. I felt the levels rise so high that any hope of rational reasoning was out of the question. I took several deep breaths, got into my truck, and dove back. Only when I made the left turn onto the Highway 38, towards Redlands, my hands stopped shaking.

* * *

The Redlands Police building's basement greeted me with a stale, grave-like air. I waited for a few minutes until the AM watch commander sent down an officer with a key to unlock the storage room, Rich and I had converted into a temporary office.

The young detective was not here yet. In his absence, I looked through the diagram of the crime scene. I could see the progression of the attack. Clearly, the assassins came from the courtyard of the building. They discharged a rocket-propelled grenade into one of the stretch jobs and, firing their MP5 submachine guns, pinned down the four parking lot bodyguards behind the second Cadillac. Then, three of them climbed to the third floor and tossed a hand grenade into the Bobby's suite. When they followed in to mop up, Bobby and I repelled them. The crew on the parking lot had better luck, or skills. They flanked the bodyguards and finished them off. The only question I had was about the avenue of their exit.

My watch showed 8:03 AM when Rich came in with a dozen donuts and two paper cups with coffee. I took out my leather cigar case and offered him an Arturo Fuentes Churchill. He took it without hesitation. I picked one out also and we lit up. Both of us sat for a few minutes, sipping lukewarm coffee and enjoying the Dominican Republic tobacco.

"What are we starting with this morning?' Rich asked.

"We'll take all printable evidence, such as weapons and papers, and have your lab lift prints. We will also visit the morgue and see the dead bodies. Their clothing may give us some clue about who the suspects and the victims are," I said.

"We know the ID on at least one of the victims," Rich said. "But I was thinking last night that it is extremely weird that the Treasury and the Secret Service are not all over our asses about the dead body of Jose Gonzalez. After all, they usually want to take over any one-eighty-seven case involving their own agents"

"You know, you're right," I said. "It's unusual. But the whole crime is unusual. I was going through the diagram, we drew yesterday, and it raised at least one interesting tactical question."

"What do you mean?" Rich asked intrigued.

"The progression of the attack shows that that the bad guys came from the courtyard. It means that they had camped out there lying in wait before the victims and I got there. Now, they could have arrived much earlier and used one of the ground floor offices for concealment. My question is about their escape avenue, because I did not see any strange vehicles coming in or going out."

"Are you sure, Marty?" Rich asked. "You took an explosion head on and then you had to fight your way out. Is it possible that you missed something?"

I examined my memories for a few minutes. "Well ..." I started to say but let the word hang because I remembered the white Ford Crown Victoria. It drove up with the Cadillac stretch jobs but was not there when I came down after the explosion.

"Nothing comes to mind," I lied because I needed to think about this one further.

Rich and I went through the boxes and dropped off the guns and several manila folders with a lab tech. I also gave him the VIN number to Judy's Explorer and her phone number, witch I lifted from the memory of my cell phone.

Then, we got into the young detective's Chevy truck. As it sped up the I-10 Freeway, I dialed the morgue's number. "Albert, this is Marty. How are you?" I greeted Alberto Morones, assistant pathologist and an acquaintance of mine.

"Hey, Marty. Make it quick because I have a room full of stiffs from Redlands I'm processing," he said in a hurried tone.

"Good, because I'm on my way to see you about these bodies," I said.

"Oh, no!" Albert exclaimed mockingly. "It'll cost you a cigar. And not one of the dry supermarket horse droppings, I want the real stuff you smoke yourself."

"Okay," I said and clicked off.

Albert emptied the contents of my five-cigar leather case when we arrived. Then, he led us to his office. "I will spare you the scientific technical crap," he said. "We have no unusual causes of death. Your stiffs died from gunshot wounds, explosive device's fragments, or both. What's unusual is that two Feds in sunshades came in yesterday and collected all of the stiffs' belongings, clothing and all. They had the Homeland Security ID's which checked out."

"Do you have anything but the obvious for us?" Rich asked frowning.

Albert locked his eyes with mine. He seemed to be asking if he could talk freely in the young detective's presence. I shook my head ever so slightly.

"Not really," Albert said.

"Rich, would you wait outside for a minute or so?" I asked.

The detective said nothing, but left the room. I could not tell if my request slighted him.

"What do you have Albert?" I asked.

"I took some digital pictures of the stiffs you may find amusing," he said. "I can e-mail them to you, if you wish."

"Do that," I said, shook Albert's hand, and left his office.

* * *

Our next stop was at the U.S. Secret Service office in the City of Riverside, some twenty miles from San Bernardino. We took the 215 Freeway and got off at the Market Street exit. Rich guided his truck into the parking structure adjacent to the tall, by the Southern California standards, office tower. The elevator took us to the right floor quickly and we were greeted by two unsmiling men in white shirts and black trousers of the Secret Service uniformed guard division.

"Do you have an appointment, gentlemen?" one of them asked in a drone voice, his gold five-point badge gleaming from the chest.

"I'd like to see the special agent in charge," said Rich and produced a badge of his own.

The older Secret Service agent studied it carefully and gave it back. "What do you want to see him about?" he asked.

"Jose Gonzalez," I said.

My words made both of the agents frown. "Wait here," the older agent said and left through one of the back doors. We did not have to wait long for him to come back. Another man, dressed in a gray suit and a gray tie, came with him.

"I'm Special Agent Abrams and I am the acting special agent in charge," he introduced himself without offering his hand for a shake.

"May I ask you a few questions?" Rich inquired in a friendly voice.

"Detective Mendoza, my office has no direct involvement in the unfortunate situation within your jurisdiction," Abrams squeezed the words through his teeth with an obvious effort. "At the time of his death, Special Agent Gonzalez was on an extended leave of absence."

"Is your office conducting a parallel inquiry into his one-eighty-seven?" Rich asked.

Abrams squinted but said nothing. We stood in silence a while.

"Good day, detectives," Abrams said finally and disappeared through the back door of the reception area.

Now, the uniformed agents looked like two pit bulls ready to tear us apart. Without saying a word, Rich and I boarded the next elevator down.

"What do you think he meant?" Rich asked me as soon as the double doors slid shut.

"He received orders from Washington not to touch our multiple with a ten-foot pole," I said.

"Why?"

"If I had to guess, it is because our situation seems to have political implications," I explained. "Your lieutenant would do the same if he could."

What I did not say out loud was that Lt. Cook contracted me, in a way, to make the whole case go way from him too.

* * *

As soon as we returned to the Redlands Police Building, Lt. Cook called us in his office.

"Have we ID'ed of the dead suspects yet?" he asked briskly.

"Work in progress," I replied.

"Marty, you were recommended as a miracle maker," Cook said. "I don't want to be disappointed. Time isn't on our side."

I nodded without saying anything.

"The chief is on my ass. We need a resolution for this investigation in a few days—arrests, the whole nine yards. We need to look great, we need to shine. If the Sheriff's Department or the Feds take over, there'll be hell to pay," he said making it obvious that our meeting was over.

Rich and I walked to a local eatery and he bought us some unmemorable Chinese food. We ate in silence.

"Give me two hours to do a couple of things," I told him after my belly was full. "I will find you. I have a few situations to check out."

"Marty, be honest," Rich asked when we walked back to the station. "Do you have any idea about what's going on?"

"I think I do," I lied with a straight face. "We'll talk more later."

I stopped by the lab and asked about the VIN and the phone numbers, I gave to the tech earlier in the morning. What I got back was a report about the stretch jobs and the suspects' gun serial numbers. He also gave me a faded printout for the Judy's Ford VIN with a handwritten notation about her phone number. I tucked the papers under my arm and went to the best place to study important documents—the crapper. I discovered many years ago that my thoughts became crystal clear in these establishments.

Instead of clearing things up and pointing me in the right direction, however, the report made the crime even odder than it appeared before. The limos' last registration was in Las Vegas and had expired in 1995. A limo service had leased them and then bought the cars out. They had not been registered since.

Furthermore, ATF had no record of the two German-made Heckler & Koch MP5 sub-machinegun serial numbers. According to the report, the tech called the manufacturer's rep in Washington D.C. who informed him that their database showed both guns to have been manufactured in 1996 and sold subsequently to the NATO's strategic reserve in Europe.

I read the notes about Judy's Ford and the telephone number last. The California DMV listed the registered owner for the 1991 Ford Explorer as AST Research. I knew what this company was. Among other services to the intelligence community, tt provided a legend for the spooks in deep cover. Her phone was assigned to a cell service provider specializing in prepaid phone cards.

I washed my hands before leaving the men's room and called the cell company. A rude woman, on the other end, told me that they did not keep track of the subscribers' names. The limo company was next. The owner of the Las Vegas-based Good Wishes Livery Co. was much more informative. I dictated the VIN numbers to him over the phone and the man promised to call me back. He rang my cell phone ten minutes later. "I sold the cars to an exporter thirteen years ago," he said. "A car carrier picked both Cadillacs up on November 19, 1994. Do you want me fax you the bill of lading?"

I thank him and gave my fax number at home.

On my way down to the basement, I ran into Rich walking up. He gave me a questioning look.

"Do you have a PC with an Internet connection I can use?" I asked.

"Sure, you can use mine," Rich said and took me to his desk.

I found the pictures, Albert e-mailed. He had to send eight messages to accommodate the transfer volume. The photographs depicted the dead bodies in various positions on the morgue's gurneys. My eyes stopped at the picture of a nude shoulder belonging to a suspect. The shoulder had a tattoo of an anchor superimposed on a globe, Marine Corps insignia. Below it, I saw the tattooed words, "The Old Breed" with a number "1" over the skull and bones.

Now I was getting somewhere. "The Old Breed" was a nickname for the First Marine Division stationed at Camp Pendleton. The skull and bones with a number "1" had to be a regimental badge, I decided. The e-world revealed the secret of this tattoo on my third try. It belonged to the First Renascence Battalion attached to the First Marine Division.

"Now I know where to look, you stupid jarheads," I muttered under my breath.

The pictures of the other suspect's nude body produced no interesting information. The sharp images of their camouflage fatigues, however, gave me more than I expected. The tunic belonging to the tattooed corpse had the gunnery sergeant's stripes and a faded, sawed on, nametag with the name "D.Raven " clearly visible. The other tunic showed the corporal's stripes and a nametag which read, "R.Sooner." I took my notebook out and jotted down the information. One discovery, however, left me puzzled. Both tunics bore a shoulder patch with four letters "N.A.H.P." I searched the Internet for it, but found no relevant references.

I picked up my cell phone to call the Camp Pendleton Provost Marshal. I held it in my hands for a few moments, put it down, and dialed from a Redlands Police telephone. If the Provost Marshal's office had phone ID capability, it was to my advantage to be cloaked in the law enforcement air.

"Captain Rumsey," a deep voice answered on the second ring.

"My name is Marty Greenblatt and I am calling from the Redlands Police Department," I said, choosing my words carefully to give the impression of an official police business, but not to misrepresent myself as a cop.

"Marty Greenblatt. I know of one Marty Greenblatt, but that man is not a Redlands police officer. He's a private dick," Rumsey spoke slowly. "I'm one and the same Greenblatt," I said, ignoring the slight, and asked. "Do we know each other?"

"No, but I know who you are."

"I hope you can help me," I said in a business like way, my internal alarms going off. "The Redlands P.D. contracted me to help with a multiple one-eighty-seven in their jurisdiction and some of my leads point to Oceanside."

"What do you have, Greenblatt?" nothing friendly in Rumsey's raspy voice.

"I'd like to interview the C.O. of Gunny Raven and Corporal Sooner from the First Recon," I said.

Rumsey grunted and asked, "Why?"

"Their dead bodies are in the San Bernardino morgue. They were killed during a commission of the one-eighty-seven. I believe that they are part of the seven- or eight-men crew."

"Greenblatt, I need to talk to you in person," Rumsey said as if laboring to stifle expletives.

"I can be in your office within three hours, depending on traffic," said I.

"I'll notify the gate," said Rumsey and hung up.

I found Rich and told him that we needed to take off to Oceanside. The dash clock of his truck showed 2:09 PM when got in it. As we drove, I told Rich about my progress.

"Why wouldn't Rumsey talk on the phone?" he asked.

"We are walking on the edge of something big. I sense some major politics which go beyond our county or even the state," I said. "For all we know, Rumsey is knee deep in these guys."

"So, what's out plan?"

"We conduct this investigation as any other. We need to interview the dead leathernecks' C.O. to find out their circle of contacts. Once we do that, we will see the whole crew. If we are lucky, one of them will turn," I said.

Our trip took less than two hours, traffic did us a favor. We came to the north gate guard shack and produced our credentials.

"Please, park you truck there," a stern corporal pointed to a parking space next to the shack. "You are expected and the MP vehicle is on the way to pick you up. Please, leave all your weapons in the truck."

A few minutes later, a green Humvee drove up with two men in the desert camouflage fatigues with MP badges. The Diesel engine roared as the truck took us to the Provost Marshal's office. An officer with a nameplate reading "W.Rumsey" waited for us outside. He turned out to be a short stocky thirty-something man. His thick neck and face were of dark red color, contrasting sharply with the pale skin of his freckled forearms. Captain's crew cut revealed receding red hair.

"Let's take a walk, detectives," the man said without preambles, introductions, or handshakes. "I'm talking to you off the record. Raven and Sooner can't be in your morgue because they died in a helicopter crash six years ago."

Rich looked surprised, but I was used to these things. "This fact explains a lot," I said. If the guys in the morgue were working for Pentagon or Langley off the books, the crash record could have been faked with ease.

Rumsey looked at me in a measuring way, squinting. His body language was unmistakable; he wanted to talk but did not know how to start.

"Rich, let me have a private chat with the Captain," I said.

"No problem, Marty. I'm getting used to being kicked out of conversations around you," he said with a smile and walked away.

"You were with the Eighty-Second in Fort Bragg, am I right?" Rumsey asked once Rich was beyond the hearing range.

"Blue Falcons, Third Battalion, sir," I replied crisply in my best military voice. After all, he was a commissioned officer and my last pay grade, at the time of my discharge from the Army, was that of a master sergeant.

"I checked on you and I was told that you're a straight shooter. I was also told that you never went civilian," Captain's blue eyes bore into mine.

I said nothing but nodded slightly.

"Have you ever heard of Mark Foxtrot?" he asked.

I had no idea who or what it was, but said nothing. Rumsey looked at my poker face as if trying to decide something.

"Did she contact you?" he asked.

I guess my face betrayed something because he smiled. "Tell her to come in. Tell her that there is no other way. Tell her that she needs to tell us where the unauthorized beacon is."

Nothing else was said. Captain and I shook hands good-bye and the same Humvee took us back to the gate. As Rich and I drove off, I saw a white Ford sedan follow us for a few miles.

"Watch your ass from now on," I told Rich when we were back on the parking lot of the Redlands Police building. "This one-eighty-seven involves some hard people."

"I figured it was not your local gang-banger crowd," Rich gave me a half-smile. "Watch yourself too."

My pocket chronometer showed 7:56 PM when I turned onto the Highway 38. A pair of headlight dogged me for about ten miles. I decided to see who it was by breaking hard after veering abruptly to the shoulder. The headlights passed me by; they belonged to a white Crown Victoria without license plates.

When the intersection with the Silver Springs Avenue was only a mile away I dialed Judy's number.

"Hi, Marty. Where are you?" she asked cheerfully.

"Judy, are the birds nesting, running, or flying?"

"Oh. What birds?" she asked surprised, but caught herself quickly. "Those birds are still nesting. Why?"

"If it is so, go to the porch now," I said.

"... and every sword was against the other, so that there was very great confusion ..."

Bible: Hebrew, 1 Samuel 14:20.

January 2008

Chapter Fourteen

I Save Judy

udy waited for me on the porch as I instructed.

"You are as paranoid as I knew you would be," she said and put her arms around my neck cautiously.

I pulled Judy close and kissed her on the mouth hard. There was nothing cautious about the French kiss she gave me back. When we walked into my home holding hands, I caught the smell of something delicious coming from the kitchen.

"Even though you've been a mean Sasquatch to me," she said in a fake submissive voice, "Your little missy will treat you like a pasha."

She walked me into the bathroom where, to my absolute surprise, an apple-scented bubble bath waited. A dozen candles lit the small room. What happened next is embarrassing to describe. I don't remember ever being bathed. I am sure that my mom gave me baths when I was a toddler, but it must have been before the child's brain has the capacity to remember. Well, Judy bathed me! First, she undressed me and guided me into the bathtub. Then, her gentle fingers scrubbed my whole body softly, even the most private parts. By the time she was done, I didn't care if she was to kill me on the spot. The experience was worth it!

"Did you like your bath?" I heard Judy's whisper while she dried my back after I stepped out of the bathtub. Instead of answering verbally, put my arms around her and held her close for what seemed to be an eternity.

"I cooked you a few things," Judy said finally and handed me a robe.

I have never owned a robe in my life. Putting this dark blue garment on was a new experience. "I bought it for you. I decided that if I am to make you fall in love with me, my job would be so much easier if you were to become a bit more housebroken," she said.

I had no retort because the food on the kitchen table diverted my attention. She had fried some zucchini with garlic and served it with a little dish of blue cheese dressing. Next to it, Judy put a plate full of grilled bell peppers, a skillet with the whole slew of deep fried chicken gizzards, and a bowl of sauerkraut. All these things were my dream food. My mom used to make such delicacies, as appetizers, for the big-to-do Sunday dinners when I was a kid. I have not seen these dishes, together on one table, in many years.

"Judy, you are a nasty girl," I said. "You just made my favorite stuff. How did you know that the path to my heart goes right through my belly?"

"I researched you," Judy said giggling. "But don't be so smug. All smart women know that the man's heart, stomach, and one other organ are all interconnected."

* * *

My old Datsun pickup fired up without complaints when the sun started to rise next morning. The Duke Ellington's "Take the 'A' Train" tune caressed my eardrums while the residual memory of Judy's throaty moans of pleasure, which I caused earlier in the morning, blended in with the music. The sounds of horns and saxes reverberated throughout my body. The drum's beat, however, warned me about the real world just at the right time. The corner of my left eye noted a white Ford Crown Victoria parked at the intersection of Silver Springs Avenue and Highway 38. It sat at the same spot where I had waited for Judy two days ago.

I turned onto the Highway 38 and drove for another fifty feet. The drums would not let me slip back into the lover's daze and my gray matter turned on the internal alarm system finally. I realized that the Crown Victoria contained four men in green camouflage fatigues. My sideways glance had registered one of the shoulder patches clearly. It read "N.A.H.P."

N.A.H.P.!!!

I looked into my side mirror and saw the Crown Victoria drive up the Silver Springs Avenue towards my house. My hands jerked the steering wheel on pure instinct and whipped the pickup into a u-turn so hard that it stalled. I turned the key but the battery refused to juice the starter to the proper power. It whined without firing up. I tried again.

No go!

My hand pulled the .357 Magnum Colt Python from the glove compartment and the blue finish on its six-inch barrel helped me see what I needed to do. I left my truck in the middle of the highway and ran up the hill. I took my favorite old footpath which traversed the steep slope and passed in the back of my property. The adrenaline circulated in my bloodstream freely while my legs moved. "One, two, three—inhale," my mouth counted. "One, two, three—exhale."

Before I knew it, the back of my house loomed in front of me. I slowed down and checked the ammo in the gun. The six hollow-pointed rounds expressed their eagerness to do their deadly business on my command.

I circled the garage and peeked from behind two large pines. I could see my driveway clearly from this position. The white Crown Victoria occupied the space in front of my garage arrogantly, next to Judy's green Explorer. As I looked on, two men in camouflage fatigues got into the Explorer and backed it out. Another two men, dressed the same, came out of my house with Judy between them. She walked with a forlorn expression on her face, hands handcuffed behind her back. This crew made a huge tactical mistake, however. They focused their attention on what was in front of the house. I was in the back of it and had the advantage of surprise.

I waited until they were within fifteen feet of the Crown Victoria and made my move. The time slowed down for me; as it always does in the face of extreme danger. I took a deep breath in, made five steps, stopped, aimed, and fired twice—on exhale—into the first camouflaged forehead.

FOUR ROUNDS LEFT.

Then, I took more air in, side stepped, aimed, and fired once more, this time into the second camouflaged forehead. The magnum load explosions jolted my body, filling me up with energy and calming me down.

THREE ROUNDS LEFT.

"Do I have enough time to finish all of them off?" I asked myself. Instead of bothering to think such rhetorical question through, however, I filled my lungs full of air once again. My legs made an about face, while my arms aimed the gun and my right hand squeezed the trigger again. A single hollow-point slug slammed—with joyful malice, I imagined—into a man in the driver's seat of the Explorer. His limp torso fell on the steering wheel.

TWO ROUNDS LEFT.

The passenger got out and used the vehicle for cover. His submachine gun sprayed nine-millimeter slugs in my general direction. Same mistake as in Bobby's office, I thought. The poor bastard could aim the first round only; the rest of the lead went all over the place.

I dropped to the ground and caught his left foot in my gun sites, under the Explorer. The next squeeze of the trigger made the man scream out loud. He fell to the ground holding his ankle.

ONE ROUND LEFT.

Air in. Without moving an inch, I shifted the sites onto the thrashing head and fired. I did not have to see my target to know that I hit him. He stopped screaming abruptly.

I got up to my feet and looked at Judy. She stood motionless, her eyes and her mouth wide open. Her face and the body language showed fear mixed with something else. I've seen this something else before. It is an odd forlorn-like emotion which overcomes some people who witness violence often, can not do anything about it but refuse to get used to it.

"Close you eyes," I ordered curtly.

Judy's eyelids went down instantly.

"Are you going to shoot me too?" she asked, her voice trembling.

"No."

I picked up Heckler & Koch MP5, taking it from the dead hands of the camouflaged man I shot with my first two rounds. I moved the selector to the single fire setting and fired twice into his head.

Judy jumped when she heard the report.

"Keep your eyes closed," I told her again.

Then, I walked to the other three bodies in camouflage and shot each one of them in the back of the head two times.

Judy's hands were still handcuffed behind her back and eyes shut when I came to her and gave her a kiss on the mouth. Her body shook uncontrollably as she tried to reciprocate. Her cold trembling lips, however, would not obey. As Judy began to sob, I picked her up, slang her over my shoulder, and carried her into the bedroom. There, I tore the jeans and the panties off her, spread her soft round thighs, and entered her.

My body moved hard with the predatory energy. My every thrust brought more and more color to Judy's face until it glowed in the crimson flush of carnal ecstasy. "Please, kiss me, Marty," she moaned. I put my lips to hers and growled. As she growled back, both of us thrashed at the top of our lust.

"Marty, what was that?" Judy asked after we separated from each other and caught our breaths. "How can you be so vile and so precious all at the same time?"

I stared at her face silently. She looked back at me with her wonderful green eyes full of a powerful emotion. All my adult life I wished for a woman to look at me like that. Even though the handcuffs still bound Judy's hands behind her semi-naked body, she had me now. And the worst part of it was that she knew it.

"Are you going to keep me tied up forever like some love slave?" she asked provocatively. "Careful, my mean Sasquatch, I may grow to like this rough side of you and demand more of it."

"Are you going to tell me now about what's going on?" I asked.

"I can't, Marty." She said softly. "Don't be angry with me and take the handcuffs off."

"In this case, before I undo these things, I will look you over for clues to who you are," I said.

My hands took the rest of her clothing off. Some of it bunched up at the handcuffed wrists. Then, I began a methodical examination. The soft, well-cared for skin of her torso and hips was of a pleasant pink color. The lower part of her thighs and upper parts of the calves showed a nice tan, however. "She likes to wear shorts and hiking boots," I made a mental note.

I found a long jagged scar on top of her head, just above the hairline.

"What happened here?" I asked.

"This is how it all began," Judy said cryptically and refused to elaborate.

The rest of her body contained no other unusual skin marking. Her earlobes were pierced with one hole in each. No earrings, however. She shaved her legs but did not trim her pubic hair. Judy was not a bikini wearer type, obviously. The appearance of her body pointed towards a woman who enjoys nature and shies away from the city's nightlife. I also found a California Drivers License in her jeans. The document expired in 1996. It showed her to be born on December 1, 1970, five-four, one hundred and thirty pounds. The name on the license read, "Judith Anne Dobiash." The address below was that of a Big Bear Lake post office box.

All through my probing, Judy issued giggles and feeble protests. After I was done, I tried to take the handcuffs off her using my own standard police key. It did not fit. I had to search the dead bodies outside to find the right key.

As soon as she was free, Judy slapped my face and said, "This is for scaring me outside earlier. I thought you were going to shoot me too."

I stood still, waiting to see what she was going to do next.

Judy put her arms around my neck, and—visibly enjoying her absolute control—gave me a long French kiss.

"And this is for saving my life, my knight in shining armor," she cooed.

"Take a shower and dress," I said. "We have a long day ahead of us."

"What are we going to do?"

"Many interesting things," I answered honestly because I had a plan now.

"...How many facts we have fallen through
And still the old façade glimmers there,
A mirage, but permanent. We must first
trick the idea ..."

John Ashbery (b. 1927), U.S. poet, critic. "Flowering Death."

January 2008

Chapter Fifteen

I Save the Day

hile Judy took her shower, I examined the ID cards I collected from the corpses outside. They were made out of white plastic with large block letters "N.A.H.P." on top and smaller lettering which read "Pacific Habitats Security Services" below. Each ID had the owner's color face mug shot with the name on the front and magnetic strip on the back.

I also examined the dog tags I took off the bodies. They looked like the regular U.S. military issue with the wearer's name, serial number, and blood type. I noted a few differences also. The religion of preference stamp was gone and the stamp "N.A.H.P" was added at the bottom. I recorded the information from the ID cards and the dog tags into my notebook and put them in a brown paper bag. Then, I dialed the Redlands Police.

"Lt. Cook speaking," he baritoned on the third ring.

Andrei V. Lefebvre

"Clay, this is Marty. Your problems are over. I closed your case and made you look good," I said cheerfully. "You have to play ball obviously."

"What do you mean? What happened?" he asked in a worried voice.

"Take yourself and one of your trusted men," I said stressing the word trusted. "... and rendezvous at my home at your earliest. I will explain when you get here."

After Cook acknowledged, I clicked off and dialed Detective Eddie Sobaleff at the Sheriff's Department.

"Rendezvous at my house code three," I said after he answered his cell phone.

"What's up, Marty?" he asked.

"Remember our conversation a few days ago about the Redlands situation?"

"Yes. What about it?"

"I made a few moves and the situation is just about to go away. I need your help to make sure that everything is airtight," I said.

While I waited for Cook and Eddie to arrive, my fingers typed up two pages of text. When my printer finished printing the last page, Judy came out of the bathroom.

"Stay in the bedroom with the door closed," I told her. "This house is going to be full of cops in a few minutes."

"Did you neighbors call because of the shooting?" she asked.

"No. There are no neighbors around in the winter. All of the surrounding houses are summer homes. I am the only one who lives here full time." I said.

Almost as soon as she closed the bedroom door, Eddie walked into the house through the open front door, gun in his hand.

"What did you do to those people outside?" he asked and holstered his weapon.

Instead of answering I gave him the two pages I wrote. He read the text and scratched the back of his head. "Is Redlands P.D. going to play ball on this one?" he asked.

"They are here. Let's ask them," I said because I saw a Redlands Police cruiser drive up to the Judy's Explorer. Rich was behind the steering wheel and Cook rode shotgun.

They got out and surveyed the carnage in front of my garage. They walked up to me with the identical frowns on their faces. I gave Cook the same two pages Eddie just read. The man read them and passed the paper to Rich. While he examined my text, Cook shook Eddie's hand but said nothing. They obviously knew each other.

"If everybody agrees," I said after Rich put down the pages. "I will handle the press and you'll handle the stiffs."

"Okay, Marty," said Cook. "Call the press. This is not perfect but will have to do under the circumstances."

He went back to the police cruiser with Rich. I saw them discussing something for a short time. Their conversation ended when the young detective lifted the police radio microphone and spoke into it. In the mean time, Eddie flipped his cell phone open and began explaining to the Sheriff's dispatcher what he wanted done.

Within thirty minutes, my property teemed with the sheriff's deputies, crime techs, and the coroner vans. Eddie and Lt. Cook directed this law enforcement convention with ease. By the time the dead bodies were carted off to the county morgue and the last police car left my driveway, my clock showed 2:06 PM.

The Sheriff's department impounded Judy's Explorer and the bad guys' Crown Victoria. I walked down to the Highway 38 and brought my truck back. The battery, miraculously, had enough juice to crank it up.

I had my part to do now. I faxed the pages, I typed up earlier, to the San Bernardino News-Record newspaper. Then, I picked up the phone and dialed Barry Roberts, the newspaper's city desk editor.

Extortion Gangsters Die In Wild Hail of Bullets

By William Smith
News-Record Staff Writer

The Redlands Police officers gunned down four gang members in a Wild West style shootout this morning. The hail of bullets also killed an innocent bystander.

The confrontation took place after the police cornered the gangsters in a remote wooded hillside near the Highway 38. After a prolonged firefight, the police killed the four suspects while sustaining no casualties among officers.

Redlands Police officials refused to discuss the case on the record. Off the record, however, one of the detectives close to the investigation, believes that the dead suspects are responsible for the Lugonia Avenue murders three days ago. Apparently, the killings came about as part of an extortion demand gone bad.

The San Bernardino Sheriff's Department (SBSD), in which jurisdiction the shooting took place, praised the Redlands officers.

"(They) behaved professionally and followed proper police procedures," Det. Eddie Sobaleff of SBSD said. He went on to commend the Redlands officers for their restraint and tactical skills which prevented any casualties among the law enforcement personnel.

Police had not revealed the dead suspects' names at the time the story went to print. They, however, identified the dead bystander as Judith Dobiash, 36, of Big Bear Lake.

"...O my lost love bounced from a good home ..."

Dylan Thomas (1914–1953), Welsh poet. "If my head hurt a hair's foot."

January 2008

Chapter Sixteen

A Note From Judy

had to move quick now. I suspected that whoever was behind the crew I killed was going to show up at the morgue, just like they did the last time. I rented a motel room near the county morgue's building and told Judy to stay inside. Then, I found my friend Albert the assistant pathologist.

"I need a fresh Caucasian Jane Dow in her thirties," I told him and gave him ten one-hundred-dollar bills.

Albert took the money casually and showed me three bodies to choose from. I rejected two of them because of excessive tattoos. The third body looked perfect for my purpose. She was a victim of a hit-and-run driver. The body seemed to be about the same size as Judy's and the face was gone as a result of the accident. I had Albert enter the corpse into his log as Judy Dobiash.

Then, I waited patiently. At 4:48 PM I observed a man wearing an ill-fitting black suit enter the morgue's front office. I recognized him right away. He was that stocky Marine Provost Marshal, Capt. Rumsey.

I came behind him and said, "You got your wish, she's dead now. And I had to take care of your crew. No one knows what really happened."

The man almost jumped when he heard my voice.

"Here are their ID's and the dog tags," I said and gave him the brown paper bag with these items. "She did not have any ID."

"Did she tell you where the unauthorized beacon is?" he asked anxiously.

"No."

"I don't care about the grunts, but I needed her alive," he said angrily. "She knew where it was and you blew it."

The beacon again. I had no idea what he was talking about, but was not ready to confess my ignorance.

We stood with our eyes locked in an unfriendly "who blinks first" contest. He lost and looked away.

"Some people in the Security Services will not be happy," Rumsey said. "I know that everything in A1 looks so far away, but I wouldn't piss the Partnership off if I were you. Your A1 did and you know what happened to him. I want to think that you are wiser than him."

I did not understand his references neither to "A1" nor to the "Partnership" and the "Security Services." The thought of asking him about these terms crossed my mind for a millisecond and disappeared. I said nothing.

"So, what are you going to do now?" he asked.

"Same thing I always do," I said in a non-committal tone.

"Since she's dead, you better find that beacon quick or you may find yourself on the sharp end of a termination warrant," said Rumsey.

He walked to the reception window and showed his Homeland Security identification card to Albert. Then, Rumsey asked to see the bodies. He looked them over casually and collected all the uniforms from the men I killed. The naked body of Jane Dow held his attention for almost two full minutes according to my pocket watch.

"Where is her stuff?" he asked finally.

"I took care of that," I said.

"This is not you job." Rumsey frowned.

"Just throw me under the bus," I smiled.

"I plan to do that anyway," Captain laughed and left the building.

* * *

Judy greeted me with a kiss when I walked into the motel room. "Are we going to stay here tonight?" she asked.

"Yes, until I figure out what's going on," I said and gave Judy my best interrogation stare.

She laughed.

"What is an unauthorized beacon?" I asked.

Judy's face went sad. She lowered her gaze down to the floor, just like a little girl who has been caught doing something she shouldn't have.

"Marty, I love you. You saved my life and I trust you completely. But other people are involved. I gave my word not to discuss the beacon," she said in a quiet whisper-like voice.

She brought up her soft green eyes to mine and I could not bring myself to get angry with her. We went to bed early and held each other until the sleep came.

My nightmare was back. The bad guy pointed his gun at Sean Smith and I saw him fire it. The muzzle's orange ball woke me up. As the sleep left me, I knew instantly that something went wrong. Judy was not in the room.

I jumped off the bed and turned the lights on. My watch showed 5:54 AM. Right under the chronometer a piece of paper caught my attention. It was a note from Judy.

It said, *"I am putting you in danger by being with you. They will catch on to the fact that I am not dead soon. I am going back. My mean hairy Sasquatch, please don't try to find me. I am sorry, I thought I could live the life of someone else. I can't! You better forget me as soon as you can. Just pretend I was a dream. I love you forever."*

The note was singed *"Your Little Missy."*

I took my time taking a shower and putting my clothing on. Her note was an obvious plea for help. She wanted me to follow her. But where? I went down to my truck.

It was gone!

I checked my pockets and the motel room for the keys. The keys were gone too! Judy had taken my truck.

Part Three

Crossing the Highway

"...The Past—the dark unfathom'd
retrospect!
The teeming gulf—the sleepers and the
shadows!
The past! the infinite greatness of the past!
For what is the present after all but a
growth out of the past?"

**Walt Whitman (1819–1892), U.S. poet. Passage to India,
verse 1.**

March 2010

Chapter Seventeen

Phone Call From the Past

Two years and three months flew by. My life returned to normal as if Judy had never appeared on my doorstep and the men in green camouflage fatigues had never terrorized the San Bernardino County. Bobby DiCesare came back a week after Judy had taken my truck, which I found parked in my driveway with the keys inside. I also got my Pathfinder back from the police tow yard.

When I tried to ask Bobby about our adventure, he shrugged his shoulders and said, "Marty, think of it as just another mission. You shined. You solved the problem here and allowed me to solve the problem in..." he paused. "...the other problems. File it away into the round file and move on."

"But I never found that unauthorized beacon I was contracted to track down," I told him.

"It's not important right now, move on," he said.

Bobby has been a life-long buddy of mine. We have been putting our lives in each other's hands casually for many years now. We had become more than friends. No single word in the English language can describe the trust which develops between two combat veterans. It goes beyond the sloppy sentimental gibberish of the today's pop culture. The feminized observers of our time call it "male bonding." To those who use these words, I suggest spending some time in a firefight, just an hour or two. While enjoying this activity, I further suggest to look into the void of a gun's' muzzle, held by a man trying to kill you. And, when a stranger to your side—with a reckless abandon to his own safety—puts a round or two in the bad guy's skull, I propose that the emotion you might feel after that would go beyond gratitude, comradeship, or "bonding."

But I digress...

I ignored Bobby's advice and researched Judy anyway. My dear reader, how could I have gone on and not looked for her? She came at me from the left field and bewitched me. I hate discussing sentiments; but when you deal with females, you can't escape. The ladies thrive on penetrating the most sensitive parts of our hearts. And, when they find the right strings... Well... They play, and play, and play. Normal men have no counter moves. This is how we are created. Good Lord blessed the "stronger sex" with high stature, strong limbs, and brave heart. But, when he took our rib out and made Eve, He gave her the ability to overcome any man's brawn with kindness and intrigue.

With ease, Judy had overran my defenses. The move—she used—was of the lowest difficulty. She was just nice and caring. That was that! She hooked me. Now I missed her every morning, afternoon, and evening. And if this makes me a sentimental chump of a pussywhipped variety, so be it.

I had spent two sleepless months on line. I found out that she was from Buffalo, New York; at least a birth certificate in her name was issued there. She got her drivers' license in New York when she was eighteen. She obtained a California Drivers' License a year later with an address on the Silver Springs College campus. She earned her Masters Degree from that school and then disappeared off the face of the Earth in 1993. Her drivers' license expired in 1996 and she had not renewed it since.

Both of her parents died ten years ago and I discovered no other relatives. In her school records, I found the names of her professors. I tracked down all of them. Some did not remember her, but the ones who did, had not seen her since 1993.

After a while, I set aside my notes about Judy Dobiash. I knew that this investigation has to sit in the shadows for a time. I learned, in my forty-sex years in this world, that some things need to ripen in my brain before the solutions become obvious.

The break came from an unexpected direction.

* * *

My cell phone's jingle woke me up one Spring evening. The alarm clock showed 11:01 PM. I pressed the green button and tried to speak. My voice was still asleep and only a faint whisper came out.

"Greenblatt," I said after clearing my throat.

"Hi, sir," I heard a man's voice with an unmistakably Asian accent. "I am sorry to wake you, but I need to talk to you."

"Who are you?"

"You know me. I'm Mr. Lee from the convenience store where you buy your cigars," the man said.

"Oh, hi Mr. Lee. Are you alright?"

"I am. But you, Mr. Greenblatt, have trouble. I talked to a lawyer and he said that you need my help," Lee said.

"Who is your lawyer?"

"Mr. Ralph Oberman."

I felt chill go down my spine. "Ralph Oberman" was not a lawyer or a person. This was a password from the old operation Remove Claws.

"Ralph and I don't do business anymore," I came back with the counter.

"No matter, the president's men are on their way to get you. You have to focus, " Mr. Lee said and hung up. The "presidents men" had only one meaning: the U.S. Government had a problem with me. But why? The operation Remove Claws—which had crossed to the south of legal—has been over for many years now. "Obviously it is not over," I corrected myself.

Within fifteen minutes of the call, I saw two silver Chevrolet Impala sedans park in the street, half a block downhill from my house. My night vision glasses made the world glow amber. I kept my left eye closed in case an intense light would render my right eye blind for a time. I stood on my porch with a Ruger Mini 14 semi-automatic assault rifle at ready.

I could see four agents, two per car. I also spied a female figure in the back seat of the second Impala. Humans were not the only visitors I had tonight. My night vision glasses showed a bright amber shape of a mountain lion, secreted behind an old pine, not far from the sedans.

"Stay in the cars," I yelled in my sternest voice. "I have you covered. Only one of you comes to the porch."

They did not listen to me and began exiting. I fired once in the air. "I'll pick you off one by one within three seconds. Get back in and stay in!" I yelled again, adding expletives. "One of you get your ass to the porch. Now!"

The mountain lion began moving backwards slowly. He shot an angry look in my direction and I saw bright light reflecting from the mirror retinas of his eyes. I also saw my visitors' confusion. I surmised that they—whoever these Feds were—did not have a warrant for my arrest nor a search warrant. If they did, they would have brought local sheriff's deputies. I heard them talk to each other, but could not make out the words.

"Stand down, Greenblatt," one of them yelled finally. "I am coming to your porch. Hold your fire."

As he walked up, the rest of the Feds got back into their cars.

"This is far enough," I told him when he was within fifteen feet. "Keep your hands where I can see them and tell me what you want."

"We just want to talk to you," the man said in a calm voice.

"I have a phone," said I.

"I'd like you to come with us and talk in our office."

"Do you have a warrant for my arrest?"

"No. But I can get one tomorrow if I need to," the Fed said soothingly.

"Okay, what's so important?"

"Jose Rodriguez was a friend of yours, wasn't he?" the man asked.

"Yes."

"Well, he was working a counterfeit case. You seemed to be involved somehow, but he did his best to shield you. Now, we have a suspect in custody."

"So..."

"She said that she knows you."

"What's her name?" I asked.

"Joanna Greenblatt."

You could have knocked me over with a feather. Joanna Greenblatt was the name of my grandmother.

"Well, you seem to be surprised," the Fed chuckled.

"What's your name?"

"Special Agent Williams, United States Treasury" he said and showed me his star-shaped Secret Service badge. "I find it strange that you show up in the middle of our investigations regularly. First, we find your prints on the bad money. Then you are found to be present when Jose Gonzales was killed. Now, we have a break in the case which Jose worked on, and the suspect is asking for you by name."

"Okay, Williams," I am standing down. "As long as you guys don't try any funny stuff, I am harmless."

"Deal."

We walked to the Impalas. I looked inside the second Secret Service sedan and saw a teenage girl in the back seat. I recognized her immediately. She was the older girl in that strange wagon, which disappeared into the silver cloud more than two years ago.

"Why have you arrested this girl?" I asked.

"We got her in commission of passing bad currency," Williams said.

"Where are you taking her?"

"This is weird. Almost as soon as we reported the arrest, the Homeland Security contacted our Special Agent in Charge. They want to pick her up tomorrow," Williams agent said. "Why do you ask? Do you know her?"

"I don't know yet," I answered. "Where is she going to spend the night?"

"We are making arrangements with the Silver Springs Sheriff's station since she's a minor," Williams said.

"Okay, how can I help you? I'm willing to cooperate," I lied with a straight face.

"Be in our office tomorrow at nine hundred hours sharp. If you don't show up, we'll be back with warrants, tanks, helicopters, and nuclear weapons if we have to," Williams said in a stern voice.

* * *

After the Secret Service sedans left with the girl, I drove my Pathfinder to Mr. Lee's Convenience Market. Mr. Lee stood behind the counter as always.

"Are you in Mark Foxtrot confidence?" he asked me without saying hello.

"No. I have no idea what you are talking about," I answered.

"You need to gain confidence quick."

"How do I do that and why do I need to do that?" I asked.

"I've been in neutral for a long time," Mr. Lee said. "My orders were to observe and repot only. For many years, I had nothing to report. Now, Secret Service is getting too close."

"Too close to what?"

"Take care of the girl and gain confidence," said Mr. Lee with a sad smile. "The original Mr. Ralph Oberman's followers are virtually non existent anymore. I knew of you by chance only. You should know that Remove Claws operation did not end. It continued under a different name."

"Why is the girl important?"

"Two reasons. She does not belong in this world," Lee said and hesitated, trying to find the right words. "She's important to you in another way. Personal way."

"Does the name Judy Dobiash ring through this situation?" I asked because my gut told me that Judy was in the middle of this mess.

"You are on your own," Lee said without addressing my question verbally. His head, however, nodded just slightly. Then, he made a hand motion to follow him. We walked through the back door and walked down the hill into a ravine. There, I saw a horse harnessed to a cart made from the copy of my old truck. The cabin, the engine, and the transmission were gone. Only the bed and the front seat remained.

"Dispose of this," Mr. Lee said pointing to the horse with the cart. "Then, take care of the girl. Secret Service traced the bills, she had been spending, to a bank. The bank traced the money to the businesses along the Highway 38. Secret Service staked out the highway and got her. Right now, they are as clueless as you are. But, they can't be enlightened."

"What about you?"

"You will never see me again."

* * *

The bay gelding stood still under the dark sky. He sniffed my ear when I came close and took the rains. I walked him across the Highway 38. The wagon-slash-old-truck, loaded with boxes of canned food, rolled noiselessly behind the horse. One of my neighbors had been bringing his Arabs to Silver Springs in the summer. He had built several stalls and a large turn out area behind his summer house. In the winter, he lived in Marina Del Ray and never showed up here.

I came to this deserted house, undid the leather harness, and let the horse into the fenced turn out area. As soon as the gelding sensed freedom, he kicked out and ran several circles. After that, he sniffed the ground and began feeding on the frozen weeds.

My Nissan Pathfinder waited for me patiently at the convenience store. The small building was dark now and Mr. Lee's car was gone. The dashboard clock showed 12:36 AM. I dialed Eddie Sobaleff's cell phone number.

"Who is it this late at night?" asked Eddie, his voice hoarse. I had woken him up.

"Greenblatt here," I said cheerfully. "Are you awake enough to talk?"

"Yes," Eddie coughed several times. "What are you up to, Marty?"

"You and your people owe me for several situations I helped you with. Am I wrong?" I asked.

"You're not wrong," said Eddie. I knew that he was completely awake now and listening carefully. "What's going on?"

"Meet me at the convenience market at Highway 38 and Silver Springs Avenue," I said. "Do you think you can be here in a thirty minutes."

"Okay, Marty," said Eddie and clicked off.

My clock glowed 12:51 AM when his Chevy Tahoe parked next to my Pathfinder in such a way that our driver's side windows faced each other.

"There is a girl in the Silver Springs Sheriff's sub-station," I said without preliminaries. "Her name is Joanna Greenblatt. Secret Service brought her there two hours ago. They are transferring her away in the morning. It will not be good for her."

Eddie's face maintained a blank expression as he listened to me.

"It would be preferable if the Sheriff's Department would release her in my custody. She's a minor, you see," I said.

"Is she related to you?" asked Eddie.

"Let's say she is," I said.

"Okay, such thing may be possible."

I followed Eddie's Tahoe to the station. As he parked in the "employees only" paring space, I stopped my Pathfinder half a block away. I turned the lights off but let the engine run. A few minutes later, my cell phone rang.

"Marty, we have two Secret Service agents guarding her. I put together a release form and you signed it already," Eddie said. He was letting me know that he forged my signature. "I'm going to distract the Feds. As soon as I hang up, time exactly three minutes and get to the employees' entrance."

Eddie clicked off when my dashboard clock showed 1:23 AM.

At exactly 1:26 AM. I stopped by the door with the "Employees Only" sign. The door opened and the girl jumped into my passenger seat. I kept my headlights off and drove slowly, avoiding using the breaks. When we were two blocks away from the Sheriff's sub-station, I turned on the headlights and put the hammer down. Only then, I glanced at the girl. She stared back at me.

"Thank you, sir," she said.

"Is your name really Joanna Greenblatt?" I asked.

"Yes."

"Are we related?"

"Yes."

"How?"

"I am your daughter, in a way," said Joanna.

"What?"

"Well, I am not really your daughter but in a way I still am," Joanna's voice betrayed confusion.

"Do I know your mother?" I asked.

"Yes," she said.

"What is your mother's name?"

"Judith Greenblatt," Joanna said

"Who is your real father?" I asked.

"You are, I think," she said.

"How could that be?"

"I don't know," said Joanna, kept looking at me, and whispered. "So this is how my dad would have looked like."

When we parked in front of the deserted summer home where I left the gelding, I heard the horse's loud neighing. I told Joanna to stay in the Pathfinder and ran to the back with my Colt in hand. What I saw was something one never forgets. My old friend mountain lion hunted the gelding. The big cat kept his body low to the ground, slowly advancing forward. The horse stood still in the middle of the turnout area. When the mountain lion sprang forward finally, the gelding turned around and delivered a vicious rear leg kick to the cat's head. He followed it up with the front hoofs. After he was done, the lifeless body of the mountain lion lay on the cold ground. I jumped over the fence and fired my Colt once into the cat's head.

Just then, I heard Joanna's footsteps. She, too, jumped over the fence and rushed to the horse. "My poor little Buckie," she cooed while caressing the gelding. Her voice sounded exactly like Judy's.

I helped Joanna put the harness back on Buckie and she drove the wagon to the old abandoned stretch of the highway. I sat next to her and said nothing until we were nearing the rockslide. We stopped. In silence she gave me a thick white card with a large blue dot in the middle. It felt like an oversized credit card. I gave Joanna a questioning look.

"Just press on the dot," she said.

"What is it?" I asked and pressed.

Before Joanna had a chance to answer, a cloud of thick silvery mist enveloped us.

"...Other people's harvests are always the best harvests, but one's own children are always the best children ..."

Chinese proverb

March 2010

Chapter Eighteen

Beyond the Silver Mist

The senses returned slowly. First, my ears woke up. I heard the birds chirping, wind blowing through the trees, and my own labored breathing.

Next, I felt the morning's breeze on my face and I discovered that my head rested on a chunk of broken concrete. Then, my mouth reported a foul taste of bile. After that, my nose woke up and detected clear cold air with a faint odor of Cordite. My eyes came back last.

I opened them slowly. My pupils focused unhappily on a stretch of some deserted highway. The old road nestled in a small canyon between two hills covered with winter brush and sparse pine trees. I was flat on my back, behind a large boulder on the side of the highway. The hardtop showed no evidence of motorized travel for quite some time. The plant life had overtaken a good part of the concrete. A few tumbleweeds rolled lazily to and fro, slaves to the whims of the unsure wind gusts. Here and there, rusted hulks of what used to be cars and trucks littered the road. Some had grown into the surface, others sprawled on the highway like the carcasses of some prehistoric animals. Most of them showed signs of fire and many were dotted with bullet holes.

As I struggled to sit up, my body issued a protest. A dull pain in my joints and spine made any movement difficult. I ignored the pain and got up to my feet. The highway appeared to be completely abandoned except for a commotion of the morning birds. A sudden wind gust brought a smell of manure mixed with burning wood. I turned my head to see the source. Several faint columns of smoke plumed up the hill towards the rising sun. I tried to make a step but lost my balance right away. On my way down, and just before passing out again, the memory of how I got here hit me...

I remembered the mist and the feeling of nausea. I also remembered a group of men running uphill towards our wagon, their sub-machine guns spewing led at us. I jumped down and told Joanna to drive as fast as she could.

I found cover behind a large boulder. From there I fired my Mini 14. I think I got two of the bad guys. The others started to flank me. I was trapped between the boulder and a steep hill. Just when the things looked hopeless, several explosions rocked the air. I recognized the sound of mortar fire. Whoever was firing the mortar was correcting, getting closer to my assailants. Before I found out what happened, one of the mortar rounds went off near me. The last thing I remembered was a blinding flash.

When I woke up again, the sun stood high. I got up to my feet with some difficulty and looked around. The road was still the same. Now, I saw the bodies of three men in green camouflage fatigues sprawled on the hardtop about one hundred feet away from me. Further down, I saw several fresh craters in the road and more green-clad bodies.

Suddenly, I recognized the canyon. This was that abandoned stretch of the Highway 38. It was not the quite the same, however.

The rockslide was not there!

Instead, the road snaked forward unobstructed and disappeared into a curve behind a steep hill.

I patted myself down, checking for injuries and discovered a bulge in my breast pocket. Inside, I found the thick plastic card with the large blue dot. I pressed on the dot. A feeling of nausea came right away and the familiar cloud of silver mist enveloped me. It brought total darkness and a freefall sensation.

I don't know how long the experience lasted. When it was over, my dear reader, I still stood in the same spot. Instead of the sun, though, dark clouds dispensed a cold sprinkle of fine mist. The abandoned stretch of the highway looked like it has always looked since the rockslide, which was back by the way. No leftovers of cars and trucks were within sight anymore. The dead bodies and the explosion craters vanished as well.

* * *

I walked back to my home. Special Agent Williams and his Secret Service crew waited for me.

"We have to arrest you," Williams said.

"On what charge?" I asked.

"Adding and abetting the escape of a federal prisoner," he said.

They took away my Mini 14, handcuffed my hands behind my back, and drove me to the Riverside Secret Service headquarters. Still handcuffed, I found myself in a small interrogation room.

Even though the chair was hard, my recent adventures took a toll me—I fell asleep.

"Wake up Greenblatt!"

A rude voice yanked me out of my slumber some time later. I opened my eyes and saw the infuriated face of Capt. Rumsey.

"Where is she?" he snarled and kicked me in the stomach with his right field boot. I fell off the chair and looked up. My combat instincts were up to the task, thankfully. The abdominal muscles flexed just as the boot connected and protected my internal organs form any damage.

"I need to know where you hid the girl." Rumsey yelled, spit coming out of the mouth.

He towered over me in his desert camouflage fatigues. For a few moments he stood still, his eyes boring into mine. Then, he picked me up by the collar of my jacket and threw my body against a wall. Rumsey underestimated me. I bounced off the wall and kicked him in the groin. Since my hands were still handcuffed behind my back, I could not follow up with my fists. My knees, however, worked fine. As he stood there, bent over, holding on to his privates, I kicked him in the nose with my right knee. He straitened up, his hands on his face now. Without missing a beat, I produced a picture perfect side kick to his jaw. Rumsey's unconscious body folded down to the floor like a cheap blow up doll with the air gone.

Just then, the door to the interrogation room opened and a hoard of the Secret Service agents separated me from Rumsey. The last to enter was Acting Special Agent in Charge Abrams.

"Take the handcuffs off me," I told him in a quiet voice. "If you want to talk to me, treat me with respect."

Abrams did not look like a man who wants any violence. He unlocked my handcuffs himself.

"You shouldn't have done that," he said pointing at Rumsey who was still unconscious.

"He didn't leave me much choice," I said.

"Okay, let's go to my office," he said and motioned for Williams to follow us.

I eased into a soft armchair in his office. Williams sat in the other one while Abrams took his place behind a desk.

"Now, Greenblatt, tell me what you know about Gonzalez' death and the girl you sprang form us," Abrams said. Even though his voice was of a demanding nature, I detected no force, no real desire to find out.

"Agent Abrams, have you ever had a feeling that you are asleep and just about to wake up Matrix style?" I asked.

Neither Abrams nor Williams said anything.

"I know no more than you do. People, some of them dangerous, think that I am a cog in some conspiracy. The fact is that I am trying to find out what's going on myself," I said and was pleased to see that the Secret Service agents listened intently. They projected a desire of wanting nothing to do with my situation. "My best guess is that we have found ourselves in the way of an 'off the books' operation. I don't know what it is yet. But I am convinced that your agency's involvement is incidental. Rumsey is off the reservation. This much I do know. You don't have to cooperate with him."

"I like you better than Rumsey," Abrams said. "But he carries the weight of the Homeland Security and the Marine Corps. What weight do you carry?"

I had nothing to say. All my credentials were "off the books."

"Let me ask you a question," I said. "If I was just a pedestrian, would I have gotten away with your prisoner that easy? You checked on me. You know that my civilian status is a veneer."

Andrei V. Lefebvre

"A veneer for what?" Abrams asked with a genuine curiosity. "This office has been working a counterfeit case for ten years now. Some of the bad money has you prints on it. What is more puzzling is that the same bills have prints of one of your associates."

"Who?"

"We matched the prints to someone by the name of Sean Smith. We know that you worked with him," Abrams said.

"Sean has been dead for almost sixteen years now," said I.

"Yes, we found records to this fact. However, your people ..." Abrams hesitated. "... people in your business are not always dead when the paperwork says that they should be."

"I assure you that he is gone because I saw him die from a gunshot to his heart with my own eyes," I said.

Silence.

"Jose told me that the fake money was so good, it could have been real. Is that true?" I asked.

"Yes. It is an amazingly good forgery," Abrams said.

"How do you know that the fake money is fake and not the bills you compare it to?" I asked.

"We thought about it. We had the money in the ATF evidence analyzed too. We have no answer to this question," Abrams said biting his lips. "Actually, both batches look so real that they should be real. However, the duplicating serial numbers make this possibility impossible."

"So, what do we do now?" I asked.

"You tell us," Abrams retorted. "I don't want to be involved with whatever 'off the books' operation you and Rumsey are involved in."

"Kick both of us, me and Rumsey, out of your office and wash your hands. If you need to put the counterfeit operation on hold, do that. Rumsey has no juice to go over your head. If he had such power, you would have heard from Washington already," said I.

"...Our most important decisions are made while we are thinking about something else ..."

Mason Cooley (b. 1927), U.S. aphorist. City Aphorisms, Second Selection, New York (1985).

March 2010

Chapter Nineteen

Something Which Defies Any Explanation

Taxicab took me back to Silver Springs. I asked the cabbie to drop me off on the side of the Highway 38, about two miles away from my house. I had a paranoid suspicion that someone unpleasant may be waiting for me. When I got to my house, using the footpath to the back of my property, I found that my suspicions were only partially justified. Someone had been in my home not long ago and created a mess. The furniture had been tossed around and my closets had been emptied. I looked in the garage and found it ransacked as well.

As I analyzed what has been done to my residence, I understood that whoever did the tossing was looking for Joanna more than likely. The bookshelves, my desk, and the file cabinets were not touched. In the garage, someone had moved a stack of storage boxes, but did not go through each one.

I spent three hours putting my house back in order. Then, I put on Scarlatti's classical guitar CD and filled my bathtub with hot water. While the guitar strings caressed my eardrums, I eased my body into the scorching water and let my mind wonder.

Sleep took me over. I saw my mom and dad holding hands as they walked up some mountain trail. In the dream, they were young, just like in the picture next to my alarm radio clock. That faded photograph showed them in their mountain exploration outfits. In it, my dad has his arm around my mom and she shows a happy loving expression on her face. This snapshot had been taken, my mom told many times over the years, when she was pregnant with me. In the dream, my parents turned around and smiled. "Don't follow us, Marty," Dad said in a clear loud voice. "You always do your best if you make it your own way." Mom said nothing but her lips formed a happy smile, just like in the picture, and waived at me.

Her smile and her eyes were telling me something. I knew that it was "the something" which I should recognize. I strained my gray matter and it came to me. Joanna's eyes and smile looked exactly like my mom's. My emotions surged and woke me up. The watch reported 3:01 PM. The bathtub's water was cool now. I got out and dried my body with a large towel. Then, I took out the classical guitar CD out and put on a Benny Goodman album. His clarinet brought up the memory of Judy. I could almost feel her body curled up next to me.

I sat in my armchair, lost in daydreams. While the big band sound cut through the reality, my sentimental mood turned more practical. The events of the last few days passed through my mind. I understood that I was faced with a situation to which simple logic could not be applied. I remembered something Under Secretary Greene told me six years ago. His exact words, as he put a piece of paper in my breast pocket, had been, "If you run into something which defies any explanation on the global level, see the man whose info is in your pocket now."

My old notebook held the paper now; I had taped it to the one of the pages for safekeeping. I went to my den and fished it out from the safe. The paper had a name "Walter Kurz" on it. Below, I found a local phone number. I wavered for a moment, deciding whether my situation defied explanation on the "global level." Then I slapped my forehead, knocking all the doubts out, and reached for the cell phone.

http://www.WhosWhoinScience.org

Walter Alexander Kurz, American/Austrian Physicist

Walter Kurz was born in Vienna, Austria on 2 September, 1922. He attended the University of Vienna in the late 1930s, until Nazi Germany annexed Austria in 1938. Prior to the annexation, 16-year-old Kurz wrote a letter to Otto Stern, Nobel Prize Winner in physics, asking his reaction to his Diesseitig Vervielfältigung (Temporal Duplication) Theory. Stern showed high regard towards the young man's abilities but suggested to Kurz to avail himself of basics before tackling such a complex issue.

Nazi war research machine enlisted young Kurz into one of its weapon development centers. He worked on a controversial Abweichung Project. The project, (translated literally as "Divergence"), was to create a "super weapon." Few records of this project have survived the World War II. What is known, however, is that the German researchers had believed that they could develop a device which would defy conventional rules of physics and propel weapons to any point in the universe. In 1944, Gestapo investigated Kurtz and found that his father was Jewish. He was arrested and shipped to Chełmno concentration camp.

In 1945, advancing Soviet Army freed the surviving inhabitants of Chełmno and took twenty-two-year-old Kurz to Moscow where he conducted his research under the tutelage of Vladimir Foch, world-renowned Soviet physicist. No information is available about the directions of his scientific studies, except that they were related to the sub-atomic theory.

In 1962 Kurz moved to Leipzig, East Germany. Later the same year, he moved again, this time to an undisclosed city in the United States. It is believed that the CIA had engineered his escape across the Iron Curtain.

California-based Silver Springs College invited Kurz to join the Physics Department in 1974. His theoretical research in quantum Mechanics won praises from such Nobel Prize notables in the American community of physicists as Eugene Wigner and Hugh Everett.

Kurz is semi-retired and lives with his wife Roberta in Big Bear Lake, California.

"...Genius (which means transcendent capacity of taking trouble, first of all) ..."

Thomas Carlyle (1795–1881), Scottish essayist, historian. The History of Frederick II of Prussia, bk. 4, ch. 3 (1858-1865).

March 2010

Chapter Twenty

I Meet Walter Kurz

r. Kurz' home looked much like my own. It hid in the thickness of pine trees and was protected by a long, barely navigable, dirt driveway. The town of Big Bear Lake sits at 7,000 feet and sports thick layers of snow every winter. Even now, the runoff did not melt all of the pack. The icy slush covered the driveway. My watch showed 6:17 PM as I walked up carefully. The smell of burning wood hit my nostrils and I saw smoke pour freely from the chimney.

Before I reached the porch, the front door opened and a matronly woman came out. I surmised that she was Roberta, Dr. Kurz' wife. I spoke to her earlier today. As soon as she heard my name over the phone, her voice obtained an interesting quality. It sounded as if she had expected me to call for many years and had given up on waiting. Roberta suggested that I come and meet her husband as soon as I can.

Now, I made a few steps forward and waved at her.

"Mr. Greenblatt," she greeted me as if we were close friends. "I am so glad to meet you finally."

She looked to be in her late fifties with a petite frame and platinum blond hair. Her posture and her gold, tastefully diamonded, jewelry spoke of a woman used the moneyed levels of our society.

"Likewise, Mrs. Kurz," I put my most polite foot forward.

Her husband met me in the doorway and extended his handshaking hand. He pulled me in, across the doorway, with a surprising strength for a man in his late eighties.

"I am a prisoner of many superstitions, Mr. Greenblatt," he said. "One of them being that shaking hands across a threshold is unacceptable."

I said nothing, smiled, and nodded.

Roberta set up a spread of cold cuts, deviled eggs, and fresh vegetables.

"What would be your pleasure?" Dr. Kurz asked and motioned towards the liquor cabinet.

His accent had a harsh trace of German in it. His blue eyes possessed a penetrating quality of a man who is used to examining others and passing uncompromising judgments. Even in his advanced age, the power of Dr. Kurz' personality shone through. He had the air about him which could only be obtained by traveling the hard roads of life. My host was a man who did not care much what people had to say about him. I judged him to be the one who enjoyed doing unconventional things, and reveling when the "in crowd" would get scandalized by his actions. In the other words, Dr. Kurz was the drinking partner of my dreams.

"Dr. Kurz, I will drink whatever you will serve," I said.

The old man smiled and combed his thick white beard with his fingers.

"Roberta, Mr. Greenblatt and I will drink beer. Corona beer," he said, his European accent thick, and sat at the table. His wife served the beverage in the ice cold glasses and joined us. Dr. Kurz and I downed four mugs in silence, enjoying the lager and the food. Roberta did not drink with us, but made sure that the empty bottles were replaced with the full. At some point, she got up and brought a covered dish.

"One of my students went wild duck hunting and was kind enough to share some of his spoils with me," said Dr. Kurz.

He removed the cover from the dish and I saw three birds baked with sweet potatoes. The ducks were delicious. We killed another few mugs of beer and I felt a slight lightness in my head.

"Do you enjoy sauna?" Dr. Kurz asked, his face showed genuine happiness.

"Yes, I love steam."

"I spent many years in Russia. They have a high culture of steam bathing. It is an old tradition worthy of imitating," he said. "I had a steam bath built in the back of my house. Would you object to moving our conversation there?"

While Roberta stayed in the house, we undressed to our birthday suits and relaxed in a small log cabin with a brick fireplace. The bricks were so hot that when Dr. Kurz poured a mixture of beer and water on them, the liquid evaporated instantly into an invisible steam. The two tiers of wood benches semi-circled the steam room. I watched my host place a white towel on the upper bench and only then sit down. I followed his example. The invisible, scorching steam with a smell of baking bread—produced by the evaporated beer mixture—made the sweat run down my body freely.

For about twenty minutes, we basked in a hellish pleasure of the high heat. Finally, Dr. Kurz got up and walked out of the log cabin into the darkened back yard. I followed him. We came to a small round pool full of icy water. He plunged into it. I closed my eyes and jumped in too. The burning-like sensation of the thirty-three-degree water to my piping hot skin was beyond any of my past experiences. I felt the rush of blood circulating throughout my body. It brought energy, kicked the alcohol-induced lightheadedness, and cleared my mind.

"You must have found the unauthorized beacon," Dr. Kurz said after we were back in the steam room. "You must have crossed the highway into A1. This is why you are here. Isn't it?"

"I did cross something into somewhere other than what I can explain," I said and relayed to him my experience in the abandoned stretch of the Highway 38. "But I don't know what the unauthorized beacon and A1 are."

Dr. Kurz wiped the sweat of his forehead and sprinkled drops of water, mixed with beer, on the piping hot bricks again. The drops evaporated the second they touched the bricks. They produced another burning wave of steam which enveloped my body and cleared the sinuses.

"Mr. Greenblatt, you are ready to gain confidence in Mark Foxtrot," said Dr. Kurz. "Do you have any significant math of physics background?"

"No."

"No matter," Dr. Kurz said with a mild disappointment. I understood that he longed for deep scientific discussions. "You have heard of Quantum Mechanics?"

"Yes. It has something to do with wave-particle duality," I raked my brains for this long forgotten information I picked up years back.

"Yes, it is part of it. But the road I am trying to roll our discussion on is paved with the fact that subatomic particles do not behave in the same way Newtonian objects do. They seem to have a mind of their own. An observer of such particles seems to have an effect on them and makes them behave in unexpected ways. In the Newtonian world one can calculate how a physical object behaves. If you know the mass, speed, air resistance, and the gravity pull, you know where a rock, you have thrown, will end up. In the world of the subatomic particles, such predictions are guesses only. We have no ability to construct a single equation which would explain how and where the subatomic particles will end up. We can calculate a pretty good guess. But this as far as the human science has gone so far."

We left the steam room again for another plunge into the round icy pool. I felt the hoards of frigid subatomic particles attacking my overheated skin. The clarity of mind—such plunges produce—can't be overstated, however. When we climbed out from the water and went back to the steam room, my gray matter was ready to absorb anything.

"Let's continue," Dr. Kurz said as if an audience of hundreds was in front of him. "When I was a teenager, I came up with a crazy idea that we can induce a Newtonian object, i.e. physical object composed of countless trillions of subatomic particles, behave in a non-Newtonian way. My theory postulated that I can hurl our rock in such a way that the gravity and the wind resistance would be of no consequence. It is possible, using very little energy, to propel our rock from here to Vienna instantaneously. It may even arrive before we have propelled it."

I stared at Dr. Kurz in disbelief. "How can that be possible?"

"I will spare you the scientific explanation. Our universe is such that if the rock is de-constructed into its quantum parts, it will behave like a subatomic particle. I worked for a German research lab during the war on such a project. We have never gone beyond theory. After the war, the Russians nabbed me and I continued my research in Moscow. There, I was able to build a system which was supposed to do just that. I thought it would be able to hurl rocks, and other things, across the universe."

The man stopped. He stood up from the bench and dried the sweat off his body. "Let's take a shower and continue in my living room over coffee," he said.

Roberta had the coffee and the cakes ready for us. We sat at the table, exhausted from the steam, and drank the delicious coffee. I smiled but said nothing, waiting for the old scientist to continue.

"Men are arrogant creatures," Dr. Kurz spoke up finally. "We have tendency to live in our own fantasies. We see what we want to see, ignoring the facts staring us in the face."

He motioned for his wife to refresh his cup. She did so noiselessly and retreated back to a darkened part of the room into a comfortable looking loveseat.

"I was so proud of my theory, which had to do with proving that our line of time is not constant on the sub-atomic level, that I missed what my equations really meant," Dr. Kurz continued. "The time is not a singular entity. Imagine an infinite number of strait lines drawn on a piece of paper. Some are parallel some fork into more and ran parallel to others. Some of them are thick, others thin, yet others are long or short. This is how our universe is constructed. The lines represent the different timelines possible. Actually, I constructed an equation which proves that our universe possesses an infinite number of timelines. The science fiction writers had christened this phenomena as alternative universes. What my equations show is that at every point in time an infinite number of possible timelines fork from our own. Some are the same as ours except for a minor divergence, some are radically different."

"Are you telling me that I had been transported to an alternative universe yesterday?" I asked.

"Yes. You have visited another timeline. Sometime in the early Nineteen Nineties our timelines have diverged but remained connected through a series of beacons," Kurz said.

"But how?"

"In the late Fifties, the Soviets, with my help, put together a network of beacons throughout the world designed to transport physical objects in a way not unlike the beaming process in the Star Trek transporter," said Dr. Kurz. "Fortunately, for the free world, the system did not work. The objects either did not go anywhere or disappeared for good or reappeared at random locations and times. Neither I nor anyone else was able to fine tune the network. It simply did not work the way I designed it."

"Well, how do the other timelines come into play?" I asked.

"This is funny. The system, I designed, was capable of tapping into other timelines. It did it better and more reliably then when it was used for its original purpose, i.e. transporting Newtonian objects within our timeline. Whoops," Dr. Kurz chuckled. "And we did not realize what we did until someone from a parallel timeline contacted us."

His laugh turned into a coughing bout. Roberta rushed up to him with a glass of water. As he drank, she caressed his thick white hair. Genuine affection moderated the dutiful expression of her stern face. Dr. Kurz took her hand in his and straitened his shoulders. For a brief moment, I saw him as he probably appeared in his prime: a firm, tree-trunk of a man.

His penetrating blue eyes read my thoughts. "I am an important man, you see," he said as if lecturing a teenager. "Important men have to be taken care of. I've never been married before. Never saw a need to. When I came to the U.S., I became important. So ..."

His stopped talking and brought Roberta's hand to his lips and kissed it slowly, visibly savoring every moment. His wife stood still, visibly enjoying it immensely. Her demeanor, however, resembled that of a nurse rather then a wife.

"So, someone had to take care of me. Ease me into this life," Dr. Kurz continued. "This is where Mrs. Kurz became Mrs. Kurz. You, Mr. Greenblatt, and my wife have much in common."

"The birds are nesting, my sweetie," Roberta said, kissed the old man on his lips and continued. "Mr. Greenblatt does not care. He knows how things are. And I do love you, you know."

"I know," said Dr. Kurz and let go of his wife.

Roberta pulled up a chair to the table and looked me in the eyes. Her blue pupils had a cold distant quality. She was not a woman to take lightly, I decided.

"We refer to the other timeline as A1," she said. "They think that they are the proper timeline and our divergent line is an aberration. Their history forked away from our timeline in a radical way."

I took out my cigar case but Roberta shook her head slightly and I put it back into my jacket.

"Marty, both of us work for Ralph Oberman," she said enjoying my surprise. "My affections for my husband are real McCoy but it was an arranged marriage because Dr. Kurz and Ralph Oberman are one and the same. Operation Remove Claws was designed to track down and deactivate the Soviet beacon system my husband invented. Somehow, when A1 timeline and A2 timeline forked, we remained connected through the series of windows. It took my husband two years to find that the connection was because of the duality of beacons."

"Duality of beacons?" I asked.

Dr. Kurz smiled, "When our timelines forked—we call this phenomena divergence—the network was powered up. For the reason, only a complicated equation can illustrate, windows remained between the timelines. I found that the window effect took place when the beacons in both timelines were within few miles of each other in their respective worlds. Since everything diverged, i.e. duplicated, the duplicated beacons produced the windows."

"So, the Operation Remove Claws was never about particle weapons, wasn't it?" I asked.

"Yes, the operation's goal was to destroy the beacons. You and your people have eliminated almost all but a handful," Dr. Kurz said. "The history in A1 timeline has not been kind to them. We, in our timeline, want to sever all of the contacts with them. This decision was made on the highest levels of our government. So high, as the matter of fact, that the President of the United States may not even be in confidence of Mark Foxtrot."

"Confidence? Mark Foxtrot?" I asked again.

"Mark Foxtrot is the point of divergence, point where our timelines have forked," Dr. Kurz explained. "Confidence is another euphemism for knowing something which is kept secret from most. Only a handful of people, a few hundred at the most, know about A1. Once we destroy all of the beacons, our timeline will roll along as if the divergence was never more then an obscure scientific speculation."

"I seem to be in the middle of it all," I said. "Do I have a role?"

"Mr. Greenblatt," said Dr. Kurz smiling. "Most people in our country believe that we have a structured government which does its business according to a set of rules which can be codified. To some degree they are right because this is our tradition inherited from the Western European history. However, such model is static and conflicts with the variables of human nature. Our officials do not create policy. They tend to rubberstamp the decisions which are obvious already."

"Okay, who makes those obvious decisions of policy?" I asked.

"No one man or official body of men make it. The decisions are formulated by the consensus of the social groups in power. And I don't mean official power. Every society on Earth, including ours, has its own elite, i.e. people with power and money. When the elites are huge, like in the U.S., the people enjoy reasonable amount of economic and intellectual freedom. When such elites are small, as in the poor countries without middle classes and a large underclass, the members of such elites are forced to close down the freedoms to maintain their power. What I am getting at is that within these elites the decisions grow during their informal socializing such as playing golf, attending fundraisers, and so on. No one speaks about any particular situation in depth or at length. Nevertheless, after the issues receive reactions during such informal discourse, the elites' majority formulates an opinion. Just like people formulate an opinion on the fashions every year. No one designer invents it. Many compete, but some become popular and some don't. The political ideas receive the same treatment."

"I understand," said I.

"So, my dear Mr. Greenblatt," Dr. Kurz chuckled. "You are at the brunt of the decision making process. You have to act in a certain way. You know which way to act because you can guess what the informal opinion on the situation is. No one can order you to do anything. Whatever you do will determine what the future will be. If you understand what the right decisions are, someone will backdate your actions as a successful operation and will assign a catchy name to it. If you won't be able to sell your actions as a success, you will suffer the indignity of being a failure. And those who are opined as such, are treated harshly."

"Rough, isn't it?" I smiled happily in contrast to my words for Dr. Kurz offered me my liberty. He handed me my freedom of action.

"We will be cheering for you," said Roberta. "I have a personal stake in seeing you succeed."

"How, so?" I asked.

"You know Judy Dobiash, don't you?" she asked with a mischievous smile.

"Hmmm... yes," I said taken aback.

"She's my niece," said Roberta.

The woman no longer smiled. Her face took a hard expression one usually associates with the violent men. "She's a creature of A1. Judy of our timeline is no longer. I want the one who's left here. Or her children at least," she said quietly. "Mr. Greenblatt, I know that you are not impartial to my niece. If nothing else, take care of her and her girls."

Roberta's demeanor changed again. Instead of hardness, I saw a worried woman now. "Other than my husband, Judy is the only close relative I have left," she said and wiped the tears from her eyes.

"...Hiding places there are innumerable, escape is only one, but possibilities of escape, again, are as many as hiding places ..."

Franz Kafka (1883–1924), Prague German Jewish author, novelist. The Third Notebook, November 18, 1917. The Blue Octavo Notebooks, ed. Max Brod, trans. by Ernst Kaiser and Eithne Wilkins. Exact Change, Cambridge, MA (1991). Dearest Father: Stories and Other Writings, trans. by Ernst Kaiser and Eithne Wilkins, New York, Schocken Books (1954).

March 2010

Chapter Twenty-One

The Escape

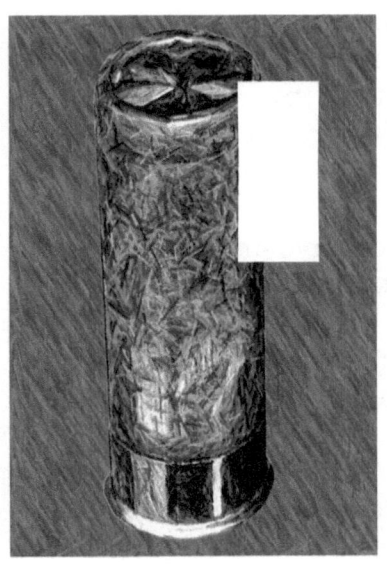

woke up in a darkened motel room next morning. My watch showed 5:57 AM. A few moments passed before I remembered where I was. Last night, I left Dr. Kurz' house shortly after midnight. The beer and the steam room relaxed my body to the point where I did not want to drive back home. Instead, I checked into a local motel.

The small room smelled of mildew. While I took a shower in the tiny bathroom, the last night's conversation circulated in my gray matter. Walter Kurz had answered all of my questions. The parallel timeline explained the duplication of currency and the fact that Joanna thought I was her father. Since she claimed her mother to be Judy, an interesting possibility opened up. Could it be that mine and Judy's counterparts, in another timeline, met and produced a child?

The bath towel proved to be too small to dry me properly. I tossed the soaked piece of cloth on the floor and ripped the sheet off the bed. The cotton fabric finished the job. When I happened to glance at my unshaved mug in the mirror, my eyes stopped at my cell phone in the breast pocket. I flipped it open and almost turned it on.

After a few moments of contemplation, I decided against powering it up. I shut it off last night so no one could trace the ping. Cell phones emit signals every so often when they are on. Technology exists which makes it possible to locate the cell network antennae which had the contact with the cell phone last. Granted, it would be a general area of approximately one square mile, but it would be enough to compromise my whereabouts.

Instead of checking my messages through the cell phone, I used the room's landline. An automated attendant told me that I have six messages. Five of them were hang ups. The sixth was from Bobby.

"Buddy, I miss you," his crisp voice baritoned. "I went bird watching without you and saw a bald eagle in full flight. Call me back."

"Bald eagle in full flight" could have meant only one thing—the United States Government was after me big time.

"Are you on a secure phone?" was the first thing Bobby asked after picking up his office line.

"No. It is a third party landline," I said.

"Do you have a condom on you?" he asked.

It took me a few seconds to understand that he wanted me to use a voice scrambler. This device encrypts the sound into the unintelligible electronic beeps. Only a related descrambling device can turn such digital gibberish back into human speech. Without saying anything, I looked in my gym bag and found the gadget. It looked like just another receiver. I unplugged the regular receiver and plugged my gadget in.

"We can have safe sex now," I said.

Bobby chuckled. "You buddy Rumsey secured an arrest warrant for you. You are charged with hindering a Federal investigation. Flimsy charge, but the offence is a felony," he said. "I am working on it for you but it will take at least a week to sort things out."

"Who is Rumsey? Is he from A1?" I asked.

This time Bobby laughed out loud. "You gained confidence, I see. I never wanted you involved in the Mark Foxtrot project. Remove Claws was bad enough. To answer your question, Rumsey you know is our timeline's idiot. His A1, his double in A1, however, is a big honcho in his world. His power is based on the help from his A2 in our world. Without each other they are done. This is why they want to control as many beacons as possible."

"How's the game scored so far?" I asked.

"They are losing. A1 looks nothing like us. They have some severe political and economic problems on the scale of pre-World War Two Europe," Bobby said. "I am aware of only three functioning pairs of beacons. Our people control one set, Rumsey's crew has the second, and the third one is a mystery. It is the one you're looking for. Did you find it yet?"

I ignored the question. First, I am not sold on the infallibility of the scramblers; and, even though the man on the other end sounded like Bobby, my professional paranoia allowed for a possibility that I was talking to an enemy imposter. So, instead of answering, I asked, "Do we have any detecting devices to track it?"

"Not that I'm aware of. The beacons require only minimal power. I am told that they use some sort of subatomic perpetual motor in them. The beacons are always on but emit only minimal electromagnetic fields and, therefore, undetectable."

"Can you tell me what they look like at least?"

"Sorry, partner. They can look like anything. Like cell phones, radios, computers, or any other electronic gadgets," Bobby said.

"Bobby, thank you for the heads up. I am off the reservation now," I said.

"It's about time," said Bobby and hung up.

* * *

On my way down the San Bernardino Mountain, I picked up a tail. A white Chrysler PT Cruiser nestled behind my rear bumper and refused to be shaken off. I led it all the way down to Redlands. When I stopped at a gas station, PT Cruiser waiting across the street, my cell phone rang.

"Greenblatt, you are not going nowhere," Rumsey said after I answered. "Put your hands on the hood of your car and wait for my men to take you into custody."

"Who are your men?" I asked.

"I have the Homeland Security authority to arrest you. We have a Federal arrest warrant signed by a Federal judge," he yelled indignantly.

"Rumsey, are you sure you want to tangle with me?" I asked adding an expletive.

"Listen to me, Greenblatt. I eat guys like you for breakfast. Surrender now!" his voice had a note of desperation in it.

"Captain, don't get your panties all twisted now," I laughed insultingly. "Your warrant is just as good as a piece of toilet paper and you should you use it next time you wet yourself."

"I warned you!" he roared as I clicked off.

I filled up my gas tank to the brim and checked my weapons. I had a rifle, a shotgun, and a .38 caliber revolver. I also had several ammo boxes for these pieces. The presence of my arsenal calmed my nerves down.

Before the PT Cruiser sat on my tail, I was heading towards the abandoned stretch of the Highway 38 with the intention of crossing into A1. PT Cruiser foiled my plans. The last thing I wanted was to lead Rumsey's men to the window into the other timeline. I surmised that it was the one caused by the unauthorized beacon. While contemplating on my next move, I spent another two hours cruising up to Big Bear and then down past Silver Springs. The PT Cruiser refused to go away.

What I needed was a diversion. But what kind?

The answer came finally—I needed a bomb. Where would I get the bomb? After all, you can't just go to the drug store and buy one. Or can you? But of course you can, my dear reader!

I wheeled up to the closest pharmacy. There, I purchased a dozen instant ice packs. These items consist of two-layered bags, the core is full of water and the outer layer is laden with the Ammonium Nitrate crystals.

Not many people know, however, that Ammonium Nitrate is a powerful explosive agent. The energy it can produce is mind-boggling. It is totally harmless, however, unless triggered hard that is.

I got back into my Pathfinder. PT Cruiser sat arrogantly some one hundred feet away. The two men inside it smiled. I guessed that they have called for back up, and savored my apparent demise to come. I ignored their drilling eyes, cut the Instant Ice packages open carefully with a razor, and created an explosive device using an empty soda bottle and the Ammonium Nitrate crystals.

Then, I started on a detonator. It had to have a powerful kick. I found a box of 12-gage shotgun shells and pulled one of them out. Then, I cut the top off from the plastic casing and removed the buckshot. After that, I emptied the powder from eleven other shells into the casing without buckshot and sealed the top with a piece of duct tape. Now I had my detonator. I taped it at the mouth of the soda bottle.

As I finished making my bomb, a black Suburban pulled up behind PT Cruiser. I glanced at a long gun case in my back seat. There, my lever action Marlin 336 rifle with a mounted scope sat quietly, waiting for my call to duty.

I put the Pathfinder in drive and moved slowly towards the parking lot's exit into the Highway 38. I saw the men in the PT Cruiser and the Suburban look at me intently. They procrastinated; they had no plan. I guessed them to be a motley collection of the military police personal, upon who Ramsey bestowed the emergency Department of Homeland Security credentials. They did an awesome job of finding me, but now they had to take me down. They were used to the controlled conditions of the U.S. military. All of their training geared them towards containing the suspects in a small perimeter, waiting the bad guys out, and forcing them to surrender.

Since I was not confined to a controlled geographical location, I had this crew at disadvantage. Time, however, was not on my side. I needed to put some distance between us in a hurry.

I inched my Pathfinder to the highway. My right foot hammered down on the gas pedal as soon as the front wheels rolled past the parking lot's exit. A hard g-force pushed my body into the seat. I sped downhill, away from Silver Springs and the window to A1.

The Homeland Security vehicles lurched forward and followed me. I let the needle of my speedometer reach eighty-five miles per hour. When I saw my pursuers gaining, I made a hard u-turn in the middle of the highway. The Pathfinder fishtailed badly, but did not donut. I regained control quickly and sped up in the opposite direction.

The PT Cruiser's and the Suburban's tires made a loud, siren-like sound, as the drivers applied the breaks hard. Since they did not plan to turn, I won at least three minutes. By the time I neared the abandoned stretch of the Highway 38, my rear view mirror showed no one behind me. I did not turn into the abandoned stretch, but passed it and drove for another mile.

Finally, I parked my Pathfinder on the shoulder beneath a steep hill. The window to A1 was on the other side of it. I wedged the bottle with the Ammonium Nitrate in my passenger door's window in such a way that the detonator's primer faced out. I put my Smith & Wesson in the waistband and took out the Marlin rifle.

Then, I walked up the hill and chose a position behind two large pines, about two hundred feet away from the road. The rifle felt solid in my hands. I pulled the lever down and brought it back up, forcing a cartridge into the firing chamber. I peered through the scope at the bottle in the Nissan's window. I had a clear shot.

My wait proved to be short. In less than a minute, I saw Suburban brake hard and stop within just a few feet of my Pathfinder. The PT Cruiser almost ran into

Suburban but stopped in time, inches away from its rear bumper. The tires smoked from hard braking as four men poured out with their handguns pointed at my Pathfinder.

They did not approach it but went into a maneuver called the Felony Car Stop. In requires cops to take cover behind their own vehicles, order the suspects to emerge and spread eagle on the pavement for handcuffs to be applied. I heard them yelling for me to place my hands outside the drivers' side window.

Since I was not inside the Pathfinder, I brought my rifle up instead. The scope's crosshairs centered on the detonator's primer. The air filled my lungs and I let it out slowly. On the tail end of the exhale, I squeezed the trigger gently. An 150-gramm bullet left the muzzle of my Marlin at 2,300 feet per second and slammed into the detonator's primer. The primer sparked the powder inside

the modified shotgun shell causing it to explode hard.

The Ammonium Nitrate refused to take this insult calmly. It exploded angrily into a hot ball of fire. The shock waive sent reverberations through my body. One of the Homeland Security men fell, while the rest backed up. Terrific fire engulfed the Pathfinder. I figured that they will be busy with the explosion for a few hours before realizing that I was not inside the vehicle.

As I turned around and made my way uphill on foot, I heard the gas tank blow.

"...Time present and time past
Are both perhaps present in time future,
And time future contained in time past.
If all time is eternally present
All time is unredeemable ..."

T.S. (Thomas Stearns) Eliot (1888–1965), Anglo-American critic, poet. Burnt Norton (Four Quartets).

March 2010

Chapter Twenty-Two

The Other Timeline

The silver mist appeared by the rockslide dutifully and enveloped me. The feeling of nausea, it produced, was not as bad this time around. Soon, I emerged from the dark freefall into a torrential downpour. The weather in A1 differed radically. I decided that if I ever see Walter Kurz again, I will ask him about it.

The bodies, I left behind during my last visit, were gone. Someone filled in one of the mortar shell carters and drew a cross in the dirt covering it. I guessed it to be where the bodies went.

I looked up the hill. The heavy rain produced a torrent of water streaming down the highway. Now I had a decision to make; do I go up the road or down? Since walking down requires less energy, I started downhill towards Redlands.

When I passed the location where, in my timeline, the new Highway 38 forked away to hug the hill on the other side, I found a steep mountainside only. Here, no one had changed the direction of the highway.

In another two hundred yards, I came to the spot where the Silver Springs Avenue crossed the highway in my world. I found the street, but with difficulty. The weeds and the small trees had broken through the hardtop and made the road virtually indistinguishable from the surrounding hillside. I decided not to go up the Silver Springs Avenue to see if my home existed in A1. My professional paranoia suggested that if someone was to lay a trap for me, that location stood out like a sore thumb. Rumsey's methods were somewhat primitive, but his straightforward approach did not make him a fool. Only a doofus would assume that he did not allow for the possibility of my crossing into this world.

I continued down the highway for another hour. I saw no one and heard nothing but the sound of falling rain. The highway's hardtop had eroded considerably. In some areas, the mud and the rocks covered it so thick that they obscured all vestiges of human engineering. I also noted traces of recent fighting. Spent small arms casings littered the road in places and I passed a number of explosion craters. In one spot, a barricade of burned cars and trucks blocked the highway. I had to climb up the hill to go around it.

When I came down to the highway again, a loud sound of Diesel engines greeted me. Three Humvee trucks, painted in desert camouflage colors, drove up to the barricade on the other side. Six men in green field fatigues got out and pointed their Heckler & Koch G3 Rifles in my face.

"¡Manos arriba!(hands up)" ordered one of them in Spanish, loud but not yelling. He had a deep red scar across his forehead. All of the men had an air of the old salts who knew their way around combat about them.

As I reached for the sky slowly, the round shoulder patches of Mexican *Grupo Aeromóvil de Fuerzas Especiales* caught my eye. They were the south-of-the-border equivalent of the United States Rangers.

"Esta bien (it's okay)," I said, thankful that my gray matter released this bit of Spanish. "Somos amigos (we are friends)."

"Feasible (possibly)," the same man said without moving the business end of his rifle from my chest, "¿Eres Jack Perez? (Are you Jack Perez?)"

"No. Yo es la persona otro (No, I'm another man)," I said.

"Okay, put your hands down and come over," the man said in flawless English now and the whole group seemed to relax. I realized why the same instant because I heard a slight nose, muffled by the rain, behind me. Two Mexican soldiers stood a few yards up the hill, giving their comrades in front an "all clear" hand signal. I could read them like a book. They were in a hostile territory and, fearing ambush, sent a two-man team to circle around. These two men took up sentry duty on the side of the hill now and the rest of the soldiers surrounded me.

"You don't have to admit it. I know Jack Perez when I see one," said the man with the scar. "I rather like you guys. But you caused too many problems for El Asociación."

He spat on the ground and continued, "Me personally, I don't care. I was born here East L.A. If I wasn't with Fuerzas Especiales, I'd be with Jack Perez. But I have to take you in. Mexico City wants to be nice to El Asociación, and El Asociación wants all Jack Perez to be brought in."

The soldiers searched me and removed all my weapons. The Humvee, they put me in, was of a cargo carrier configuration. They handcuffed my hands behind me and tied my waist to a hook inside the truck's bed. I could almost hear the proverbial meowing and barking as the havens dispensed the large quantities of water. While the rain pelted me with the huge freezing drops, the three trucks turned around and started down the Highway 38. We drove for about an hour. The A1 world was different. Extremely different. Instead of busy traffic, only silence greeted me.

When we drove into Redlands—a nice growing middleclass community of 63,000 in my timeline—I saw blocks upon blocks of burned out buildings. Only the highway showed the signs of use. The cross streets fell into decay, covered by the layers of debris. While the Humvee lumbered along, I scanned the surrounding for any indications human habitation. I found none. Some homes burned to the ground, others looked demolished, and yet more stood under the rain with gaping sockets of broken windows.

A pack of stray dogs crossed the street in front of our convoy and disappeared into the ruins of some burned out apartment building. We made a left turn into the Orange Street and drove under the I-10 Freeway. The bridge had collapsed on one side. I spied two craters. Aerial bombs, I guessed. It appeared that someone had purposefully destroyed the Orange Street overpass from the air.

On the south side of the freeway, I saw a large open field where the movie theaters stood in my timeline. Orderly rows of drab green tents occupied the ground now. I estimated at least one hundred and twenty eight-man tents. A barbed wire fence with watch towers surrounded the filed. I shook my head to make sure that I saw what I saw.

My peepers eyeballed a concentration camp!

A large blue banner rose like an evil sail at the barbed wire gates. I read the white lettering on it, "The Partnership Will Make Your Life Worth Living."

I made the connection. "El Asociación" meant "The Partnership" in Spanish. The Humvees stopped at the Redlands Police building. Instead of police cruisers, however, the parking lot was full with Humvees. A barricade, consisting of sandbags with machinegun nests, surrounded the structure. A large Mexican tricolor flew over the building next to a light blue flag with green initials "N.A.H.P."

The Mexican solder with the scar got out and walked inside the building. He came back quickly, followed by two Anglo looking men in green camouflage fatigues. Without saying anything, the Mexicans let me out from the back of the truck and took the handcuffs off. The two men from the building patted me down and cuffed my hands behind my back again with their own set of manacles. Then, they walked me inside the lobby.

It was full of men in camouflage fatigues hurrying to and fro. The cacophony of their voices had a touch of the surreal, Kafkaesque, if you will, my dear reader. My guards walked me to a closed door without a sign. One of them pressed a buzzer. Instantly, the door opened and a short skinny kid in the same green camouflage fatigues— N.A.H.P. patch on the shoulder—walked out. He looked barely old enough to shave.

"J.P. in open rebellion," said one of the guards with a touch of Midwest in his voice and handed the kid a large envelope. "Fuerzas got him half way up the mountain.

The kid nodded and the guards left.

"What's your fair share number?" he asked me.

"PFC Rogers, why am I under arrest?" I asked him instead, reading the name from the sewed-on nameplate on his breast.

The kid lifted his pale blue eyes up to mine with disbelief clearly written on his face. "Listen to me Jack Perez," he said, shaking in an unexplained fury and adding a few expletives, "... if it was up to me I'd tear you head off and crap down your windpipe. Give me your fair share number!"

"And you listen to me pipsqueak," I retorted in kind. "My name is not Jack Perez and I can shove you attitude up your ass and then some, unless you tell me what's going on."

Some indecision registered on the young man's face. He looked around and then tried to sucker punch me. His round house right missed because I side-stepped. PFC Rogers lost his balance and fell to his knees. Just then, several guards ran up and jumped on me hard from behind. I protected myself the best I could. Since my hands were handcuffed behind me, this was a loosing battle. At the end, they hogtied me and took me to the basement storage area. In this timeline, it was converted into several rows of jail cells. Two guards threw me on the floor inside one of the cells. I must have passed out because when I woke up, the bindings were off. My boots and my jacket were off me as well. Two small windows at the ceiling's line illuminated my surrounding. I was inside a cell with five men. The small enclosure had no bunks, forcing all six of us to sit on the floor. A honey bucket spread its foul odor by the cell's door.

I found my missing garments quickly. A burly bearded man had my boots on and sat on top of my jacket. I got up and stretched. My body ached from the beating but I detected no major damage. I looked at the man who took my stuff. He returned my stare defiantly. I made a half step towards him as he got up. Without warning, I unleashed my fury upon this man. Two kicks and five punches later, I had my jacket and boots back. The burly man was back on the floor, bleeding from his mouth now.

The rest of the fellow inmates took no part in the fight. They huddled up in the corner of the cell and watched our struggle, staying out of the way. These men wore drab blue jumpsuits with white seven digit numbers stenciled on the back and right breast. Their faces looked thin and hair unkempt.

I claimed the portion of the floor as far away from the honey bucket as possible, closed my eyes, and fell asleep. I woke up sometime later. I had no idea what time it was, since I did not want to take my pocket watch out in front of other inmates. I deduced that it should be early morning because I felt refreshed as if I slept for many hours. My body still ached form violent yesterday. I stood up quietly as the rest of my cellmates slept on the floor. I came to the thick bars separating the cell from the hall and did isometric exercises.

About an hour later, two green-clad guards came in and banged on the bars declaring wake up time. Then, an inmate in blue jumpsuit pushed a food cart through the hallway between the rows of cells. He stopped at every cell, made inmates sign a paper on a clipboard, and dispensed the bowls of beans. When the food cart came to my cell, he had only five portions of beans. My cellmates signed the sheet on the clipboard and received their food.

"Where is my food," I asked.

"Jack, you don't have a fair share number," said the food cart man. "You won't get any chow until you get the number."

'When would that be?" I asked.

"Who knows. Soon. But you will get the number. Your name Partnership don't care about but the number they will give you," said the man and moved on to the next cell.

"You must be one radical Jack Perez if you don't even have a number," said one of my cellmates.

"Why is everybody calling me Jack Perez," I said. "It's not my name."

"All of you are Jack Perez. You guys have good intentions but you make life for the rest of us more difficult," he said.

"Why are you here?" I asked.

"Oh that," the man gave me a sad smile. "I tried to hitch a ride on a freight train south. My daughter and her kids left before you guys started fighting with the Partnership. I heard that a Durango's governor set up habitats for ADPs. She found a place for herself there."

"ADPs?" I asked.

"American Displaced Persons, you know!" exclaimed the man, visibly annoyed by my ignorance. "I didn't make it very far. They found me inside a cargo container with two other guys. I guess they'll send us to the Earth Reclamation Habitat now."

A loud clanking of the cell's door sliding interrupted our conversation. "You! Jack Perez!" a man with sergeant's stripes on his green camouflage fatigues yelled at me. He walked into the cell while two other guards stood with their belly clubs at ready outside. "Don't try no funny stuff. I'd off you as soon as look at you but our boss wants to talk to you."

"... A truth ceases to be true when more than one person believes in it ..."

Oscar Wilde (1854–1900), Anglo-Irish playwright, author.
"Phrases and Philosophies for the Use of the Young,"
Chameleon (London, Dec. 1894).

March 2010

Chapter Twenty-Three

The Light Colonel

"Y ou need to explain this crap, Jack!" yelled a heavyset man with the Lieutenant Colonel's oak leafs on his green camouflage fatigues. He had my wallet in his hands. I stood by his desk—in the corner office which was occupied by Lt. Cook in my timeline—with three guards behind me. The Light Colonel took my California drivers' license and my credit cards out.

"All of this looks like pre-Two-Nineteen garbage. The difference, though, is that your IDs and credit cards show issue dates after the DMV and the banks stopped making these things," he continued angrily. "Who are you and where did you get this crap?"

A large stylized poster, depicting a former U.S. Vice President, occupied the wall behind the desk. A quotation in bold white letters read across a dark green background:

> *"The Earth has a fever. Don't ask what the Partnership can do, ask what you can contribute to the cure..."*

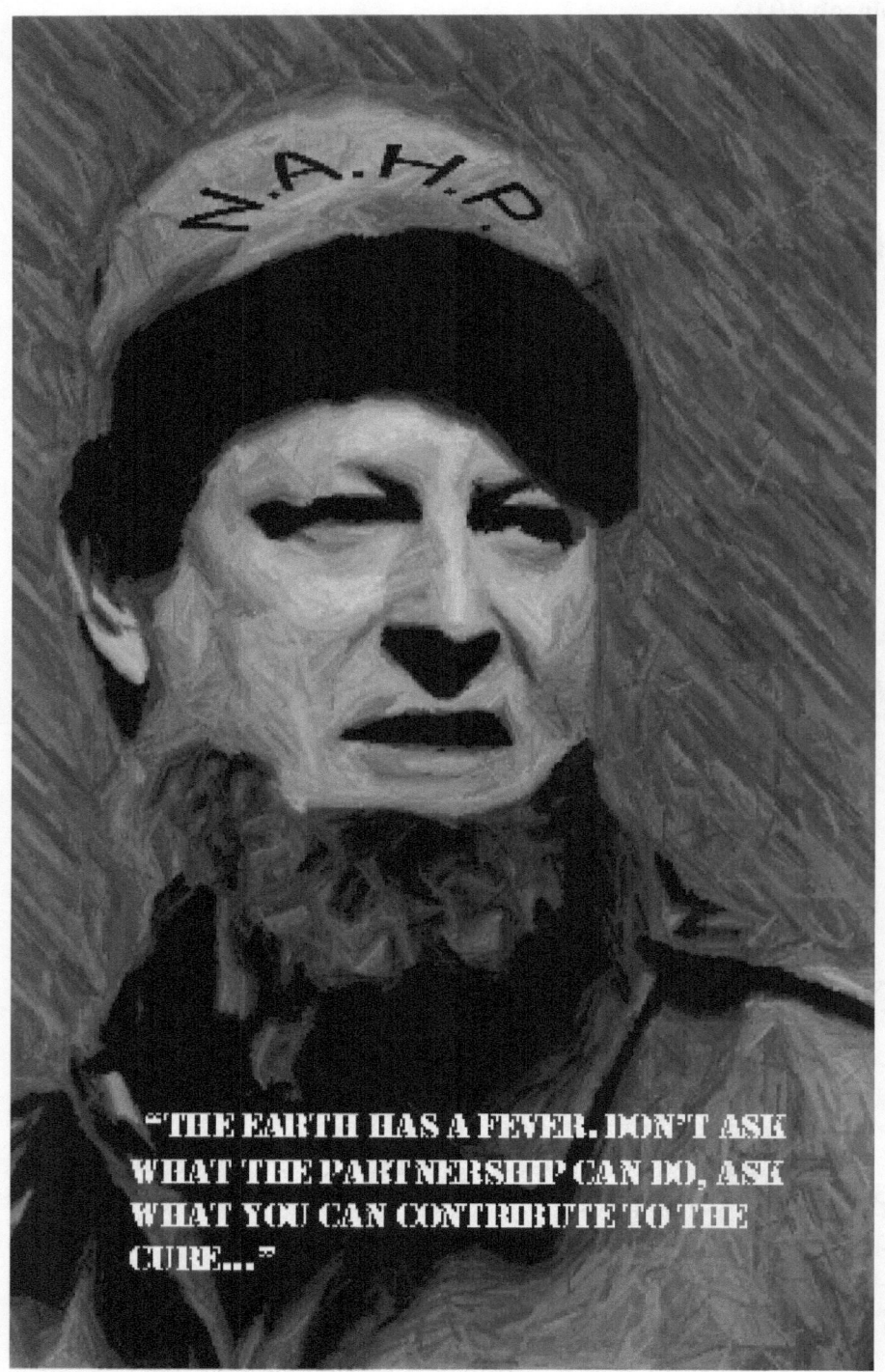

I stood in silence. My empty belly and beat up body made it difficult to decide what to say. The Light Colonel showed a twinge of insecurity behind his blister. People like that fold, if faced with brutal frontal assault usually. I pulled up a chair and sat down. The guard closest to me grabbed my left arm. I broke his hold casually.

"Okay, okay, let him be," said the Light Colonel and gave the guard a hand signal to stop.

"I need some food, real stuff not beans and water, and let's talk in private," I said.

The man thought a while before sending the guards away. Then, he pulled out a MRE ration from his desk. I opened the container and found that it was a beef stew. I ate the food cold. The Light Colonel gave me a plastic water bottle. It had no label and the water tasted awful.

"I have orders to report all people with pre-partnership IDs to Oakland," he said. "I've been here since before Jack Perez but never seen a pre-partnership ID with post-partnership dates."

"Why am I under arrest?" I asked instead of answering.

"Because you are a J.P. in open rebellion," he said.

"What do you mean in open rebellion?" I asked.

"The Fuerzas found you in the zone undesignated for human habitat with firearms," he said. "You will find your way to the ERH any which way. I can make your time there easy or hard, it will be your decision. If you talk to me honestly, I can give you a clerk's designation and a corresponding fair share number."

I understood that my interrogator was threatening me with prison but promised to help me do easy time if I was to cooperate. The A1 timeline went completely off the civilization's tracks. This was not the Southern California I grew up in.

"Lieutenant Colonel, some time we come in contact with the situations which should pass us by. You've stumbled into one of these situations now. Who I am and what I am doing has nothing to do with you or your command structure. Your best course of action is to let me go and forget you ever seen me," I said.

The man smiled and leaned back in his chair. "You talk as if we lived in the world before the Two-Nineteen. We ain't. I caught some rumors about what's going on in Big Bear. You guys just can't let go of the past. Well, it's gone! We love the Partnership now. It has maintained the law and order and prevented the Mormons and the Mexicans from taking over."

He picked up my money clip and pulled out several bills. "Why are you carrying these around? Do you people still use it?"

"Thank you, for the food," I said. "I'm just a man following certain orders. Release me. No one has to know."

This time the Light Colonel laughed. "I wish it was that simple. Your IDs say that your name is Martin Greenblatt. I checked the Partnership records. There was someone by your name with the same DOB. He was a hardcore Jack Perez, even before Jack Perez became what it is now. That Martin Greenblatt disappeared, probably died during the water riots, just after the Partnership came in. I doubt you are him. I think whoever you work with, made up the IDs in the dead man's name. But why forge pre-partnership docs with post-partnership dates?"

This was my time to laugh. "There is so much you don't know," I said.

The Light Colonel shook his head and looked me in the face. His brown eyes bore into mine as if trying to read my mind. Failing to do so, he took out a blank form and scribbled something on it.

"I sent a notification about your apprehension to Oakland. I was hoping to follow up with a complete report about who you are. As it stands now, I will charge you with wilfully traspassing on the land undesegnated for human habitat and possession of illegal weapons. The PHJC is schduled to arrive in about two weeks I have no doubts that you will end up in the ERH for an indefinite time."

"What is PHJC and this ERH?" I asked.

"You are not as smart a you look," the Light Colonel smiled. "The Public Health Justice Commissioner is the law for for those who choose not accept the Partnership. And the ERH... Where have you been? Haven't you heard about the Earth Reclamation Initiative?"

I shook my head.

"Hmmm... You are not going to like the Earth Reclamation Habitat, the ERH, I promiss you. Unless, ofcourse, you unburden your secrts to me. I'm assigning you a temporary fair share number until PHJC will send you to ERH for the rest of your miserable life," Light Colonel seemed to enjoy himself now. "The good thing, Jack, is that the rest of your life ain't going to be that long."

"... Destruction, hence, like creation, is one of Nature's mandates ..."

Marquis de Sade (1740–1814), French author. Dolmancé, in Philosophy in the Bedroom, "Dialogue the Fifth," (1795).

March 2010

Chapter Twenty-Four

The Chinook

Semper Fidelis

spent the next eight days in the basement cell. The Light Colonel was as good as his word; he issued me a number, which bought two meals a day: canned beans with corn tortillas.

This world felt like a foreign country. I listened to my cellmates for hours. Their stories were about hunger, separation from families, and longing for the world before the Partnership. Almost all of them got arrested when they tried to make their way south to Mexico. Apparently, traveling through some parts of California had turned into a heavy felony. Yet, this Southern California has become the last place where anyone wanted to be.

I was a stranger here and the last thing I wanted was for anyone to figure out how strange I really was to this world. So, I decided to listen only and asked no questions. For this reason, my dear reader, the large picture still eluded me. Where was the U.S. government? Or, did it exist any more? Why did Mexican military patrol Southern California? And, how did Jack Perez fit into all of this?

I had no answers for the first three questions. The Jack Perez situation seemed more understandable. Apparently, there was a group somewhere in the Big Bear Lake area known collectively as Jack Perez. It and the Partnership—which appeared to be the government of the day—seemed to be less than friends. For some reason, everyone was convinced that I was a member of this group. Well, not everyone; there were people in this world who knew who I was. But, I am getting ahead of myself, my dear reader.

Early in the morning of the ninth day of my incarceration, things began to happen. A loud thumping

got me out of my slumber before wake up time. As soon as the sleep left me, I understood that the thumping sound belonged to a number of men marching in step. Inside a minute I saw them—six Marines in Class B uniforms with side arms.

"Special detail..." hollered the Marine with the Gunnery Sergeant's chevrons. "Haaaaaaaaaaaaaaaa alt!"

The intensity of his vocalizing reminded me of basic training.

All six men stopped in their tacks at attention in front of my cell.

"Leeeeeeeeeft face!" the Gunny hollered again as if on the parade ground. The Marines executed the maneuver flawlessly and the thump of their right boots shook the floor.

"PFC Washington!" the Gunny yelled.

"PFC Washington," sounded off a tall lanky Marine.

"PFC Washington, overcome the cell door locking mechanism!" the Gunny articulated every syllable in a crisp precise way. I admired his virtuoso vocal control.

"Aye, eye, Gunnery Sergeant!" the tall lanky Marine sounded off again, made three marching steps forward, and came to a halt at the cell's door. He produced two tools, which looked like curved screwdrivers, and inserted them into the cell door's lock. The door unlocked with a loud click and PFC Washington slid it open.

"Mr. Martin Greenblatt," the Gunny sang out, starting low and bringing the last syllable of my last name up to a crescendo. The man had a voice like an opera singer. "Pick up your possessions and assume your position in the formation."

The Marines made several steps and opened up a place for me in the middle. The power of Gunny's singing commands were such that my legs, as if they had a mind of their own, moved me out of the cell in a marching step and positioned my body in the middle of the formation.

"Special detail!" Gunny sang his command low and then brought the end up. "Forrrwarrrrrrrd haaaaaaaaaaaaarch."

All seven of us lifted our right feet and started forward. We marched in step to the stairs, up two flights, into the lobby, and then outside the building. Everyone we passed—mostly guards in camouflage fatigues—stopped and gaped. No one made a sound but their faces had the same expression of astonishment.

Outside, a Chinook helicopter occupied most of the parking lot, its two rotors rotating in a stand by mode. It sported a dull blue paint with no identifying marks. The Marines and I marched to the chopper and entered it through a rear ramp. As soon as the last Marine got inside, the ramp closed with a hydraulic hiss. The whine of the turbines rose and the bird lifted off the ground. We were airborne.

"Mr. Greenblatt move to the front," Gunny said and pointed to the door separating the cargo hall from the forward compartment. There, I found four rows of empty seats. I sat into one. The Marines did not relax, three sat behind me and one in front. Gunny and PFC Washington remained standing with their eyeballs fixed on me. The forward compartment lacked portholes so I had no idea where we were headed.

Now I had time to think. Several incongruities came to the surface right way. The first was my escort's uniforms. The Marines wore class B's. However, instead of shoes they wore black combat boots under the trousers. Also, I remembered that when they stood at attention their fingers were pointing straight down rather then be in a natural curled position. My gut feeling told me that they were imposters.

"Gunnery Sergeant," I barked at the Gunny in my best military voice. "Permission to speak."

"Permission granted Mr. Greenblatt," the Gunny answered in his great command voice. Now, I detected something foreign in it. No, it was not an accent, my dear reader. It was the way he annunciated his syllables. Native speakers have a tendency to slur just a bit. This man's sounds came out crisp and perfect. Too perfect for someone whose first language was English.

"Gunny, you are not American," I said. "Don't get me wrong, I thank you for getting me out that crap hole. But... Tell me who you and your crew are."

Gunny stood still for a moment. Then, he winked at me.

"Mr. Greenblatt, please ask no questions. My orders are to extract you from the Partnership and escort you to a certain destination."

We flew for two hours and thirty six minutes, according to my chronometer. The hands of the pocket watch registered 7:41 AM when the sound of the rotors changed and the turbines began to whine down. Chinook touched down soon afterwards. I heard the hydraulic hiss of the back ramp and the smell of the ocean hit my nostrils. My escort got up.

"Mr. Greenblatt," the Gunny addressed me in a formal voice. "Please, join our formation."

I stood up and we marched out of the helicopter the same way we marched in. The outside greeted me with an overcast sky and a light fog. The Chinook sat on a huge deck of an aircraft carrier. I did not recognize the silhouette of a superstructure. As we marched towards it, I saw a short mast flying a white flag with two blue bars crossing it diagonally. I knew that I should know what the flag meant, but could not bring it up from my memory.

A gaggle of sailors, wearing French style sailing hats, doubled timed by our formation. As they passed, they took a number of double takes at us. The seamen wore navy blue bell-bottomed trousers and open collar tunics of the same color. At the neckline, I saw the striped t-shirts. Their hats were stenciled with Cyrillic letters. I deciphered the writing. It read "Varyag." Before I got a chance to figure out what all of this meant, we halted at the superstructure.

"About face," Gunny ordered and all seven of us turned around. "Parrrrrrrrrade rest," he barked again and I, with the rest of the men, spread my legs shoulder width and my hands went back behind my back almost by themselves. I spent so much time in active duty that obeying these simple commands became second nature.

In the mean time, the sailors ran up to the Chinook and pushed it forward a few yards. Then, they secured it to the deck with clamps. Someone, a naval NCO probably, yelled out a command in a foreign language. The sailors grouped by the bird at attention. The warning bells went off just then and the deck panel with the copter and the men sank inside the carrier. The bells chimed until the deck panel rose up again. The Chinook was gone, only the sailors came back. Now, they walked back to the superstructure leisurely and gaped at us.

When they came closer, I recognized the uniforms and understood the language they spoke. I also remembered what the word "Varyag" meant.

"...Never explain—your friends do not need it and your enemies will not believe it anyhow..."

Elbert Hubbard (1856–1915), U.S. author. "Index," vol. 1, Selected Writings (1921).

March 2010

Chapter Twenty-Five

The Tupolev

he language, the sailors spoke, was Russian and Varyag was a Kuznetsov Class aircraft carrier. In my world, the Soviets started to build it in the Eighties. When the Soviet Union fell apart, the Nikolayev South Shipyard—which laid the keel—became the property of Ukraine. This new country promptly sold the unfinished carrier to China for fifty million dollars. The Chinese towed it to Macao and turned it into a floating casino. The sale had been a huge news story among my circle of people at the time.

But that was in my world, my dear reader. In this timeline, Varyag flew the Russian naval colors and prowled the Pacific off the California coast. The vessel seemed complete and ready for action. As if to confirm this, the warning bells went off again and I saw a medium sized transport jet land on the deck. I recognized its Tupolev silhouette: TU-204 model I thought. The plane boasted the same drab blue paint as the Chinook. The Tupolev, however, had identifying numbers on the wings and flew a Russian tricolor on its vertical stabilizer.

It came to a stop in the middle of the flattop: about one hundred yards from us. The carrier's deck could fit three football fields. I had spent some time on the USS Dwight D. Eisenhower, an American Nimitz Class carrier. Varyag was about the same size. These super carriers make a man feel dwarfed by the technology. These floating metal islands are the pinnacle of the fabled

Industrial Revolution. They are the culmination of a dream: the Great Dream of Technology.

Our great-great-great grandfathers believed in iron and fire. These industrial pioneers were the visionary giants of their day. My dear reader, I am not talking about the Morgans, Rockefellers, Duponts, and such. No. The men I have in mind were the foremen, the engineers, and the inventors who did not make it into our history books but created the fabric for the Dream. Without them, our society would not have reached the critical mass of desire and knowhow to roll the progress of technology off the dead stop.

These men grew up in a primitive world. Everything, which needed to be built and maintained, had to be done by hand. If a hole in the ground needed to be dug, a hand spade would come out. If a ship needed to be unloaded, the men would put their backs—literally—into it. And so on. To them, the huge metal machines symbolized more than just technological progress. Their industrial creations were an awesome prayer. The steel and iron machines became an offering to the divinity of human victory over the chaos of random elements. The generations, who followed, forgot the meaning of the prayer. A "gee wiz" attitude towards the gadgetry replaced the visions of a breathtaking grandeur. In our "post industrial" age, we no longer pause in shock and awe when we advance new technologies. What we do is play with the new inventions a while and then mindlessly discard. But I digress ...

The gang of deckhands sprinted towards the Tupolev and began fueling it. After they finished, the Tupolev taxied past the fake Marines and I. It stopped at the far end of the flight deck and turned around. I saw a side door open and a ladder came out.

The Gunny double-timed towards the plane. He climbed inside the Tupolev and stayed there for a short while. Then, he climbed back out. I did not recognize him at first because he wore a dark suit now. He double-timed back to where I and the men in Class B's still stood at parade rest.

"Special detail! Atten-hut!" the Gunny, who was obviously something other than USMC Gunnery Sergeant, roared. Nevertheless, I will go on calling him Gunny, my dear reader, so both of us can keep track of this character.

I decided to continue playing the charade and straitened up at attention. "Maintain formation," he bellowed again in his great command voice. "... and forward haaaaaaaarch!"

I, with the fake Marines, started towards the Tupolev. The Gunny stopped us at the ladder. He ordered some of his men to climb in. Soon, one of them, now wearing a pullover sweater and faded blue jeans, came into view. He looked me in the eyes and motioned to come up.

Inside, the Tupolev had a civilian configuration. Orderly rows of empty seats filled two cabins, first class in front and coach to the rear. The plane left the aircraft carrier quickly and turned to the right, due North. I sat down in the last row—next to the window—in the first class. My escort, the men changed into civilian clothing, gave me a wide berth. Two them sat down four rows ahead of me an the rest of them disappeared in the coach compartment. We were the only passengers as far as I could see.

I looked for reading material and found a flyer in Russian with an Aeroflot logo on top only. Apparently, this plane served as a civilian carrier not long ago. Aeroflot is the largest Russian airline in my world, a hold over from the Soviet Union days. I do not speak fluent Russian, but I can read Cyrillic. Since it is a phonetic alphabet, one can pronounce the words without knowing the meaning. The airline flyer, however, did not require much knowledge of the language; it instructed the passengers on the emergency exit procedures.

As soon as the Tupolev leveled off on its way north, the Gunny came in with some food. He sat in the isle seat leaving an empty seat between us. He placed a tray full of cold cuts, boiled potatoes and smoked fish on it. Then, he produced two bottles of mineral water and gave one to me. Only now, I understood how hungry I was. For the last nine days, I survived on a modest staple of beans and corn tortillas.

I used my hands, Gunny did not bring eating utensils. Something in me demanded that I eat as much as could, as fast as I could. I overrode this impulse and ate with a

deliberate slowness. I was in a hostile territory and did not want to get sick or sleepy. Well, sleepy I got anyway after I finished; this is the way our bodies work, my dear reader.

The Gunny ate some as well and washed his food down with his bottle of mineral water. "Go to the rear head, wash up, and make yourself presentable. You will find some fresh clothing in the last row," he said after the last morsel of food disappeared.

I said nothing but nodded in acknowledgement. I have not thought about it until this moment, but I did spend a week and a half in the same garments without a shave and a shower. I touched my face and felt a healthy beard. Suddenly, I became aware of how dirty and grimy I was. So, I got up and walked to the back of the plane. I passed the men of my escort. One of them slept in a reclined seat, and two others played cards. They gave me blank looks, as I passed, without interrupting their game. But for my escort and me, the passenger compartment was empty.

Just as the Gunny promised, the last row of seats in the rear was full of clothing. Someone threw piles of blue jeans, slacks, sweaters, and other garments on the seats. I picked out a pair of gray wool trousers, light blue dress shirt, and camel hair sports jacket. I also fished out several unopened packages of brand new white t-shirts, boxers, and black socks. A pair of black wingtips caught my eye. They looked about my size, so I took them.

The rear lavatory—the Gunny had referred to it by the old navy moniker: head—had no showers but a small washbasin only. I plugged it and filled it up with cold water because the hot water faucet refused to budge. Then, I undressed to my birthday suit and used a stack of paper towels as washcloth. It was not the same as taking a proper bath, but under the circumstances, it felt awesome.

I looked at the pile of my old clothing on the floor. I hated to loose my jeans and plaid shirt, so I refilled the basin with clean water and did my best to launder the garments. After I wrung them out, I hung them to dry on a hook above the mirror. Only then, I walked outside and found the Gunny in a flight attendants' jump seat.

"You need to find another change of clothing for yourself. While you do that, let me find a suitcase for you," he said as I put my new duds on. He got up and went fore only to come back quickly with a blue gym bag.

"This is all I have for now," he said.

I put another pair of slacks and two shirts—which I liberated from the back row pile—in the bag. I also put my cowboy boots there.

"Now, you look like you belong," the Gunny said.

"Belong to what?" I could not help myself asking.

Instead of answering he gave me a crooked grin and walked me back to the first class.

"...Whose game was empires and whose stakes were thrones,
Whose table earth, whose dice were human bones ..."

George Gordon Noel Byron, Lord Byron (1788–1824), Age of Bronze. Stanza 3.

March 2010

Chapter Twenty-Six

I Play the Game

y chronometer showed 5:48 PM when we landed on another aircraft carrier. I slept for a few hours and missed the time when the morning turned into the evening. Now, a beautiful Pacific sunset made the ocean glow in a deep red hue. While my escort and I sat inside the plane, the Russian deckhands refueled it. I could not see the name of the vessel and I did not recognize the superstructure silhouette. Soon, we taxied to the far end of the flattop. The Tupolev turned around and stopped.

All of a sudden, I heard loud voices in the coach cabin. Two men sitting in front of me in the first class jumped up and ran through the curtains separating the compartments. I got up too and looked through the curtains. The Gunny and three men, I have not seen before, argued in Russian loudly. The new men stood by the open door and I heard shouting coming from the outside. Without warning, one of the new men shoved the Gunny back and produced a black semiautomatic pistol.

The Gunny and his crew responded with a lightening speed. The Gunny kicked the gun out the man's hand and four of my escorts fell on the three new men. They overpowered them with ease. Then, Gunny closed the door. As he sealed it with a long lever, which he semi-circled down, one of his men ran past me into the cockpit. Within seconds, the turbines came to life and pushed the Tupolev up the flight deck and off into the air.

"Meester Greenblatt," I heard a Russian accented voice behind me. I turned and saw one of the Gunny's Marine imposters—now wearing an ill-fitting black suit—motioning for me to sit down. I did and the man sat next to me. He betrayed some tension as if he wanted to say something but held it back. The silence lasted for half an hour, until the plane climbed above the cloud cover.

"May I call you Marty?" my companion spoke up again after the Tupolev leveled off.

I nodded.

"Not everything comes out the way you plan it," his accented English was fluent. "We completed the extraction according to plan. Yet, our mission will end only after we deliver you to a prearranged rendezvous point. We were assured that the details of our mission were secure on the highest levels of our command. As you may have seen, we were compromised."

The man in the black suit stopped talking and fixed his bright blue eyes upon me. Even though his face maintained—what we have christened in our trade—an "Evil Russian Stare," I knew from experience that this hostile blank look meant nothing but a wait for my reaction. Russians do not smile much in a way of politeness. Many years ago, I was part of a team debriefing a Soviet defector who told us—among many other things—that Russians look at smiling as a sign of simplemindedness. I am sure some academic egghead could explain the psychological differences in our cultures which lead to such a perception. Since I find most people in academia ill prepared to discuss topics in non-politically correct ways, I accepted this anthropological curiosity's existence and did my best not to over-think it.

"What is our rendezvous point?" I asked.

"Khmmm..." he cleared his throat and his "Evil Russian Stare" became even more evil. Yet, his bright blue eyes laughed. Yes, my dear reader, he laughed at me without making a sound or exhibiting the corresponding facial expressions. I could read the message in his peepers loud and clear: I will not get the answer without working for it. However, he wanted something from me too, otherwise he would not have sat down next to me. I figured that he must be a commanding officer of this crew, which I guessed to be one of the Russian special assignment teams.

The best known is Spetsgruppa Alfa. I was also aware of a few others, which had no names but code designations only. Even though, my knowledge came from my world, I decided that these Russians could not be that much different. For this reason, I asked no more questions. If the man wanted something from me, he had to ask. Also, I knew that if I satisfy his curiosity without asking for something back, I would lose his respect. If he wanted my input, he would have to give something up. This is why his eyes laughed. The bargaining had began. I made a mistake by setting my price first without knowing what he wanted from me. In his mind, he had an advantage.

"You are in a difficult situation Meester Greenblatt," the black-suited man said in a severe tone. His eyes, however, continued laughing. "Up until just a few days ago, the Partnership wanted you bad. Now they can care less; your people assassinated William Rumsey. He headed the Pacific Habitat's Security Services and placed a price on your head personally. With his death, no one in North America cares about you. But, as the Partnership lost interest, some important people in my country got a whiff of your presence here. Some of them are willing to pay a great deal of money for you to disappear..."

The man let his words trail. The harsh tones of his Russian voice accentuated the chill his statement brought on. I said nothing and continued looking him in the eyes. Such was a risky move. Russians could interpret eye to eye contact as a challenge. I learned this hard way many years ago. This man, however, did not react in any way. As we studied each other, his "Evil Russian Stare" softened. While his facial expression became friendlier, his eyes stopped laughing and his pupils became hard, with some unpleasant edge to it.

"We need to keep you alive until I can hand you off," he said business like. "Pray that we do. There is an attempt by a rival agency to stop us. You won't like the alternative. While we chat, my team is interrogating the idiots who tried to attack us. I doubt that we will get much information from them but every little bit can help."

"If you rivals see me die, won't that slow them down?" I asked.

My companion's eyes flashed with a strange expression.

"Are any of the men, your people are interrogating, about my size?" I purposely phrased this question in a statement like way.

His eyes flashed another strange expression and he nodded slowly.

* * *

We flew for six more hours and the Tupolev landed once more, this time on a darkened island airstrip. I saw colorless silhouettes, outside the plane, refuel it and we were airborne again. The Gunny brought me more cold cuts and mineral water but did not sit down and eat with me.

The food made me drowsy and I fell asleep again in the comfortable first class seat. When I woke up, my pocket watch showed 4:57 AM and the world outside the Tupolev's window basked in the bright sunlight. We no longer flew over water. I saw a great expanse of greenery, crisscrossed by the blue lines of streams, beneath the plane. My ears popped and I felt the Tupolev's descent.

On the way down, we hit some turbulence which shook and rolled the plane. When the worst of it passed, my new friend in the black suit came up to my seat.

"Follow me," he said.

We walked into the coach section. There, I saw the rest of the fake Marines with the three new Russians. One of them looked badly hurt. He stretched across four seats, his face pale with blank eyes staring at the ceiling. The man's body twitched every so often. Another new man looked unhurt but sat in the seat with a sour look on his face, hands tied behind his back. The third new man stopped me in my tracks. He was about the same height and build as I. He wore my jeans and plaid shirt. His hair looked freshly cut to resemble what my barber had done to me three weeks ago. From fifteen feet away, even I could have mistaken him for me at first glance.

I came close to the man and looked into his eyes. The pupils were constricted and his face had a detached, faraway expression. Even without proper examination, I could tell that this man was pumped full of barbiturates.

"Meester Greenblatt, we don't nave much time," my black-suited companion said. "I picked out a uniform for you. Put it on."

He held a set of blue pilots' digs on a hanger. I changed right there in the isle. The pants were a bit loose and a tad short. The shirt and the jacket were a size too small. My companion, however, remained satisfied after he looked me over. The Gunny helped me with the tie and pinned a Russian flag pin on my lapel.

Then, Gunny said something to the black suit in Russian. The only words I understood was "*evo morda,*" which translated as "his snout" in English. Yet, something told me that these men would not use these worlds in their dictionary meanings. I suspected that they spoke in some colorful colloquial contexts.

"Why are you talking about my *morda*?" I asked intrigued, hoping to trigger some laughs. Laughing could bring their guard down, I figured, and would give me a chance to learn more about what they have planned. My plot worked to a degree. Both, Gunny and the black suit, grinned when they heard me.

"Well, your *morda* looks too American," said the Gunny. "We need to make you look more like a Russian."

I nodded and grinned too because I began to understand what they wanted to do. Just then, the pilot activated the landing chimes. Everyone sat down into the economy class seats.

We made two passes over some city. It snaked along a waterfront with a huge harbor. The Tupolev flew over a large number of concrete block apartment buildings. I have seen similar architecture in the old Warsaw Block countries.

The plane landed without incident. When it started to taxi across the airfield, the Gunny motioned for me to go into the lavatory and handed me a blue disposable razor. "Shave your face but leave your mustache along," he said.

Cold water shaving is not much fun. But, I did as he asked. When I finished, Gunny produced a huge makeup kit. "Theater actors use this," he said in response to my questioning look. The box was the size of a briefcase and contained multitudes of brushes, paints, glosses, and other things for which I had no name.

The Gunny and another man—the one who changed from Class B's into the faded jeans and sweater—started on my face. They clipped my eye brows and applied red dye to them. Then, they brushed my face with something cold and wet. Within few minutes, my mug became of a sickly pale color with dark freckles sprinkled feely across my nose and cheekbones. After that, I heard a loud buzzing sound. Before I had time to protest, the man in faded jeans removed all my hair off my head with wireless clippers. As the last dark brown strand fell on the floor, the Gunny placed a wig on my—now bare—scalp. He adjusted it and brushed it with a large comb.

"Okay, this should fool anyone for a while," he mumbled as he stepped back examined me. Now I detected a trace of Brooklyn in his intonations.

Curious, I gave myself a once over in the mirror. Well, my dear reader, I had difficulty recognizing myself. Instead of my tanned round-faced mug with dark receding hair, a thinner face of a pale redheaded man stared back. My eyebrows and my mustache were light red, almost blond, and my head was covered by a wig of bright red hair, carelessly parted on the right side.

"Take this," the Gunny handed me a blue pilots cap. As I put it on, the disguise became complete. From the lavatory mirror, an unmistakably Russian face of a man in pilot's uniform stared back at me.

I turned around and saw another man in a Russian pilot's uniform standing at the doorway to the lavatory. A few seconds passed before I recognized the—formerly—black-suited man.

"Showtime!" the Gunny's opera voice sang out behind me.

The plane had managed to stop while he had been putting the makeup on me.

"Meester Greenblatt, let my boys exit first. We will walk ten to fifteen meters behind them," the black-suited man said. "No matter what happens, stay with me and don't speak. Just do what I ask and I promise to keep you alive."

I watched the men, who rescued me, walk down a boarding ramp. They kept my lookalike between them. The black-suited man looked at his wrist watch and his lips moved as if he was counting seconds.

"Let's go. You walk down first," he said. "When we are down, we will walk side-by-side with you slightly behind me."

A nice cool breeze touched my face as soon as I stepped outside the plane. I enjoyed its ocean smell as I walked down the boarding ramp to the black surface of a tarmac. About three hundred feet away, stood a large glass building with a huge sign in Russian, English, and Chinese, "Welcome to Vladivostok."

In my world, Vladivostok was the largest Russian port city in the Pacific. It had a huge naval base. During the Soviet Union days it had been closed to foreigners. Even after the Soviet Union broke apart, the new Russian government did not encourage non-Russians from visiting

this city. In this world, however, the Vladivostok's tarmac was full with the passenger jets from Japan, China, India, and several other carriers whose origins I did not recognize.

By the time my feet touched the blacktop, the first group of men approached a pair of large double doors on the side of the glass building. What happened next took a few seconds only. A dark figure ran up from the inside of the double doors as soon as they slid open. Instantly, I recognized the tall thin frame of the imposter Marine who went by the name of PFC Washington; he was the man who had picked the lock to my basement cell yesterday.

Something bright flashed in his right hand and a sharp reverberating concussion of a magnum load report touched my eardrums. It bounced around my sinuses and died in my throat. I saw the back of my look-alike's head explode in red and his body fell forward. The rest of the men fell on PFC Washington and wrestled him to the ground.

Meanwhile, my black-suited companion came down the boarding ramp and started towards the glass building at a leisurely pace. I remembered his instructions and kept slightly behind him. I noted that he purposefully positioned himself between the glass building and me.

By the time we approached the dead body of my lookalike, a detachment of Russians, in military uniforms with sub-machine guns, surrounded the scene. One of the uniforms barked something in Russian to the black-suited man and I. My companion nodded and turned around. I said nothing and followed him. We walked to the other side of the glass building. While we walked, I looked at our reflection in the glass. We appeared to be just two pilots in identical blue uniforms and with identical blue gym bags in our hands.

We entered the building through a small side door on the other side. An uniformed guard—with an AK-47 assault rifle carelessly slang to his side—walked up to us in a lazy shuffle. My companion reached into his breast pocket and produced a blue identification book. The guard studied it for a moment and then lifted his eyelids to look us over. I produced my best version of the "Evil Russian Stare" as his peepers eyeballed me. Then, the guard shifted his gaze to my companion again. Without saying anything, he handed the identification book back and waved us through.

We passed several passport control checkpoints. My companion simply waved his identification book and the security men simply ignored us. Finally, we made it to the main waiting area. Without stopping, my companion walked up a small staircase leading to a gallery above the floor. There, I saw several bars and restaurants. We passed all of them by and stopped in front of an unmarked door. He pressed a small button to the side. Instantly, the door opened with a loud buzz. Inside, I saw a narrow crevasse of a poorly lit corridor. As soon as we entered, the door closed noiselessly. We marched forward on the gray linoleum floor. The corridor made a sharp left turn and a sharp right turn after that. Then, it ended abruptly in front of another unmarked door. My companion stopped three feet in front of it and waited. I waited three feet behind him. We stood still for about two minutes.

When I say "two minutes," my dear reader, it sounds like a fairly short measure of time. When you wait in front of some random Russian door in semi-darkness, however, the time crawls by so slow that these two minutes could have been two centuries.

Finally, the door opened and a tall man with the flat face of a professional fighter motioned with his enormous paw for us to come in.

The big man gave me a look over and squinted.

"Sit down, Mr. Greenblatt," his said in flawless American English. "We need to change your appearance again."

He asked me take my jacket and shirt off. Then, he removed my red wig and worked on my face with the brushes and other tools of makeup. When the man finished, he produced several of wigs of his own. He picked out one after some contemplation. It had light brown hair mixed with silver. He placed it on my head carefully.

"Now you look like a local," he said and took out a small mirror. I looked at my face; much older man with bags under his eyes and an alcoholic nose looked back at me from the mirror. Only my eyes reminded me of myself.

I changed into the dark suit I had packed into the blue gym bag on the plane. The big man looked at the bag with a frown.

"You can't use this thing anymore. It does not fit your new persona," he said as if he was a movie director critiquing an actor. An old beat up suitcase came up from somewhere and I put the blue bag into it.

After that, the big man worked on my companion. He turned him into another older man whose face bespoke of an intimate familiarity with the bottle.

Thirty minutes later, we got into a cab and headed out of the airport. My companion said nothing about our destination. I did not ask either. I needed time to get my bearings. I am used to be in command of situations. In order to master my current state of affairs, I had to learn how this world operated. Such a foundation would give me the ability to make decisions based on facts.

I already gained some power to influence event around me. I had suggested to use one of the captured Russians as a decoy. It came as a pleasant surprise when the fake Marines had done just that. Their quick, bold actions convinced me that they were true professionals. Since they have been treating me like a VIP rather than a hostage, I surmised that whoever waited for me at the rendezvous point did not want to be my foe.

Vladivostok Airport stood about fifteen miles outside the city limits. The cab driver wheeled his small Toyota sedan, I did not recognize the model, onto a four-lane highway. It looked new, with fresh blacktop and bright billboards—advertising everything from beer to women's lingerie—on both sides of the road.

Our cab raced through a rough Siberian landscape. Even with the summer approaching, the snow clang to the ground in the large dirty patches. Its filthy leftovers contrasted sharply with a gentle beauty of the early spring flowers poking their innocent pastel-colored buds through the rotting leftovers of a last year's vegetation. The scenery's nuanced contradictions looked so inspiring that I wished for a talent of verse making because this visual screamed for a gifted poet to draw poignant parallels between it and the cosmos of human existence.

But I digress...

"... If all the world must see the world
  As the world the world hath seen,
Then it were better for the world
  That the world had never been ..."

Charles Godfrey Leland (1824–1903), *The World and the*
World.

April 2010

Another World

ersistent knocking on my hotel door—three short, one long, two short, one long—woke me up. This was a prearranged signal from Alex, the name my new black-suited friend had introduced himself by two days ago.

I got up and glanced at my watch—6:37 AM. I had spent two days in the Pacific Siberia Hotel. It catered to merchant marines from all over the world. The small suite turned out to be clean, warm, and dry. I was able to take a long shower for the first time in two weeks. I also caught up on my sleep. Since Alex did not want me to leave the room, he had brought two bags full of smoked sausage, dried fish, and several loafs of delicious French style bread. He also left a case of Russian mineral water and warned me against drinking from the tap.

More knocking: three short, one long, two short, one long. Any other type of knocking meant trouble. I opened the door. Alex's familiar mug came into view. Slightly behind him, another man stood with his eyes fixed on my face. I recognized Bobby DiCesare's kisser instantly. A split second before I let a greeting smile curl the corners of my mouth up, I saw that the man was not Bobby from my world. The gent who stood at the door looked exactly like my pal but...

His eyes gave him away. My Bobby had a bright spark in his pupils which could turn into scorching fire before you knew what hit you. This man's eyes looked cold: extinguished and emptied by sorrow. Shivers went down my spine when I tried to imagine what sort of calamity could turn Bobby's flamethrowers into a frostbitten, barren world I spied behind his peepers.

"Hi buddy," I said and extended my shaking hand to this frozen eyes Bobby. When he gripped it with his cold paw, I pulled him towards me and gave him a bear hug for a second. Then I slapped him on his back and let go.

"I am so glad to see you!" I exclaimed and looked at his face. I wanted a reaction to understand what kind of a man this frozen eyes Bobby had become.

"You are one conniving son of a two-dollar whore," he retorted and laughed. "I have not seen you here for many years and I forgot what a piece of work you have been."

While Bobby's mouth laughed heartily, his ice-laced eyes became even colder. This man was much different from my friend back home. No empathy! This is what this Bobby's eyes lacked. My Bobby had a huge heart. This one projected no more compassion than a shard of ice.

We arranged ourselves around a small table in the corner of the room. A dim light from an overcast sky came through the window in pastel grays. The world became black and white and the frost of Bobby's eyes brought chill into the room. We drank the Russian mineral water in silence. Neither I nor Bobby looked at each other. Alex sat still, eyeballing both of us with suspicion. When the silence became ridiculous, he got up abruptly and left the room without saying anything.

As soon as the door closed behind him, I felt Bobby's frigid gaze. I lifted my eyes to his face, avoiding his pupils at all costs, and forced myself into a polite smile.

"Okay, Marty," Bobby said. Even his voice seemed to be devoid of warmth. "I have been against brining you from A2. My belief is that contacts between our worlds will come to no good."

He stopped and took a pull from a mineral water bottle as if it contained distilled spirits.

"Why are you here?" he asked.

I did not answer right away for I was not sure I could trust this man as much as I would trust my Bobby.

"What happened to this world?" I asked instead of answering his question. He seemed to have waited for this question and the story just poured out. The tale he told was both horrible and fascinating

The United States was no more. An entity with the initials N.A.H.P. had taken over. The letters stood for the North American Habitat Partnership. It all started when a coordinated nuclear attack by the Islamist terrorists had wiped out the scores of American cities in 1994. Washington D.C. and the New York City took the first hit. A few days later, Philadelphia, Boston, and Detroit also perished in the mushroom clouds. Our forces struck back. American nuclear warheads hit Baghdad and Teheran. Next, the radical Islamists escalated the conflict by blowing up Tel Aviv and Haifa. Israel seized to exist, but not before nuking Mecca, Medina and Riyadh in Saudi Arabia.

At this point, the Western Europeans—ostensibly Great Brittan and Germany—came in contact with the midlevel officers of the United States armed forces. The Federal Government and the top Pentagon brass had been vaporized. The U.S. military, thanks to the Cold War planning, stood together as an organized force still. The Europeans and the officers decided against recreating the Union. Instead, they put together a temporary governing entity under the auspices of the United Nations. Thus, N.A.H.P. had been born. This executive body was to administer the geography of what used to be the United States on a temporary basis. Just like many other "temporary" government plans, this one had become permanent.

The Partnership, an all-encompassing moniker for N.A.H.P., ruled its subjects with the gusto of a New Age tyranny. It reveled in its unchallenged power and rewrote history. As you may have guessed already, my dear reader, the United States had the villain's part in it.

In addition to rewriting history, the Partnership created a network of open-air camps, calling them "Habitat Centers." There, nuclear survivors received medical help as well as food and water. Millions of displaced Americans huddled in these centers. Chaos and lawlessness permeated at first, until the Partnership declared marshal law and began summery executions. These actions helped some, but did not provide for a long-term solution.

The American economy died with the nuclear blasts. The once invincible U.S. dollar became no more than a novel piece of paper, destined to turn into a collector's item sometime in the future. The Partnership's Fair Share Vouchers had replaced the greenbacks.

Thirteen years later, the situation remained dire. Diseases, famine, and violence still ruled supreme. Some parts of the former United States achieved relative autonomy and closed their borders to the rest of the population. The Utah Brotherhood of Habitats and the United Texas Habitats turned into authoritarian states. Both of these entities had important votes in the N.A.H.P.

Southern California faced a sad situation. The former states of California, Oregon, and Washington created an administrative body called the Union of Pacific Habitats with Oakland as its governing center. They quickly came into conflict with the United Texas Habitats and the Utah Brotherhood of Habitats over religious issues. Oakland had blown up the Hoover Dam to destroy what was left of Southern Nevada and to create a desert buffer between California and the unified forces of Texas and Utah. The Texans promptly bombed the Colorado River canals into history and stopped the water from flowing west. If that had not been bad enough, Oakland politicians—following a historic dislike of Southern California—had blocked the flow of water south from Northern California.

Without irrigation, the land turned into desert quickly. Los Angeles and surrounding counties depopulated within just a few months. In 1997, Mexican Army marched in and—under the pretext of humanitarian effort—began looting the abandoned homes and businesses. The Partnership did nothing since it had invited the Mexicans in the first place.

This is when a group of Marine pilots, led by bull Lieutenant Jack Perez of the Third Marine Aircraft Wing, had enough. They convinced the commander of the Fortieth Mechanized Infantry Division of the California National Guard to join them. The combination proved effective. They succeeded in rolling the Mexican Army back and won the geography from Kern County to the Mexican border.

The military operations took six months to complete. Jack Perez rose as an undisputed leader and the soul of the rebellion. His name became the name of the whole affair. When one spoke of Jack Perez now, he spoke of anyone who refused to recognize N.A.H.P. as a legal political force.

Jack Perez the man, however, realized quickly that most of the coastal areas became uninhabitable due to the lack of water. He had no ability to bring irrigation; so, he dispersed his followers in the mountains from San Bernardino to Mammoth Lakes. He reached out for help to the old world. Only Russia was receptive. Kremlin politicians saw a chance to gain a foothold in the North America and supplied Jack Perez movement with arms and oil.

The Russians also recognized the United States Government in Transition. Please, my dear reader, don't mistake it for the real thing. This group of former Washington D.C. functionaries took residence in Alaska. It had been affected the least by the nuclear catastrophe and found itself in a schizophrenic situation. On one hand, it proclaimed itself as an independent nation; at the same time, however, Alaskan politicians showed loud vocal support for the restoration of the United States. Their deeds, apparently, did not match the volume of their rhetoric. They tolerated the United State Government in Transition but did not press the rest of the world to recognize it. Ironically, only the former Warsaw

Pact countries granted the members of the transition government diplomatic status.

The Partnership came back hard in 1999, but was unable to dislodge Jack Perez forces. Some of the Partnership units, drafted from the former U.S. military, joined with the California rebels. This is when Oakland asked Mexico for help again.

Mexico City had its misgivings about entering California again. Jack Perez mauled their forces badly the first time around and they faced economic and political turmoil within their own borders.

After much political posturing, our south-of-the-border neighbors provided only one division, their elite *Grupo Aeromóvil de Fuerzas Especiales*. They became known as "the Fuerzas." Interestingly, the Fuerzas stabilized the situation. Their command showed to be independent and concluded an unofficial piece treaty with the Jack Perez forces. Mexicans seemed to be content in leaving the Californians be, as long as they did not interfere with a huge reclamation project conducted in the costal areas.

The Partnership started a systematic removal of all signs of an industrial civilization from Los Angeles to San Diego. Their propaganda goal was to turn this land "back to the wild life." In addition to the lofty slogans, Oakland politicians made huge profits from selling salvaged lumber, metals and other commodities.

The Partnershp horded tens of thousands of former Americans to work in a network of work camps, christened Earth Reclamation Habitats. At first, they sold the idea of working in the camps to the refugees from the nuclear blast areas. However, the rumors of prison-like conditions dried up the supply of volunteers quickly. Now, the Partnership filled up the camps with male convicts and captured Jack Perez.

Furthermore, Oakland outlawed all petroleum products and prohibited most internal combastion engines. The only allowed civilian use powerplants had to ran on bio fuels. Since no distribution system for such fuels existed, this decree reduced most of the Pacific Habitats residents to subsistence level and made them totally dependant on the Partnership.

Bobby spoke for over an hour. At times, his story sounded like a confession. I had not interrupted him even once. When he finished, we sat in silence for quite a while because I needed time to digest what he had said. Many questions came to the tip of my tongue, but I stopped all of them from leaving my mouth.

"What is your place in this world?" I asked finally.

"I am the Director of the Office of Intelligence," he said. "The U.S. Government in Transition appointed me to head their intelligence arm."

"Is it anything like the CIA?" I asked.

"No. It is more like makebelieve," Bobby's mouth laughed while his eyes chilled the room by another few degrees. "Well, not all of it is a sharade. Contacts with A2 are real enough and we have some real capabilities, especially when it comes to covert operations. There is no shortage of quality well-trained volunteers. What we lack are recourses. We lost the bottomless purse of the American taxpayers. The Russians have been helpful, but its a loveless marriage."

"Why are you against contacts with the A2?" I asked.

"Our histories roll along on two different highways. I don't see your people willing to accept our realities. We are getting along as well as we can. I know that the Partnership is here to stay. It has too much support from the Europeans and even the people in the North American Habitats. Neither they, nor anybody else who matters throughout the world, want the restoration of the U.S. the way it was in its heyday. The Islamists managed to evaporate our cultural centers in the North-East. This is where most of the people who believed in the Union existed. People in the South and the West have other ideas."

I said nothing and took a swallow of the Russian mineral water. I was born on the West Coast and knew how ridiculous the pompous East Coast politicians came off to the people residing west of the Rockies.

"I don't miss the layers of Washington pencil pushers," Bobby continued, on the roll again. His face flushed while his eyes lost their frigid forlorn emotion and filled with a slow burn of disgust, "I see no reason to bring these leaches back into the decision making process. They screwed up our country once already in this world. Their retarded games made the Two-Nineteen possible."

"Two-Nineteen?" I asked.

"The United States ended on February 19, 1994," Bobby said. "We turned out to be a paper tiger: a sitting duck for a few dedicated fanatics. How could the Washington idiots miss what was going to happen is beyond me. We had spent billions upon billions of dollars on the state of the art weapons, communication surveillance tech, and then some. And for what? To be outsmarted by some bonehead whose ideas came straight from the Middle Ages."

"What bonehead? Who are you referring to?" I asked.

"Racheed al Jared!" Bobby explained. "He is the bonehead who will go down in history as the man who masterminded the Two-Nineteen."

"What happened to him?" I asked.

"Al Jared is alive and well," Bobby said. "He is a holy man of sorts now."

"A holly man of sorts?"

"You will have a hard time believing what I tell you ..." Bobby's face obtained a strange expression: an amalgamation of incredulity and sadness. He regained control over himself quickly and laughed heartily. "Al Jared lives in Frisco now. He has become a spiritual advisor to the Partnership,"

"Hahh?" the words refused to come out of my mouth as I struggled to understand what I heard. "The man who blew up America lives in California and advises the government on the spiritual matters?"

"Yes."

"But..." I could not think of how to phrase the questions which bottlenecked my ability to speak.

"Al Jared's real name is Richard Gordon. His group committed the suicide nuclear bombings. Somehow, they obtained Soviet-made tactical nukes, drove them to their targets, and went boom. Al Jared was to blow up Frisco. But, his piece of crap detonator did not detonate. So, he unloaded the nukes on the steps of the San Francisco City Hall," Bobby grinned.

He saw my shock and knew exactly what I wanted to ask. "I will spare you the long and idiotic story about how he received a vision from t5he havens to build a sanctuary around this live nuclear device. But, the Partnership did just that: they built a temple of sorts around the Soviet tactical nuke. It is very appealing; it looks like it came straight from the Arabian Nights. Since Mecca and Medina are vaporized now, Frisco has become a holly city for Muslims and they pilgrim there by millions every year. It is believed that when al Jared dies, he will be revered as the second coming of Prophet Mohammed."

"Why is this man still alive? Why wasn't he arrested and tried? And, I would think that after what he had done, many a man would want to..." I could not find the right expletive to fully express myself.

"This is why I don't want to mix our worlds. Unless you roll down our road, you'd never understand why no one wants to try or to kill him," Bobby laughed.

He was right, I did not understand this logic. What I did understand at that moment, my dear reader, was that I was more than just a stranger here... I was an alien from the outer space!

"Who is this man, was he born in a Muslim country and brought his Jihad here?" I asked after a short pause.

Bobby laughed out loud. He shook his head and said, "No, the man was born in Chicago to a normal middleclass family. He converted to the radical Islam in his teens. He grew up loving the U.S. so much he blew it up. Literally."

"... But why were there not among the generations before you those possessing understanding, who should have forbidden the making of mischief in the earth, except a few of those whom We delivered from among them? And those who were unjust went after what they are made to enjoy of plenty, and they were guilty ..."

The Holy Qur'an, *11.116*.

April 2010

Chapter Twenty-Eight

Racheed al Jared

efore Bobby left, he gave me a thick manila folder. My first impulse was to dive into it right away. I held myself back, however. I wanted to enjoy reading it to its fullest. So, a bit of delayed gratification was in order, my dear reader. I know that this mindset is truly un-American today. Please, don't judge me too hard. I do repent because I understand that by refusing to satisfy my desires the very moment the urge arises, I endanger the survival of our popular culture and weaken the pillars upon which our economy rests. Nevertheless, I sliced some cold cuts along with French bread and made a sandwich. I wished for some mayo and mustard. The sandwich jinn were off today, however, so I had to settle for what I had at hand. After finishing the food, I plugged in a small electric pot. When the water boiled, I poured

February 2004 Issue

$1.75

TIME

Al Jared Exclusive!

The Modern Day Prophet Shares His Wisdom on   the 10th Aniversary of the New Era!

the liquid into a Styrofoam cup into which I had emptied the contents of an instant coffee baggie. While it brewed, I opened the manila folder and thumbed through it. It contained print media clippings and documents printed on an eclectic variety of letterheads.

I looked through the papers; the clippings and the official memoranda spelled out in detail what Bobby had told me. After an hour, I was ready to close the folder when an old issue of Time Magazine fell out. I picked it up and was just about to put it back, when my eyes stopped at the front cover. It showed a man's head. This was a February 2004 issue; apparently, this periodical had become a monthly rather than a weekly publication in this word. A huge headline screamed, "Al Jared Exclusive! The Modern Day Prophet Shares His Wisdom on the 10th Anniversary of the New Era!"

The face looked familiar. I examined it carefully. The recognition came slowly. My heart began to race and I had to get up and walk around the room to calm myself down.

The eyes from my persistent nightmares stared at me from the Time Magazine cover. I looked at the picture again, hoping to be wrong. No, I was not. This was the man who, many years ago, had killed my best friend Sean Smith in my world!

The memory of that day overwhelmed me. Just as if it happened a few minutes ago, I remembered running out from the back door of an abandoned clinic and straight into a silver fog. The recall of nausea and the realization, of what I had seen, hit me like a two-by-four! That silver fog was the same cloud I saw when I crossed into this universe. I also remembered seeing the multiple reflections of Sean, al Jared, and I. Were those images reflections? Or, could they have been the actual reality, in the other timelines, projected somehow by the silver fog? I did not know. The implication of the possible answers, however, made me sit down into a chair. The recognition, that I may have witnessed the point when the timelines split, made me feel lightheaded.

"...The mission is too important to allow you to jeopardize it ..."

Stanley Kubrick (1928 - 1999), U.S. director, screenwriter. HAL computer (voice of Douglas Rains), 2001: A Space Odyssey, explaining why he won't let the spaceship commander back on board (1968), Adapted from Arthur C. Clarke's short story "The Sentinel."

April 2010

Chapter Twenty-Nine

The High Altitude Insertion

he next morning, Bobby came back with two Russian operatives. They did not identify themselves in any way, not even by their first names. The men, however, carried themselves with a certain air which pegged them as spooks immediately. They also spoke excellent English. For four hours, the men interrogated me. My initial fear, that they would pry into the areas which I could not discuss, dissipated quickly. The operatives did not seem to be interested in any of the U.S. operations in my world; they only queried about their own country in A2. They wanted to know the names of the current leaders and asked me, in detail, about how these men rose to power. I told them what I knew from the news accounts and other sources.

At the end of the interrogation, they thanked me and started towards the front door. Just before exiting, one of them turned around and asked, "What are your plans for the immediate future?"

I did not say anything.

When the silence became too long for comfort, I asked a question of my own, "Do you have any suggestions?"

"Yes, Mr. Greenblatt," the man said and now both of them faced me. "You are a foreign entity here. And I don't mean on the Russian soil only."

I said nothing and kept my eyes on his face.

"We destroyed all beacons in Russia," the other man said. "There is an opinion that all remaining beacons have to be destroyed too."

"I agree," said I after a short pause.

"Your people had deactivated two out of the three remaining beacons in the U.S. One more remains."

"I am aware of it," I said.

"Yes, we know," the first Russian said.

They looked at each other and then the second Russian fixed his unfriendly gaze upon me. "Do you have any reason to remain in A1?" he asked,

"No," I said.

"Do you have any reason to keep a window open between A1 and A2 after you are gone?"

"No," I said again.

Bobby cleared his throat. "As far as my people are concerned, this Greenblatt does not exist," he said slowly, enunciating every syllable with care. "Actually, he is no more than a figment of the Partnership's imagination."

Bobby stopped talking and gave the Russians the "Evil Russian Stare." Their faces obtained the same expression instantly.

"I can tell you even more," he continued. "Soon, your people will intercept a detailed report—marked top secret by the U.S. Government in Transition—which will examine this Greenblatt phenomena in detail and will conclude that the whole A2 myth is a calculated attempt by the Oakland counter intelligence department to ferret out moles within their own organization."

The Russian faces looked menacingly blank now. Their eyes, however, had the same jovial expression I had seen in Alex's peepers on the plane. They nodded in unison and one of them put his hand on the front door's handle.

"One more thing," Bobby said almost at a whisper. Both Russians froze in place listening. "The man who does not exist has been trained in high altitude parachute insertion."

The Russians did not react in any way and left.

When the door closed behind them, Bobby extended his right hand. After I shook it he pulled me close, gave me a bear hug, and walked out of the room. I could have sworn that his eyes shone with tears.

* * *

The drone of the plane's engines relaxed me. After refueling on a small island somewhere in the Pacific, we climbed high above the cloud cover and cruised away under a huge black sky. The full moon's small disc sat high above the horizon. Its cold light could not penetrate the eternal darkness of the moment. The clouds below, however, basked in the moonlight and resembled a surreal caricature of a stormy ocean. I closed my eyes and let the sleep take over.

When Alex woke me up, my pocket chronometer—which I kept set at the Pacific Standard Time—showed 3:52 AM. I've been asleep for the last four hours. He helped me put on a Russian-made pressure suit. This was the KKO-15 model, designed by the Soviet Air Force in the Nineteen Eighties. I turned the oxygen on and its refreshing coldness made me a bit lightheaded. I fastened a utility belt over the pressure suit. Then, Alex helped me into a parachute harness. After that, I turned on the GPS receiver on my belt and waited for the screen to light up. I had another forty minutes before reaching the drop zone.

Last night, after Bobby left, Alex came with some of his crew and transported me—blindfolded—to some airfield. They gave me one hour to familiarize myself with the pressure suit and to fold the chute. After that, Alex and I boarded the plane which carried us now. Its silhouette reminded me of the interceptors from the Sukhoi Design Bureau. It sported two huge jet engines on a compact fuselage. The jet had a small passenger compartment which could seat five men. The cockpit looked like a finely shaped glass drop on top of the fuselage. It had the appearnce of a perfect high altitude insertion vehicle.

Now, I had to keep my eyes on the GPS screen. It was not as elaborate as some of the gadgets in my world, but it did the job. When the GPS showed that we were within a few miles of the drop zone, I tapped Alex on the shoulder.

"Help me with the helmet," I said.

"I wish you a safe journey, Meester Greenblatt," he said in his harsh Russian voice. "You have to complete your mission and go back home. I have nothing against you, but I have orders to terminate you if you surface in this world again."

I nodded. Alex put a full face helmet over my head and sealed it to the pressure suit. After that, he pressed a large red button next to a side door. The warning bells went off. The plane tilted up. I knew that the pilot pulled back on the stick to reduce our airspeed before my jump. Then, the red light above the side door turned green. The airspeed speed must have gone down to a safe open air departure level, I thought. I checked the pressure suit for the last time as Alex disengaged the door's locks. He had an oxygen mask on now. The door slid up in a fluid slow motion, opening a gaping hole. I took a deep breath and stepped into the void.

Skydiving in a pressure suit has its perils. Your ears and mouth are hermetically packed; you can not guide yourself by tasting the wind and listening to the air. Thankfully, this was not my first barbeque. I had gone through the HALO training and had done a few high altitude jumps afterwards.

As soon as I stepped out, the plane disappeared completely. It had to have been clipping close to three hundred miles per hour while my body hurried to achieve the downward speed of one hundred and twenty miles per hour—the terminal velosity. A distance of more than a mile developed between the plane and I within the first fifteen seconds.

I glanced at the altimeter as I jumped; it showed a hair over 27,000 feet. My first order of business was to control the freefall. I used my legs to stop the slow body rotation to my left and worked myself into the Arch position. The skydivers call it such because to get into it, your belly has to parallel to the surface of the Earth and your back has to arch while your four limbs are spread eagle, to be used as stabilizers.

I looked at the GPS screen and lowered my right leg. My body rotated to the left and faced my target: the City of Big Bear. Even though, no one spelled it out to me in bold letters, the fine print of my conversation, with Bobby and his two Russian buddies, had directed me to get out of this timeline and seal the window behind me. They obviously knew that the unauthorized beacon was located somewhere in the San Bernardino Mountain area. It was not a coincidence that, on a moment's notice, they had dispatched a sophisticated high altitude transport aircraft just to deliver me to this precise location. I wondered if they knew about Judy or cared about her, even if they did know.

In the final analysis, none of it made any difference because their wishes paralleled my own. I was only too happy to get out of here as soon as I could and to destroy the window connecting our timelines. The only wrinkle was that I had to find the unauthorized beacon still. I knew where the window opened, but I needed to locate the instrument which made it happen. Somehow, I was not worried. My gut told me that I would be able to get that information out of Judy. The most obvious place to find her was the City of Big Bear Lake.

Now, this city was forty-five miles due south-east and 25,000 feet below. When the altimeter showed 21,000 feet, I pulled the cord. The T10 square canopy unfolded dutifully and yanked me up. The three and one-half Gs slowed my descent to a mere twelve-mile per hour within seconds.

From this point on, I had a chance to enjoy my jump. The adrenaline circulated freely through my bloodstream, making everything around me look crisp and freshly-made. The dark Earth below me was illuminated by the full moon, which looked huge now. Over the years, more than one man had tried to explain to me why the human eyes perceives the moon at different sizes. To tell you the truth, my dear reader, I never understood the explanations.

I glided over the Lake Arrowhead. However, I saw the dark void only where the water should have been. I looked down searching for the bright lights of San Bernardino and other Inland Empire cities. Nothing. A few ambers were lit in the area where the City of Redlands once was. Further ahead, however, the City of Big Bear Lake illuminated the early morning darkness.

Now I was at 16,000 feet and about eight miles north of the city. This is when the trouble began. A strong gust of wind came from nowhere and almost collapsed my canopy. I pulled the line on the right side hard and kept the cruciform inflated. More gusts followed, but I was ready for them and kept the chute expanded.

When I looked at the altimeter again, I was surprised to find that I gained altitude. I was at 20,000 feet. Also, the wind pushed me too far to the east and I was missing my target by five miles. I pulled on the left line, creating a sharp, controlled dive towards the Big Bear Lake. When I descended below 17,000 feet, however, the wind gusts hit me again. Once more, I fought to keep my canopy inflated. The wind turned me around. When I finally fixed my location, I found that I was still at 17,000 feet but about thirty miles too far to the east. I fought more wind gusts and did my best to glide towards the Big Bear Lake. However, I was now over the Morongo Valley and a steady eastwardly breeze would not let me glide west.

Soon, the altimeter informed me that I was at six thousand feet. I gave up trying to get to the Big Bear Lake—the city was above me now—and started looking for a suitable landing zone. Thankfully, I knew the area well. Morongo Valley is dotted with natural hot springs gushing up from the depth of the earth. The Morongo Indians, who own the Morongo Valley, had turned them into resorts.

My parents had taken me there every winter when I was a child.

My GPS did not have a detailed street map capability. It, nevertheless, gave me enough information to maintain a general direction. I wanted land as close to the City of Desert Hot Springs as possible.

Finally, I descended below two thousand feet. The bright moonlight gave me enough illumination to see the grid of streets. I spied not a one sparkle of man-made light. At fourteen hundred feet, I recognized the empty line of the I-10 freeway. I steered along it for some time, until I came up to a major highway forking away. I looked to my left and saw a large land expanse which no one could have mistaken for anything else but a golf course. It must be the Mission Lakes Country Club, I decided. I don't play golf but I knew this place well. The reason I recognized it is because my dad liked to tell a story of how he and his buddies got kicked out of it once. The reason for the eighty-six changed with every telling. I suspect that the actual event may not even had taken place. Yet, I had enjoyed listening to the story as a kid, and still enjoyed remembering my dad's tale.

The Earth came at me quick. I pulled hard on the right and then to the left lines to reach Palm Drive. I succeeded because I landed right in the middle of a Pierson Boulevard and Palm Drive intersection.

In my world, this area has been built up. Mini-malls and fast food joints infested it. In A1, however, the Dot Com bubble of the late Nineties and the real estate balloon of the Twenty First Century's first decade never happened. I saw a bare desert only on all four sides.

I landed harder than I wanted. I fell and the impact knocked the wind out of me. I sat up quickly, nevertheless, unsnapped the canopy, and removed the helmet. A familiar smell of the desert made me smile.

The Southern California air has a distinct odor. No, my dear reader, I didn't refer to the exhaust fumes. Smartass! The dry air has a special flavor which I inhale like perfume every time I come back home from overseas.

It brings tears to my eyes and makes me happy. Funny, how a piece of arid dirt can stimulate such a strong emotional attachment. But I digress ...

When I started to get up on my feet, the deserted intersection swayed from side to side and I sat back down again. I rested for half an hour. Finally, I regained my ability to balance and got up. I was in the middle of a ghost town. From the air, I saw a grid of streets and outlines of buildings. The view from the ground level differed radically.

The only reason I knew that I was standing in the middle of a major intersection was because of an old, worn out street sign. I could barely make out the faded letters. The dirt and the sand covered the hard top. It differed little from the rest of the desert. I rolled up the canopy and started north on Palm Drive. I passed dark, burned out ruins of two resorts. I checked each for water. The many years of neglect, however, filled the pools with dry dirt. The sky to the east began to lighten. I needed to find shelter before long. Even in April, the sun can do much damage in low desert.

Soon, I came up on more resort ruins. The building itself was completely covered by sand. The only vestige of human architecture, a partially burned wall, stuck out from a cactus covered dune. What made this ruin different was the fact that I saw water. This resort had been built on the crest of a hill and the elements spared one of the pools. The water filled it to the top and overflowed into a short creek which faded into the sand, half way down the hill. I decided to set up camp and rest. I pulled out pieces of burned two-by-fours from the wall and rigged a tent using the parachute's canopy.

After I finished, I took the pressure suit off and sat down. As I let my body relax, the adrenaline levels subsided and stopped blocking the pain. My clumsy landing left the left side of my body aching. The dull pain drilled the joint of my left hip and the ribs—on the same side—every time I took the air in.

"...Thou shalt not covet thy neighbour's wife ..."

Deuteronomy 5:21, Douay-Rheims Bible

April 2010

Chapter Thirty

Me and I

he sun cleared the horizon. It looked harmless through a thick layer of the morning's haze. I knew, however, that it will stop playing possum soon and will unleash a relentless assault of the desert heat soon. Yet, a slow breeze felt rather cold. I guessed the air temperature to be in the low fifties.

I checked the water in the pool. It looked clear and felt hot to the touch. I shed the combat boots and green camouflage fatigues, Alex had given me back in Siberia. Then, I lowered my beat up body into the pool slowly. The hot water pulled me in and began its healing magic.

My dad had instilled in me an unrelenting interest in ancient history. As a teenager, I had read tons of books about the Greeks and the Romans. I could lose myself in the stories of pagan myths for hours. As my body floated freely in this random desert spring, the tale of Hypnos came to my mind. This ancient god of sleep would help people ease themselves into slumber and see the things which can not be seen during the waking hours.

I felt his presence now. I heard his soft whisper in the wind gusts and I let my mind float with his chant.

The world around me changed. I found that I was not along in the pool any more. Another man sat across from me.

He, too, nursed his aches and pains in the healing embrace of the hot water. He looked familiar. For a moment I thought that he might be my dad. Yet, he looked different somehow.

"Hi, Marty. I never thought I get a chance to meet you," the man said in a low raspy voice. The understanding of who he was came slowly.

He was me. The me from this world.

"Hi," I answered tentatively. I was not ready for this meeting.

"You sure got yourself in one hell of a bind this time," he chuckled and took a swig form a large bottle of Jack Daniels. After swallowing the dark brown liquid with visible pleasure he passed the bottle to me. I also took a large swallow. The whiskey did not burn my throat as much as I thought it would. The liquor, however, took away the haze and brought him into better focus. He looked younger and thinner than I. A number of healed scars covered his body. I shared some of them but he had many others I did not. "What does a man have to go through to get banged up like that?" I wondered out loud.

"Crap happens," he shrugged.

A bowl of fried chicken gizzards and zucchini came up from somewhere. We drank more Jack Daniels, ate the food, and talked about Joe Greenblatt, our dad. We told and retold stories of our shared childhood and the happiness of being with this Marty filled me.

He started to leave much sooner than I wanted. "I have to go now," he said and fixed my own hazel peepers on mine. I got the taste of what I have been dishing out to others for many years. His gaze pierced through the most protected parts of my soul. "Promise me that you will take care of your wife and daughters,"

"But they are your family," I replied, feeling tremendously guilty of bedding this man's wife.

"No, you are a married man with kids now," he laughed heartily. "You can't change this history because I am you and you are me."

"…The woods are lovely, dark and deep.
But I have promises to keep,
And miles to go before I sleep,
And miles to go before I sleep …"

**Robert Frost (1874 – 1963), American Poet, from Stopping
By Woods on a Snowy Evening.**

April 2010

Chapter Thirty-One

Miles to Go

hiked along the leftovers of the I-10 freeway for two days. Actually, I walked during the night and slept during the day hours to avoid the desert's merciless sun. The wind had blown me seventy miles east from the San Bernardino Mountain.

The freeway had decayed into a little more than a memory. From the air, in the moonlight, I had seen the outline of the six lane freeway clearly. Form the ground, however, I saw none of its magnificence. The desert had claimed this monument to the internal combustion engine. The dirt covered the eastbound lanes entirely. The westbound half of the I-10 had become a one-lane road with only a faint signs of use. I had seen no traffic going in either direction. In some places, the debris covered the freeway's concrete so completely that the path became a dirt road, without a hint of its past grandeur. Most underpasses, however, survived intact. They made perfect camping spots because the massive slabs of concrete kept a cool shade during the scorching daytime.

By the time I came up on them, the sun had not started its daily rise over the horizon yet. I ran out of water by then and welcomed the sight of other humans. From the distance, I saw a moon illuminated campsite: three tents and three Humvees just south of I-10. I nursed some hope, as I walked towards the camp, that these might be the Jack Perez people. When I came close, however, I saw the letters N.A.H.P. stenciled prominently on the trucks.

Instantly, combat instincts took over. I climbed up a small hill about two hundred yards from the camp. The moon was behind me and it would have been difficult for the lookouts to spot me. I spent some time studying the tents and the trucks. I also scanned the desert surrounding the campsite for sentries. I could see no one and wished for some night vision equipment or a pair of field glasses. Since I had neither, I peered into darkness for a while, closed my eyes to rest them for a spell, then lifted my eyelids and examined the camp again.

I sat on the hill for good twenty minutes, until the wind shifted and came at me from the camp's direction. It brought the faint sounds of laughter. Some of the voices belonged to women. I examined at the camp again. It resembled a civilian outing. The trucks were parked carelessly and the tents were too far from each other to be protected by a coherent security perimeter.

I knew what to do instantly. I walked to the camp quickly. Loud laughing and giggling came from the tents. I got into one of the Humvees and pushed the starter button. The Diesel came to life instantly. I put the truck in gear and drove away from the I-10 into the desert. A few minutes later I heard a dull booming of firearms behind me and the loud thuds of bullets hitting the Humvee. I hammered the accelerator and began zigzagging through the desert landscape to become a harder target to hit. The fatigue of two walking days in the desert got to me. I misjudged the steepness of a small hill and flipped the Humvee. I did not remember rolling it but when I came to, I was inside the truck on its ceiling, which became its floor now. Thick cobwebs filled my cranial cavity and my limbs protested when I tried to move. I climbed out of the truck through an open window and attempted to walk. My body had other ideas. The desert came at me quick and everything went blank.

The world got back into focus again some time later. Now, I was face down with my hands handcuffed behind my back. I saw two sets of combat boots standing next to me.

"He's awake," I heard a woman's voice. "Turn the son of a whore over."

An unceremonious kick to my side rolled me over to my back.

"I thought we had an agreement with you guys," the same woman's voice continued. Its owner was a thin short-haired blond with captain's bars on her green fatigues. I had a hard time telling her age in the morning's twilight: late thirties, early forties. The woman's attractive face had an outdoor weathered look and she had an easy posture of a person who is used to command. She looked strangely familiar but I could not put my finger on where I could have seen her.

"You didn't have that agreement with me," I squeezed the words through my parched mouth. I had not spoken for two days and I had drunk my last swallow of water almost a day ago.

"I thought so," the lady Captain frowned. "You don't look like a Morongo."

She must have referred the Morongo Indians. When I looked at the GPS last—before I stole the truck—I was passing through the Morongo Reservation.

"What you look like is a stupid hillbilly Jack Perez," she continued. The lady Captain peered into my eyes and examined the rest of my body with a practiced professionalism of an experience street cop.

"I don't even think you are Jack Perez," she concluded. "They don't dress like that and none of those motherless idiots would steal a truck on the Morongo Habitat. Why did you ruin our R and R?"

She spat on the ground and pursed her lips in contemplation. Her hands held my GPS and altimeter.

"Where did you get these?" she asked.

"I found them," I said.

The lady Captain laughed.

"You remind me of the thickos I knew before the Two-Nineteen. There is something about you that is not right," she said and giggled.

The giggle gave her away. I was at the feet of Deedee Wilson from this world. My Deedee was a soft oversexed vixen with voluptuous body and some rather radical erotic preferences. This Deedee was thin and hard. Yet, I could see the carefully hidden vestiges of passion behind the steely cover of her blue eyes.

"Deedee, you should let me go," I said.

She recoiled from my words as if I was a striking rattler.

"What did you just call me?" she asked, her eyes wide open.

I said nothing but smiled.

"Do you know this man Debbie?" I heard a deep raspy voice. To my right, a large jealous man in green fatigues with master sergeant's chevrons looked like he was just about to kill me.

"Relax Sarge, I never met your woman before nor do I have any designs on her now," I said.

Some laughter came from somewhere behind me. I could not see the people but they seemed to enjoy a bewildered facial expression of the Deedee's obvious lover.

"I have not been called Deedee for more years than I care to admit. Who in the hell are you?" she asked.

"If I tell, you'll never believe me," I gave her the honest answer.

* * *

Six hours later, I was back where I began my A1 adventures. Deedee's sergeant boyfriend drove me to the Redlands Police Station. I had given them a fake name. It did not help, however, because as soon as the Sergeant walked me inside the lobby, we ran into the Light Colonel. At first, he walked by with just a causal glance. Deedee's boyfriend and I stood at the long counter, waiting for a man with the corporal's stripes to finish processing another arrestee. Within a few minutes, however, the Light Colonel came back. When the Sergeant saw him, he straightened up at attention and saluted.

"At ease," the Light Colonel said briskly. He came very close and examined my face.

"I have your ass now," he whispered and added a few expletives. "After your Russian buddies helped you escape. I almost ended up in the ERH myself. I asked for an Executive Termination Order. I did not get it. Apparently someone in Oakland wants you alive. But, I am not going to let you go."

Light Colonel's face showed a desire to rip me apart as he continued his low voice rant, "You embarrassed me and almost caused me to lose my command. I am not going to have you go up north to be traded back to Russia for some of our spies."

I understood that he was convinced that I was a Russian agent. I thought of saying something but held my words back. This man was beyond reason.

"You know what I am going to do?" Light Colonel asked an obviously rhetorical question. "I am going to use my executive privilege under the articles of the Habitat Health and Safety Initiative and classify you as Unredeemable."

He looked smug now.

"Do you know what it means for you?" he asked another questions without expecting an answer. "It means that you will spend the rest of your life in the ERH!"

* * *

Three guards walked me out of the building, my hands handcuffed behind my back. The afternoon's bright sun replaced the morning's haze. The clear air let me see a magnificent view. As the three men in green fatigues walked me towards the prison camp—I spied two weeks ago from the Fuerzas' Humvee—the San Bernardino and the San Gabriel mountain ranges showed off their steep slopes. The deep blue sky vaulted my spirits and the furnace-hot son burned my face.

We marched down—what used to be—Redlands Boulevard. Now debris covered the roadway, leaving a narrow passage only. I walked at a brisk pace, making the guards pant. Twice, they told me to slow down through their puffing. Both times, I complied only to accelerated back to my cruising speed gradually.

Soon, I had to stop at the gates to the camp. Two camp guards, also in green camouflage fatigues, came out. The uniforms bore shoulder patches depicting a blue globe with the letters "N.A.H.P." above and the words "Earth Reclamation Security" below.

"Welcome to the Earth Reclamation Habitat Number Forty-Six," said the camp guard with the lieutenant's bars on his lapels. His voice had nothing welcoming in it.

The other camp guard, with the sergeant's chevrons, took the handcuffs off and gave them back to my escort. They made a lazy about face and walked away.

"Put your hands behind your head and spread your legs," the Lieutenant ordered.

I complied without saying a word. The camp's sergeant patted me down carefully, took my watch away, and put it in his own pocket. I didn't say anything since it wouldn't have gotten the watch back but would have showed weakness on my part. I decided to lay low for now.

After finishing the pat down, the Sergeant asked me to take my hiking boots off. He picked them up and tucked them under his arm.

"He's clean," he said

The guards walked me inside the camp barefoot to a prefabricated building with a large "Receiving" sign. There, I was told to undress and surrender all my clothing but for my boxers.

"You're assigned to the tent twenty-four," said the Sergeant. "You come with a bad rep already. We don't tolerate any of the Jack Perez crap in here. You'll spend your first three days in the hole."

The expression on his face told that he wanted me to protest. If I had done so, he would emjoyed dispensing more punishment and humiliation. Both guards looked disappointed when I smiled and said, "Take me away. I always liked being stuck in the holes."

My poor attempt at a double-entendre, however, fell flat. The guards had too much contempt for the social class of inmates—to which I belonged in their eyes—to react to my words with anything more than disdain.

* * *

Andrei V. Lefebvre

I have no memory of the last two days in the hole, which was a literal hole in the dirt covered by the plywood sheets with a trap door in the middle. My only companions had been a plastic jag of stale water and a honey bucket. I nursed the water for as long as I could. At some point, I heard the trap door open.

"Are you alive, Forty-Fix-Fifty-Nine?" I heard a barking voice from agbove. The numbers, apparently, had replaced my human name.

"Ye....." I cleared my parched throat. "Yes, I am."

"You will refer to me and other earth reclamation staff as Habitat Partner," the voice said.

"Yes, Habitat Partner."

"You can come out now, Forty-Six-Fifty-Nine," said the voice.

When I climbed out from the hole, the sun hit my eyes like a hammer. After I adjusted to the light, two guards in green came into view. I was issued an ill-fitting blue jumpsuit with "ERH No 46" stenciled on the back and a pair of old military style boots. They also gave me a plastic card with the number 20220-4659 and my thumb print on it.

"Find the tent number twenty-four. The other UTAs will show you what to do," said the guard.

I found the tent quickly. Someone stenciled the numbers in white on its faded green canvas. It was a regulation U.S. Army eight-men tent. When I opened the flap, however, I counted fourteen bodies inside.

"Mr. Greenblatt is that you?" I heard someone ask.

The man got up from the floor and cracked his knuckles. I focused on his young face which appeared familiar.

"I'm Jake Robertson," the young man said. "My dad and my brother Andrew came to see you five years ago on the other... I mean we were waiting for you on the porch when you drove up. Remember?"

I remembered...

Andrei V. Lefebvre

Part Four

Highway Home

"...Turning, for them who pass, the common dust
Of servile opportunity to gold ..."

William Wordsworth (1770–1850), *Desultory Stanza.*

August 2010

Chapter Thirty-Two

Earth Reclamation Habitat

The August sun stood high in the cloudless Southern California sky. I walked briskly to the mess tent. My crew saved my lunch rations. It consisted of canned pork and beans with three corn tortillas. The other men waited until I finished and we walked back to our work area together. Walking along was not safe.

I have been living in the ERH Camp Number 46 for almost five months now. Brutal rules reigned supreme here. The camp housed about 2,000 inmates. They separated themselves in the order of the pre-Partnership prison gangs. About a third belonged to the Mexican Mafia, one-fifth called themselves Arian Brotherhood, and another twenty percent consisted of black inmates united under a red and blue Bloodcripps banner. The rest of the inmates classified themselves as Jack Perez. These men consisted of the actual Jack Perez POWs and anyone else, without criminal affiliations, who refused to hail the Partnership as his savior.

Today, we worked on a neighborhood close to, what used to be, the City of Riverside downtown. A convoy of fifty Diesel trucks brought us here from Redlands this morning. We traveled on the remnants of the 215 freeway. Only the westbound side of the freeway remained passable. Collapsed overpasses and aerial bomb craters destroyed much of the eastbound side.

The guards set up a perimeter and the inmates put up temporary shelters. Each of the four prison groups guarded their water and food rations jealously. The guards never interfered as long as we met the reclamation schedule. Our job consisted of going from structure to structure and taking it apart literally. We loaded all salvaged lumber, pipes, and wiring in the pick up area. A team of Partnership auditors catalogued everything and trucks took it away to the rail station.

Once in a while, we would find personal belongings such as jewelry, firearms, and other things of value. A strict decree demanded that we had to turn these items in. Obviously, much of such valuables we kept for ourselves.

After three hours of digging out metal piping, I sat down to rest on a weathered, partially burned, couch. I was inside a large Victorian home, charred by an old blaze. Jake Robertson sat down next to me and brought a water flask to his mouth.

"Want some?" he asked and offered me the water. His was a generous gesture since the water was in short supply.

"No, thanks," I said, tapping on my own canteen, "I have enough."

"This used to be a nice home," Jake said and stomped his boot on the scorched floorboards.

His foot produced a hollow sound. Both of us got up at the same time. We moved the couch leftovers out of the way and examined the floor carefully. I heard the other inmates hammering on something in close proximity. A wall of debris, however, separated us from the direct line of sight.

"It's a trap door," Jake exclaimed.

When we lifted it, I saw a staircase leading down. I entered it first. My eyes adjusted to the darkness quickly. The basement turned out to be a small room ten feet below the floor. Since Southern California architects almost never designed basements, this find was unusual. I realized quickly that our find was extraordinary. The basement turned out to be a private armory. I found a truckload of shotguns, hunting rifles, handguns, and many ammunition boxes.

"We have enough firepower to outfit a platoon," Jake said with excitement in his voice.

"Are you thinking what I am thinking?" I asked Jake.

"Yea. I am," he said. "Let's get our guys in here and head for the hills."

"Good thought. How many we can trust though?" I asked.

My question made him think. Even though, several hundred inmates were lumped under the Jack Perez banner, only a few were POWs like Jake.

"Well, I donno..." he scratched his head.

"If we are to do this, we need to move fast. Any moment the Skinheads or Bloodcripps can come upon us," I said. "You know Jack Perez men better then me. Find five or six guys—trust your intuition—and bring them here in a hurry."

* * *

Sometimes Lady Fortuna plays coy. Just like a spoiled teenybopper, this girl likes to flirt and tease a lot. Today was not one of those times. Not unlike some adult women I know, once she decided to go for it, she went all the way and then some.

Not a minute passed, since Jake left to get the men, before I heard an explosion. Five more rocked the still desert air in quick succession. Then, the echoes of small arms reports chased the bursts' booming reverberations.

"Jack Perez are on the move! Back to the shelters!" I heard a megaphone-amplified voice of the head habitat partner..

An unmistakable sound of mortar fire came closer. Somewhere to the east of us, a fierce firefight raged. I picked out a pump action Mossberg shotgun from the basement and loaded it. I kept it in my right hand and took a position just outside the basement's entrance.

Within minutes, Jake came back with nine men. Without saying a word, they descended into the basement and came out armed.

"What now?" Jake asked.

"First, we need to break through the perimeter," I said. "Then, we link up with Jack Perez to the east."

We moved out in a single file. I took the point, a few yards ahead of the rest. Soon, we came up on two perimeter guards. They walked towards us briskly, their Heckler and Koch sub-machine guns at ready. My eyes registered their presence a fraction of second before they saw me. I pumped a shell into the firing chamber and blasted at the man to my right. His body fell backwards. The guard to the left lifted his gun but a shot from behind me made him drop the weapon and grab his chest. I ran up to him and cut his throat with a camp-made shank.

"Double time after me," I yelled at the men behind me and went into a run.

We cleared the perimeter and trotted for two blocks. A long ago fire left none of the structures intact. The years of the unchecked assault by harsh elements painted everything in drab brown tones. Here and there, tall weeds covered the hardtop of the street. In some places, the dirt hid the pavement completely, making it indistinguishable from the desert.

The grotesque leftovers of a five-story office structure loomed ahead. The broken glass doors led into a darkened lobby. I made a hand movement to the men behind me to enter the structure.

Jake and I climbed to the roof quickly. I scanned the panoramic view and the memory of my own world struck me hard. This was the place where I had heard about Jack Perez for the first time. I could see the location were Rose Perez' home once stood. In my timeline, this neighborhood had become a quiet haven for the middle class families with the manicured front lawns and a sport-utility vehicle in every driveway. Here, I could see nothing but charred remains of my civilization overlaid by a grid of decaying streets. In some places, I could not tell where the ruins ended and the desert began. In a few more years, I guessed, the elements will bury everything man-made and the desert will reclaim the land.

A series of loud explosions interrupted my thoughts. To the northeast of us, I saw a group of men in straw hats and baggy shorts advancing towards an abandoned gas station. Two dozen soldiers in camouflage green defended the structure. They were about two miles away.

By the time we came close to the disputed gas station, the battle was almost over. The eleven of us came at the Fuerzas from the rear. Only four Mexican soldiers were left standing. Realizing that they have been outflanked, the men got up and raised their hands to the sky.

"Don't shoot," yelled one of them in English. "We quit fighting now."

Several dozen straw-hatted men appeared from the surrounding landscape. They probed our group with unfriendly stares and seemed to be more concerned abut us than the Fuerzas.

"And who are you?" asked one of the Jack Perez men in a barking hostile voice.

"Hey, Jose," Jake yelled back. "Wipe the smoke off your eyes. It's me Jake."

"Where did you come from?" asked Jose and a smile of relief lit up his sweat-drenched face. "Didn't you die last year?"

Jake answered with a long string of expletives.

Once the firefight ended, the Fuerzas and the Jack Perez men seemed to forget that they were trying to kill each other just a short while ago. Together, they dug a large hole and buried their dead in a mass grave. One of the Mexicans said a long prayer in Latin. I noticed that a good number of Jack Perez fighters—half of the approximately fifty men—crossed themselves in a Catholic fashion afterwards.

After the funeral, all of us, Fuerzas and Jack Perez, began excavating the gas station's two gas cisterns. I wondered how we were going to transport these mammoth containers. The answer came before we finished digging. A reverberating sound of the helicopter blades came from the east. Two Chinook birds came at us at great speed and landed recklessly close to the gas

station. By that time, we excavated the first cistern and started on the second. Within two hours, both birds lifted and carried away the gasoline-laden tanks.

I asked no questions. The Jack Perez men seemed not to notice me and Jake was busy talking to his pals. After the Chinooks left, the men separated in two groups. The larger one piled into five old pickup trucks and left towards the San Bernardino Mountain. The rest of us, including Jake and other escapees, started in the same direction on foot. Fuerzas, in the mean time, melted away into the landscape.

We walked for three hours, until the sun disappeared behind the mountains. A quick desert sunset brought the darkness in. Even without the sun, the temperatures hovered around eighty degrees. The men stopped and we camped inside an abandoned warehouse. By this time, all my water was gone and my belly demanded food. Up until then, no one seemed to notice me. I, however, paid close attention. The group consisted of eighteen men including the escapees and I. A young, muscle-bound fighter appeared to be in charge. He carried himself with the easy authority of a military officer who had seen much combat.

I found a clean spot on the warm concrete and stretched out. I must have dosed off because I did not hear the muscle-bound Jack Perez officer approach.

"Are you really Martin Greenblatt?" he asked after touching my shoulder.

"Yes, I am him," I answered.

"John Bushnell," he said and shook my hand.

"Did you really come from another world?" he asked.

"What do you know about this other world?" I posed a question instead of answering.

John smiled the way old men do when they hear youngsters talk nonsense. It was a friendly grin but for his eyes. John's eyes maintained a hard expression. I've seen that look before in the eyes of combat veterans. He must have been fighting for many years and have seen many of his friends die. Most men get tired of grieving for comrades and develop a mental wall which prevents them from getting too close.

"I don't know much. Scuttlebutt primarily about some science fiction-like hole in the universe with another world on the other side," John said and sat down next to me.

He took out a plastic two-liter bottle full of water and gave it to me. He also gave me a stack of corn tortillas wrapped in a faded rag.

"These are your rations for tonight," John said. "We'll talk while you eat."

The hunger made the plain tortillas taste delicious.

"How many people know of the other world?" I asked.

"Most everyone heard the scuttlebutt. Most don't believe it. I didn't either until I saw you," he said.

"Why?"

"I knew the other Martin Greenblatt," John said with sadness. "He took care of me and other Marines after the Partnership came in. We went on a few missions together."

"What happened to him?" I asked.

"His old head wound never healed right. Aneurism, Doc said. He died in oh-three," John said. "You look just like him. When Jake told me what your name was, I put two and two together. You must be his double from the other world because he never mentioned any twin brothers."

I nodded and John smiled again. We sat in silence, submerged into the memories of the past.

"I'll take you up to Big Bear," he said and got up to his feet. "His wife... I mean your wife... I mean you know what I mean, is still there."

He started to walk away and then stopped. "I heard that that America is still America in the other world. Is it true?" he asked.

"Yes, its true," I said and added, "Keep in mind, though, America is more of a state of mind rather than government. We are all Americans here too."

John laughed and made a movement with his open right hand as if pushing my words to the side. "I hope you're right Martin. I haven't thought of myself as an American for a long, long time..."

Andrei V. Lefebvre

"...How bitter a thing it is to look into happiness through another man's eyes!"

William Shakespeare (1564–1616), *As You Like It. Act v.*
Sc. 2.

August 2010

Chapter Thirty-Three

Casa de Greenblatt

he City of Big Bear Lake welcomed me with a pleasant surprise. I expected to see more burned out landscape with starving people dressed in rags. What I found here was a bustling city of 100,000. Keep in mind, my dear reader, that in my world, the town had less then 6,000 residents. This Big Bear Lake looked like a slice from a Nineteenth Century science fiction fantasy. It coupled the modern technology with the horse drawn wagons. The city had no electricity, but boasted a Russian-made ground-to-air missile battery and an airfield full of F-18 jet fighters.

What surprised me the most, however, were the people. They looked friendly, neatly dressed, and self-confident. Men wore wide-brimmed straw hats and baggy shorts with Hawaiian cut shirts. The ladies sported cotton summer dresses—reminiscent of the 1940s fashions—with a wide variety of hats. Some women dressed just like men, but those were a minority.

The climb up the San Bernardino Mountain had taken us four days. A detachment of the Partnership security forces—former 24th Mechanized Infantry Division of Fort Riley, John Bushnell told me—blocked our advance for two days. I estimated their numbers to be at five hundred. Had they known our true strength of eighteen, we would have been dead. Bushnell, however, separated us in three teams. We used our eight mortars to shell their positions for several hours. Then, we fought back a scouting party successfully. After darkness, we used a dry bed of the Santa Ana River to pass trough their left flank.

In the morning, they realized that we moved off and called for the air support. Three AH-64 Apache birds located us quickly and rained a large caliber machine gun fire down on us. Luckily, their laser-guided guns did not aim well amidst irregular terrain full of boulders and caves. Eventually they left, low on fuel more than likely. The rest of our climb up proved to be uneventful.

Now, I marched up the Canyon Road looking for a log cabin. Bushnell told me that I could not miss it because it had a large green board with white lettering "Casa de Greenblatt" above the front door.

After walking for half an hour, I heard a sound of horse hoofs behind me. Buckie, with two girls riding bareback, trotted by lazily. I recognized Joanna instantly. The other one must be her little sister, I thought.

"Is it really you?" Joanna's eyes widened as she pulled the rains and halted the horse.

"Yes, I came for all of you," I said, walked to the horse, and squeezed the girls' hands. "Where is your mother?"

The smiles left the girls faces. "She ain't doing too good, she's awfully sick," Joanna said. Her voice had a weary adult sound to it. "She'll be happy to see you though. She's been praying that you'll find us, but she told us that you probably never will."

I started walking again and Joanna touched Buckie's sides with her heels. He began moving his legs lazily. We walked in silence until I saw a small log cabin with a large sign "Casa de Greenblatt."

Both girls jumped off the horse, handed me the rains, and ran inside the cabin yelling, "Mom, he's here! He came for us!"

Judy came to the front door before I had a chance to tie the horse to the railing. She looked pale and much thinner than I remembered. Her eyes though... Her eyes burned with the scorching green fire that made me ran up to her. I put my arms around this woman and lost myself in the delicious depth of her French kiss.

As soon as I had touched Judy, however, I knew that something went terribly wrong with her. A year and a half ago, her figure resembled that of Marilyn Monroe. Now, Judy was skin and bones only. She had difficulty standing up, so I picked her up and carried her inside. There I sat down on the couch placing her on my lap. The girls cuddled up to us on both sides.

"Marty, you met Joanna. She'll be fourteen soon," Judy said. "And the other daughter is Vicki. She's nine."

"Nine and one-half," corrected Vicki. Her vice sounded strangely familiar.

"Okay, sweetie, nine and a half. I'm sorry," Judy said with a smile and caressed her hair.

I looked around the small cabin and saw a wall full of pictures. Most of them were of Judy and me. Not of me, I corrected myself, of the other Greenblatt. However, where did he end and I began?

Judy sensed my discomforting thoughts. She touched my face and asked, "Do you think he'd be jealous of you?"

I remembered the hot springs pool.

"No, my little missy, he'd be happy," I said. "I am him and he is me. We, I mean I, just exist in different dimensions."

"So, his daughters are your daughters too?" Judy asked, her voice betrayed a fear that I would reject them.

"Of course they are," I said without hesitation. "They are also grandchildren of my parents. How can they not be my daughters?"

"I'm so happy," Judy said.

"Do you mean we can call you Dad?" asked Vicki.

"Yes, stupid," Joanna answered instead. "He is our dad."

Andrei V. Lefebvre

"...My loss may shine yet goodlier than your gain
When Time and God give judgment..."

Algernon Charles Swinburne (1837–1909), *Marini Faliero. Act. v. Sc. 2.*

August 2010

Chapter Thirty-Four

The End and The Beginning

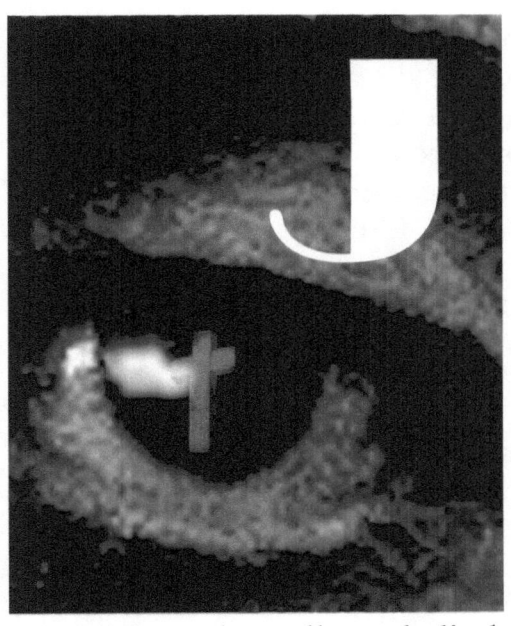

udy and I spent all evening talking about the A2 timeline. Finally, the sun disappeared behind the mountain. Judy looked exhausted. I carried her to the bed in the cornier of her one room cabin. Joanna and Vicki went to a covered back porch where—they proudly told me—their mother let them sleep during the summer.

I kissed my newly found daughters goodnight awkwardly and climbed into the bed with Judy. The air cooled down considerably. I pulled a blanket over us and held her in my arms. Her body felt cold and clammy.

"Now, my little missy, you have to tell me what's wrong with you," I said in a stern voice.

"Oh, Greenblatt," she answered happily. "I love it when you try to be mean. I know that you love me and I am not afraid that you will toss me away anymore. I never dreamt that you would actually come here."

"I did come here and stop changing the subject. Tell me what's wrong with you," I demanded.

"I don't have much time to live," Judy said. "I have advanced liver cancer. It metastasized all over my body."

I squeezed her tight and kissed her lips.

"How much time?"

"A month or two," she said with a sad smile, her green eyes on fire. "The doctor said that he can't do anything for me. He gave me a good supply of morphine to dull the pain."

"Let's go to A2, to a real hospital, to see real specialists," I said.

"My lovely Sasquatch, thank you," she said and kissed me. "I know that you'll do anything for me. This thing is not something that you can shoot and kill. It's too late. I've been to A2 doctors six years ago when you first saw me. The cancer went into remission then. It came back now. Stay with me until I die and then take our daughters to your world."

I did not protest nor did I ask for more details.

* * *

My usual nightmare woke me up early next morning. I slipped out of bed, careful not to wake Judy. She slept peacefully in the morphine-induced bliss. The image of al Jared firing his deadly gun stood in my eyes as I walked out to the front porch. I haven't had this dream since I crossed into A1. Usually, a cigar would wake me up completely and chase the nightmare's residual away. I had no cigars. Instead, I poured myself a glass of water.

I stood in front of the cabin and watched the sunrise. The water had a slight odor of pine resin. It's bitter aftertaste took the shivers of the dream away completely. A lazy wind gust brought the smells of smoke and manure. Roosters crowed and dogs barked not too far away. Then, I heard a familiar thumping of boots. A formation of young men with automatic rifles marched down the street while their drill sergeant, full of proper arrogance, called cadence. Soon afterwards, a loud roar drowned out all the other noises. An unmistakable chug-chug of the Diesel foretold the appearance of a Humvee. A drab green truck stopped in front of the cabin and the driver got out.

For a brief moment, I thought that I was still asleep and in my nightmare. The tall figure with a blond crew cut could have belonged to Sean Smith only. I've seen him die many years ago in my world. It had never occurred to me that he might still be kicking here.

"Son of a ..." Sean cussed happily and gave me a bear hug. "I heard that you showed up and came right away."

"How could you be alive?" I asked. "What happened in San Bernardino in 1993?"

"To my dying day I will carry this cross," said Sean, his face turning serious. "I wasn't quick enough and the dirtbag shot you."

"What do you mean he shot me?" I asked.

Sean smiled and shook his head. "Our Marty got shot in the head. He didn't die though. Not right away at least. He spent a year in the hospital and seemed to have recovered. He was okay for years, until..." He paused and looked me in the eyes. "Massive stroke; doctors couldn't help."

I heard the cabin's door open behind me and Judy came out.

"Hi, Sean," she said and put her head on my shoulder. "I found my Marty again."

Sean smiled. He changed since I've known him in the other world. He got older, obviously, but that was not it. His eyes lost the idealistic fire. His shed his intensity. No matter, Sean was still my best friend ever. I never stopped missing him. I knew that I let him down many years ago. The fact that he was alive in this world did not count. My Sean was dead. DEAD, DEAD, DEAD!

This world's Sean must have sensed my internal turmoil.

"What happened with me in your world?" he asked.

"I let him kill you. One bullet through the heart," I said. "I put the dirtbag out his misery quick afterwards. But it didn't bring my Sean back."

"Our dirtbag here got away," Sean said with sadness. "You probably know by now that he was the one who had masterminded the nuclear attack on the United States."

* * *

Somehow this day passed like a pleasant dream. I can't tell you, my dear reader, what I did and said exactly. What I know is that Sean was with me again and many of the men I lost touch with in my world were here. We reminisced about the old times and mourned those of us who died, here and in A2 timeline. Before I knew it, the darkness descended onto the Big Bear Lake. One by one, everyone left except Sean. The girls went to bed and Judy cuddled up to me on the couch. I gave her a generous shot of Morphine and her face shone with the deep glow of this drug.

"Are you going to seal the window to your world when you go?" asked Sean.

I nodded.

"That's what I figured," he said. "You wife and you are the only people left who know where the unauthorized beacon is."

"What about Walter Kurz?" I asked.

"I never heard of him," Sean said.

"There is something you don't know about Walter," said Judy. "I will tell you later." She, however, did not live long enough to tell me this story. It is quite a tale, my dear reader, but I will have to spin it some other time.

"Actually there are a few more people who know where it is," I said thinking about Juan Robertson and his sons. "Jack Perez also knew."

"How do you know?" asked Judy.

"He died in my world," I said.

"How did he die?" asked Sean with interest. "We have caught so many wild rumors but no one knows anything."

"Did you have a Cholera epidemic about six years ago?" I asked.

"Yes," said Sean.

"He crossed to my world looking for a cure probably," I said. "He never made it. Cops found his dead body in L.A."

Sean nodded and we stayed quiet for a while.

"This beacon kept us alive," said Judy breaking the silence.

"Your wife used to go through the window and bring supplies. Our Marty and me found a large stash of greenbacks in Redlands. They became wallpaper when the Partnership took over. In your world it was still money. Without Judy and the beacon, Jack Perez movement would not have survived," Sean said. "Too bad he died. You would have liked him."

* * *

Judy passed away two weeks later. She spent her last days sitting on my lap. I cuddled her weightless body while we talked about little things. She wanted to know how I would take care of the girls. I promised to put them to bed early, to find a good school, and to protect them from bullies. Judy got weaker and weaker. Fearing that she'll just slip away into the abyss without saying good-bye in a sober state, I did not give her any Morphine one morning. She complained of pain but I waited until the drug induced glaze left her eyes.

"Judy, my little missy, I need to talk to you," I said.

"I know what you want to know," said Judy and told me. I jotted down the directions to the unauthorized beacon on a piece of paper.

She died two days after that. More than one hundred people came to her funeral. Sean and I made a wood casket from some lumber I found in the back of the cabin. Then, we carried her to the cemetery. There, several men helped me dig the grave. A young preacher said Protestant payers. Afterwards, her friends—and she had many—came up to me with condolences. I felt numb, as if I was not me but some wax facsimile designed to shake hands and thank people for coming.

The girls had stood behind me silently all through the funeral. Before we left, I came up to Sean. Without saying anything, I gave him a hard bear hug and kissed his forehead.

"Good bye, my best friend," he said. "Give them hell in your world."

My daughters and I walked home holding hands. There, we sat down on the couch. They buried their faces in my chest and cried. I tried to squeeze tears out of my own eyes, but could not. Some heavy substance seemed to envelop me. No emotion could penetrate it.

The girls slept in Judy's bed that night.

Early next morning, we packed our belongings into my old Datsun truck-turned-horse-cart and harnessed

Buckie to it. The sun stood high by the time we reached the right spot of the Highway 38. I dug out the plastic card from under the rock, where I hid it many months ago, and pressed on the blue dot.

"... At the beginning of the cask and at the end take thy fill, but be saving in the middle; for at the bottom saving comes too late. Let the price fixed with a friend be sufficient, and even dealing with a brother call in witnesses, but laughingly ..."

Hesiod (fl. 8th cent.? B.C.), Works and Days. Line 366.

Epilogue

y infrared flashlight illuminates a thick steel door. No light penetrates this darkness. Without the flashlight, my night vision glasses would have been useless. Judy had given me good directions. I have no trouble finding the entrance into the abandoned silver mine. The narrow shaft stretches for 1,200 feet. I am inside the hill close the abandoned section of the Highway 38.

The door has a broken lock and it opens with a squeaking sound. The infrared light makes everything look like an old-time horror movie. I see a steel staircase on the other side of the door. I walk up one flight and come to another steel door with a small sign "Lab. Turn all your electronic devices off."

This is it. I know what I will find there. For three days after we crossed back into my world, I have been preparing myself for this moment. Without hesitation, I pull the door open and step over the threshold. The amber image of an abandoned science lab comes into my night vision glasses. I point the infrared flashlight around the room and see what I came here to find. An electronic device hums happily on the computer table. I press a button on its side. A little door slides open. I remove a glass cylinder from it and put it in my pocket. The hum stops. I deactivated the unauthorized beacon.

Now, I have to pay attention to the second part of my mission. On the floor, next to the stainless steel table, rests a badly decomposed body of a woman dressed in a lab coat. A large rock is imbedded into her red hair covered scull. I look around the lab and find a purse. Inside, I see an expired California drivers' license in the name of Judy Dobiash. I look at the DMV mug shot. Young Judy smiles back at me.

In A1 timeline, the rock hits Judy in the forehead and sends her to the hospital. There, she meets her Marty, who is also recuperating from a head wound.

In my timeline, my dear reader, the rock kills her. She never gets a chance to meet me. And, even if she lived, would we have cross paths? Al Jared does not shoot me in the head sixteen years ago and I have no reason to be in the hospital. In this world, we are not destined to meet.

As I let my mind burrow deep into the philosophical contemplations about the parallel worlds phenomena, my hands take a knapsack from my back and remove a black body bag from it. I put a pair of latex gloves on and load Judy's body in it. It is light, mostly bones covered with mummified skin.

The funeral of this Judy is a small affair. I invite Walter and Roberta Kurz as well as Bobby and his wife Tracy. My girls and I stand silently as the funeral crew lowers her oak casket, gleaming with the lacquer finish, into an earthmover-dug hole. A U.S. Army Chaplin, invited by Roberta, says a prayer. Dr. Kurz delivers an eloquent eulogy praising Judy for her loyalty and good nature.

"Thank you for taking her body out of the mine," Roberta tells me after the funeral service ends. "Thank you for bringing the closure to me and for bringing Judy's girls here."

I give her a polite hug without saying anything. Roberta puts her sunglasses on and straitens out her black dress.

"What do you plan to do with the girls?" she asks. "I'll be happy to take them. They are my relations."

"This makes us one family then," I say. "They are my relations too. My daughters, to be exact. Bobby is fixing the birth certificates and a plausible legend for our world. When he's done, I'll put them into school."

Roberta faces me, her features unreadable. I see a reflection of my eyes in her oversized sunglasses. After a brief awkward moment, she pats me on the face with her gloved hand and says, "Yes, Marty, we are related now. Bring the girls over as often as you can. Walter and I want to be part of their lives."

* * *

Three months fly by. Christmas season comes at us with the full force of its ancient tradition. Joanna and Vickie do well in school. They make many friends and the teachers praise their schoolwork.

I settle back into my world's life as if I had never gone through the window to A1. Everything seems fine except that the heavy substance—which turned my emotions off after Judy's death—never leaves me. Don't get me wrong, my dear reader, I am not miserable or sad. I feel nothing, however, just nothing.

On Christmas Eve, the girls and I have an early dinner. A large Christmas tree winks at us with the happy brightness of its lights and ornaments. After the meal, we light the candles on the mantle place and the girls say their prayers. They wish for expensive presents. They also pray for their mom to be happy in 'Haven. By the time I tuck the girls in, my alarm clock shows 12:07 AM of the Christmas Day.

As I close the door to the children's bedroom, something changes in the house. My old friend Hypnos takes away the protective heavy substance from me. The full weight of the outside world comes at me like a freight train. The pain of Judy's death knocks the feet from under me and I have to sit down at the kitchen table.

They join me—Judy and the other Greenblatt. The table fills up with zucchini, fried chicken gizzards, and sauerkraut. The other Marty and I drink bourbon whisky and smoke La Gloria Cubanas. Every so often, Judy and he exchange glances. The happy puppy love like expression on their faces makes me feel a bit out of place.

We talk all night. What is said I don't know. What I do know is that I can't let them go. Their presence holds back The Pain which lurks just outside the kitchen table.

"It's time to part, Marty," says Judy when the sky lightens on the east. She kisses my forehead. Before they disappear, the other Marty gives me a bear hug, just like my dad used to do.

As soon as they leave, The Pain comes at me like a wild predator. I do my best to ignore it and let my legs take me to my daughter's bedroom.

"Good morning, Daddy," whisperers Vickie, still half asleep.

The sound of her silver bell-like voice turns The Pain into tears. The salty river flows down my face. Vickie gets up and puts her little arms around me.

"Are you crying for Mom?" she asks.

I nod and Joanna hugs me from the other side. My embarrassing tears do not last long. I regain my composure quickly and we open our presents.

Later, the girls go outside to feed Buckie, who now lives in a fenced turn out area I constructed in my back yard.

I walk to the front porch to smoke a cigar. The heavy substance left me completely. Now, I feel the world around me in its full complexity. From where I stand, the sound of the near by Highway 38 hits my eardrums. Before my trip to A1 it used to irritate me. Now, I welcome it. Suddenly, I hear Judy's voice, easing through the highway's drone.

"You are such a mean Sasquatch," she giggles.

"You've been a bad little missy, my love," the other Marty's deep voice replies.

Then, I hear an audible sound of a spank and both of them laugh.

"Good-bye, Marty. We love you," they yell in unison and their voices merge with the noise of the highway.

The End

About the Author

Andrei V. Lefebvre is a transplanted European. For more than three decades, he made the Southern California his home. During these years, he had tried his hand at several careers. He pursued criminals as cop, covered news as a newspaper reporter, and published a pulp fiction magazine. Yet, his body and soul belong to the automotive business.

His non-fiction byline can be found in the Orange County Register, Daily Commercial News, and other newspapers. His short fiction appeared in the Man's Story 2 Magazine, and the Magazine of Unbelievable Stories.

He resides in Southern California with his wife and children.